The Unexpected Journey

This book was written by a woman who really appreciates life and all those people who make all the difference for the better around not only their world but others world too. She appreciates the natural essence of life, and that people are not numbers, unlike what is often shown to us daily. Everyone is important no matter their gender or colour or religion. This story is based on the real-life of an extraordinary woman and the love of a child that changed the path of her own life (of course with some added fictional details). Facing several obstacles most of her life, but always with the same claw as those of a warrior woman. This book shows that love is a wonderful feeling that can move mountains and bring people together. In this book the author shows us that love, sincerity, respect, and honesty are the main ingredients for a complete and happy life. Life should not be routine but should be lived to the fullest as if tomorrow was your last day, and whatever you do, always add a sprinkle of positivity and love, and then life will be worth living.

The incredible and unexpected life of an amazing woman.

Contents

Chapter 1

Santarém is a Portuguese city situated on a plateau, located on the right bank of the River Tagus, about 40 miles northeast of Lisbon, and surrounded by vineyards........This beautiful place is a town of historical significance and its origins can be traced back in time, as far as to Julius Caesar, who used the location as an administrative centre for Roman legions.........

Santarém was conquered from the Moors by Dom Afonso Henriques, the first king of Portugal. The period of Muslim rule ended on March 15, 1147 "XII century" with the conquest of the castle by the Portuguese king.

With the Christian reconquest by D. Afonso Henriques, Santarém became one of the most important cities of medieval times in Portugal, as can be seen from its numerous historical monuments, some of them monasteries.

Santarém has always been called the "Capital of Gothic Architecture" because of the splendour of its architectural heritage.

Entering the urban city, the occupation made over the centuries is shown and the most relevant monuments of this historic centre can be seen throughout the city.

Santarém - the Capital of Gothic Architecture - has a historic Centre," centro histórico" and at its entrance - there sits the seminar square. There is no way to miss it as it is so eye catching.

On the left is the church of 'nossa senhora da Piedade' (our lady of piety), a small church compared to all the others, in the city, and on the right the Cathedral that is one of the main attractions of the city. The Cathedral is a very big and powerful monument that was built on the remains of the Royal palace after the battle against the Moors led by Dom Afonso Henriques.

The Cathedral where the former Jesuit College was located is one of the most important monuments of Santarem's heritage.

The construction began in 1672, in the 17th century (XVII) and on the imposing facade we can read the date of completion of the works, in 1711 in the 18th century (XVIII)

With the expulsion of the Jesuits from Portugal, the building was abandoned, till in 1780, the Queen D. Maria I, in response to the need for a permanent installation of the Patriarchal Seminary, handed it over to a Cardinal Patriarch, for the purpose of the necessary adaptations.

There is another very important 'monument', a beautiful garden with a panoramic balcony view called portas do sol "the sun doors" , the most important and beautiful thing about this place is an amazing view over the River Tagus and D. Luis bridge, all the Lezírias Ribatejanas "vineyards fields", the fields of cultivation and the city of Almeirim in the foreground and Alpiarça, another small town on the left .

Portas do sol are located on the right side of the river Tagus, the place where the Alcáçova or Arab castle, one of the most important in mediaeval times, was located.

To the south and east of this garden we can see some of the old walls that used to surround the city of Santarém.

Beyond the walls that take us back in time, to mediaeval times, from south to north we can enjoy the River Tagus and the surroundings of this amazing region with another placed at the bottom of Santarém, called a Ribeira de Santarém. Ribeira de Santarém is like the back door of Santarém itself.

Just as we enter the garden, portas do sol on the south side are the Roman ruins of the ancient city and in the same square on the north side we can see the very old Church of Santa Maria da Alcáçova.

As portas do sol ('the sun doors') were landscaped in 1896, in the 19th century (XIX) and it has been the guest room of the city since then.

There is no one that visits this wonderful city, who wouldn't go to visit the portas do sol.

Another very distinctive monument of this city is the 'Torre das cabácas', in our days known by 'cabaceiro'. "The Tower of Gourds" or the Clock Tower.

The current clock tower or 'Cabaceiro', dates back to the reign of King Manuel I (1495-1521), dating from the mid-15th century (XV). It was built from a defensive structure surrounding the Porta do Alporão, which was built in the already-existing walls of the medieval village of Santarém.

The name "das Cabaças" was popularly established from the end of the 18th century (XVIII) due to the placement of eight clay gourds in an iron structure that supports a large bronze bell, cast in 1604. The people jokingly compared these gourds to the "hollow" heads of their municipal councilors.

In Santarém, we also have the Church of 'Graça' where in 1520, in the 16th century (XVI), Pedro Álvares Cabral (the Portuguese navigator and explorer who discovered Brazil) was buried.

The construction of this church started in 1380, in the 14 century (XIV) and was finished in the 15th century (XV).

The Church of Santa Maria da Graça, also known as the church of Graça or as Church of Santo Agostinho, is located in the square "Pedro Álvares Cabral" in the heart of the historic centre of the city of Santarém. The church is part of the convent of the Eremitas Calçados de Santo Agostinho and is one of the most emblematic monuments of the city, constituting one of the most important examples of Gothic art in the country.

There is another very important church called 'Milagre' (Miracle).

This beautiful church used to have a different name, 'Church of Santo Estevão', but during the 13ᵗʰ century (XIII), a miracle occurred, which reports the theft and desecration from a consecrated host by a lady who was a resident in the parish. Since then, this church's name changed from 'Santo Estêvão' to 'Miracle'. It then became a particularly devout place of worship and pilgrimage.

For so many years, Santarém has harboured several legends about its own origin and one of these legends was related to Greek - Roman mythology and tells us that Prince Abidis - the son of a relationship between King Ulysses of Itaca and Queen Calipso, (during a time that Ulysses travelled through Portuguese lands and fell in love with Calipso) - was abandoned by his grandfather, Gorgoris, King of Cunetas, who launched him in the waters of the Tagus River inside a basket.

Like a miracle, the basket that contained the Prince, landed on Santarém River beach where a servant raised him, but later the Prince Abidis was recognised by his own mother the Queen Calipso, which made him the legitimate heir, choosing Santarém as the capital of the Kingdom.

Another one of the legends most recognisable of Santarém was the 'Santa Iria' (holy Iria).

This legend tells us that Iria (a maiden) was once raped and later killed and thrown into the River Tagus. Later, her body was brought to Ribeira de Santarém, by the

current of the river and showed the waters moving away from her body. For this little miracle, as the people from Santarém describe, this maiden became 'Santa Iria', and a statue was created where she appeared.

Every year during winter, the river floods, makes life difficult for the local residents. The water never touched the Statue of the Saint's feet. Old people say that when the floods are so large that they reach the statues feet, Lisbon will fill with water too.

Santarém is a place of bullfighting, pitchforks, horses, meadows and a very rich gastronomy. The promotion of bullfighting shows started as a source of revenues dating back as far as 1825, 19th century (XIX), with the aim of collecting funds to help support the exposed in charge of the hospital.

Chapter 2

It was a lovely afternoon in mid-May 1936, the sun had a smooth shine, the sky was clear blue, a typical spring day, the birds were singing non-stop and there were children playing, mostly boys playing football, shouting and talking loudly, people coming up and down the street doing some shopping, and some groups of men talking in the corner of the tavern, women gossiping about everything and everyone, but everyone was getting along with one another without any major problem.

The tavern was a place where normally only men go to drink mainly spirit and wine. In this place, most men can spend hours drinking and going home late, and most men keep going 7 days a week and their wives can't say anything about it because if they do, they might get beaten up.

A woman's job was only to take care of the chores at home and to look after the kids and never complain about anything. Out of their houses, women would go to church every Sunday, to funerals and mass and to some shopping, most of it from the market.

For funerals, normally almost all the population of the city got together and went to pay their respects, because everyone knew everyone.

The baker's way 'travessa dos pasteleiros' was a nice place in the centre of Santarém, just behind the Church of Misericórdia. This beautiful church was built in the middle of the sixteenth century, (XVI) having been brought to fruition through the efforts of Queen D. Catarina, ruler by her grandson D. Sebastião from 1559 to 1606. After the earthquake and tsunami of 1755 that devastated Lisbon and adjoining areas, the Church lost the primitive facade, but was later replaced by another one of Baroque style.

It was around lunch time when Sara arrived by train at the bottom of Santarém, a little place called 'Ribeira'. Raquel was sat by the window, and since Sara began this journey, she was admiring the beauty of her own country's countryside. She was carrying a rectangular dark brown suitcase, that used to belong to her late parents. When approaching the place where she was supposed to exit the train, she stood up and prepared to carry her luggage. A male passenger offered himself to help her, but she declined his help immediately.

Sara got out off the train and looked around. She was badly impressed, because the railways were passing too close to the houses, and with lots of small children playing everywhere and making a lot of fuss with all arriving passengers. Sara raised one eyebrow. After the departure of the train towards Lisbon, she looked around for a bit and took a deep breath. She thought out loud 'Oh my dear God!'

Then she approached a woman and asked her where she can get up to Santarém. The woman indicated the bus stop and told her that she needed to wait for the next bus.

Sara joined other people who had come from the train, and she waited and waited and finally the old bus arrived. The journey took 15 minutes, but always going uphill. As soon as they got to town, and still travelling on the bus, she was admiring the beauty of the city. When the bus turned at the town market, she was surprised by its even greater beauty.

The market was a big white square building, but the most amazing thing was the notable set of decorative tiles all around, all in white and blue representing like a regional representation, which characterised the city itself in the early 20th century (XX). Sara's eyes couldn't be wider open, towards such a great monument

The bus was still moving, but Sara's head kept looking backwards at the market; she couldn't keep her eyes off the building.

"Oh my God, I need to come and see it properly", she thought. In Coimbra there wasn't anything similar to this.

A few minutes later the driver stopped the bus at the usual place and told all the passengers they could get off. Then the driver himself got out and went to get everyone's luggage. Sara stood up from her seat and with both hands, she straightened the back of her dress. She got out of the bus, took her suitcase and walked a few steps. She then took a deep breath and thought, 'This is real, I'm here, Sara! Have courage girl, you can do this.' Sara opened her handbag and took out a piece of paper with the address that she was about to need. She looked very carefully at the address and after a moment, she thought about asking someone because she had no idea which way to head and seeing two women talking not far from where she was standing, she decided to approach them. She asked for some information about the address that she needed to find.

The two women at first started to talk both at the same time, and Sara didn't know which one to turn to, but at least they were giving the same information. However, they didn't let her go without asking her where she was coming from.

Sara very politely told the two women that she was arriving from Coimbra, to see some family. But the two women wanted to know more about Sara, and they would not stop asking her lots of questions.

When Sara turned to these women for information, she never expected to be questioned the way she was, because she only wanted to know which way to head on to her family's place. Sara tried to avoid them asking anything else, but the women were persistent, and they finally got what they wanted to know.

She ended up telling them what brought her to Santarém.

The women knew everything about her cousin's death, they seemed to know all the details, something that left Sara impressed. How could a place like this, being so close to the capital, have people so...so... curious?!

After a good 30 minutes of questioning Sara, they eventually let her go. She couldn't believe that she was free of these two (detectives).

Sara started to walk, without looking back in case the two gossipers found another question to ask her.

Sara was walking very concentrated on the road ahead to make sure she did not break the shoe's heels, because of the sidewalk. She would be really embarrassed if that happened just before she met her family for the very first time, and thinking that made her roll her eyes, something that she often does when situations are boring to her.

Sara took the right way in the beginning, but she needed to ask again for directions. This time she asked a very old lady, with a peaceful look and this time the informant was not curious about who Sara was or what she was doing there. She found this old lady quite nice and pleasant. Sara wanted to know where Bakers Way was, because it was the address she had written on the paper.

When she got to Bakers Way, because of the way she was dressed, with a nice green dress and hat and black shoes, everyone who saw her had their mouths open. It wasn't every day that they saw a woman so well dressed and beautiful like Sara.

The women in Santarém did not dress badly but Sara was different, like a breeze of fresh air and because of her own tall height she was the kind of women that made all heads look twice, some in admiration, others in jealousy, especially women about her own age.

Sara herself, was always very friendly, modest and she had no patience or time for stupid people.

Sara was arriving from Coimbra, a place that she made home a few years back when her mother and father died, and her oldest sister took Sara to live with her in a convent when she was still very young.

Sara's sister was a mother superior in a convent in Coimbra, but Sara herself didn't want to be a nun; she wanted to study as much as possible, something that wasn't very common in a girl, but time was flying away and when she realised, she was 26 years old and continued living at the convent. For that time, it wasn't very common to see sibling like Sara and her sister, so tall. Her sister was a very big woman, and, for a nun, she was very strong, and she proved this a few times when, in the convent, they needed a man's muscle, she was always required. Sara was very tall, with dark hair and dark eyes and not as strong as her sister, but she was very elegant, a very caring and polite person.

Sara had been living in the convent since early teens age she loved Coimbra, but she didn't like living in a convent. Apart from her sister, she did not trust the other nuns, she never hid from anyone what she thought about nuns: that they are very false people and hypocritical, but now she had a very important mission to follow.

Sara had a cousin. Her name was Rosa, she married the year before, and three months ago had a baby boy, but she died while giving birth and Sara was really concerned about the wellbeing of the baby.

When Sara found out about what was going on with her family in Santarém she made the decision to travel there to see if she could help in any way, and her sister was supportive about Sara's decision.

Sara was walking very slowly and looking for the door number that she had on the piece of paper that she brought with her.

She was looking and finally she found it. She approached the house's front door and... she knocked. The door was in brown wood with an iron frame all around. It also had a black ring which was used as a door knock and door handle.

"Who is it?" A woman's voice replied from inside of the very modest house, with two vases of dead flowers on each side of the door.

"I'm Sara Martins, I'm Rosa's cousin!" At this very moment, Sara started to feel a bit uncomfortable, but she took a deep breath and tried to be natural for the woman who was going to open the door for her.

"Give me a second." she replied, and while she was waiting, Sara looked around and, to her surprise, she saw a few women peeking from the windows with their heads out. Immediately she thought that this place was full of nosy people, and sometimes these kinds of people are more interested in others' lives than in their own.

After a few seconds, the woman opened the door, and as soon as she did, she looked stunned while looking at Sara.

For a few seconds, the woman couldn't let anything out of her mouth. It was like she had been frozen because she wasn't expecting to see someone so well presented, like Sara was.

The woman was of medium height, thin, her hair was tied back in a little bun, and she had an extremely messy appearance, the aspect of a woman who cleans was not a priority for her; she was very unclean.

The two women could not look more different. It was like a beautiful summer day compared with a winter day full of thunderstorms.

Sara didn't use any perfume at all, only kept her good hygiene and clean clothes, something that impressed the woman very much indeed.

These few seconds felt like ages to Sara, and she thought to herself immediately that that woman needed to have a good wash, with lots of soap and a brush.

However, despite her opinion, Sara tried to put on a brave smile and to be relaxed.

"Hi, I'm Maria, Rosa's mother. Who did you say you are?"

The woman looked so filthy that Sara felt disgusted.

Sara was Maria's niece, but they had never met each other before.

"Do you want to come in Sara?" Maria asked.

"Yes please, if you don't mind!"

Following Maria, she went in.

The house had a humble and dark aspect, as if the windows did not let in enough light, but perhaps it was because the streets were so narrow that it did not give enough space for the sun to enter. The curtains that hung on the windows also did not facilitate the visit of the sun. They sat down at the kitchen table and the woman asked Sara if she wanted a drink, but she said no.

"I'm sorry to come to your house like this and I'm sorry about your loss!" Sara said.

"May I ask how you found out about my daughter's death?"

"It was in the convent where I live, you know, bad news always travels fast. Two of the nuns from here went to our convent a few weeks ago and one day at dinner time they started to talk about Rosa and how she died and that she left behind a baby boy. Through the conversation, it was my sister who discovered that your Rosa was our cousin. I was really shocked because I (like many other people) think that some things only happen to others but in the end, we are others too. Since then, I have been so anxious to meet the little one, and I hope you and his dad don't mind."

"Oh, Sara it was so sad I never thought in my life something like this could happen to me, it's a nightmare for a mother to see her kid die before her. God decided to take my Rosa away I do not know why! And now I have my grandson to look after because his dad is always out and busy and my daughter lost her life, and she is not here anymore to take care of her baby and one of these days my son in law gets married again and I will be stuck with his son! Sometimes I think that he should have died with his mother."

After Maria said that Sara was very badly impressed by her auntie. How could someone say a thing like that of a baby, an innocent little person that did not ask anyone to be born? If Maria is Sara's blood, how could she be so mean and so different from her? After all, Maria was Sara's mother's sister.

Many years ago, all the family used to live in the North, but Maria one day left with a new husband to live in Santarém and, after she moved, they all lost contact for a while. Even when Sara's mother died, Maria did not get in touch even to go to her sister's funeral.

After hearing Maria say that, she took a very deep breath to clear her thoughts, and she felt like going and picking up the child she hadn't yet met, and running away with him, far from this stupid aunt.

"Is the baby here with you?" Sara asked.

"Yes, do you want to see him? I was just feeding him, before you came. Follow me." Once again, she followed Maria into a tiny bedroom.

When they entered the room, the baby was in his little cot, very dirty and snotty.

When Sara saw the eyes of this little person crying, she fell in love with him. She had this feeling deep down in her heart that she could not leave him and that she needed to save him from the hands of this grandma.

Maria picked him up and with a little spoon she started to feed him with baby food. Sara was really surprised because she thought a baby about his age should have only milk, but the thing that annoyed her the most was the fact that Maria took the little spoon full of baby food first completely inside her mouth and only after to the baby's mouth. The baby cried and cried.

Sara felt sick; how could she do that?!

Sara asked Maria if she herself could try and feed the baby.

"Are you sure? This boy is very naughty when it comes to feeding times... it's always a problem with him."

"Maybe it is because he is still very young, and babies that small should be having milk, not baby food. Baby food maybe only after they reach 5 or 6 months old, and apart from their ages, babies are different from one another. And I believe babies have a connection with their mums, but our boy doesn't have one."

While Sara was talking, Maria was looking at her with a stupid and surprised face, and as soon as Sara made a little pause, Maria had the opportunity to jump into the conversation.

"Why do you know all this stuff about babies, because as far as I know, you are single, and with no children, or am I wrong?"

"You are absolutely right, I don't have children, but in the convent, I dealt with plenty. Some of them have lost their parents, others are so poor that their parents decided to give them away to the nuns because at least they can be fed and learn how to read and write. We have newborn babies and children as big as 12. Sometimes when parents start to manage their finances better, they come and pick up their kids, others never do, but when they get to 12 or 13 years old, they need to get a job and find their own ways." After saying that, Sara lifted her own eyes from the boy and looked straight into Maria's.

"By the way, does our boy have a name?"

"He is Jonny." said Maria.

Sara immediately fell in love with Jonny, and he felt so peaceful with her; it's as if he feels who really loves him. Babies can sense if the people who look after them are loving or not. Maria was really stressed, and the boy felt it too.

After a while, Maria was surprised to see the love that Sara was giving to Jonny, and she asked Sara if she wouldn't mind her popping out to do some chores.

"Please do, I have good company. Just one thing. Can I give him a bath later?"

"Sure, you can; I can do other things instead while you take care of him."

When Maria left the room, Sara lifted her middle finger and made a rude sign at Maria's back.

Sara could tell that Jonny had not had a bath for the last 3 or 4 days, but Maria wanted to show a different facade, but Sara was a very bright young woman and yet, at the same time, an old fox. No one could make a fool of her, and she could always read between the lines.

Sara cleaned the baby, changed his clothes and she could not keep away from him anymore.

After Jonny was asleep again, she tiptoed out of the room without making any noise and joined Maria, she was already in the kitchen, but soon she needed to get back to the room because Jonny started to cry.

By 6.30pm someone came through the door and started to talk to Maria in the kitchen. It was Torres, Jonny's father.

Torres was a very intelligent man for the time and place he was living in, but with a very strong personality. He was a bookbinder and no books passed by his hands without him having read them first. He learnt French by himself, and he did a few jobs for Oliveira Salazar, the Portuguese president at the time.

Torres was a very unhappy and traumatised young man who was himself the victim of a very independent mother who, considering the perception at this time, had many husbands; she had had five husbands and never had the time to care for little Torres.

For Portuguese women who are normally brunette, Torres' mother was blonde, slim, and medium height. She married very young the first time, had Torres and soon after she lost her husband, who died from the kick of a horse. She had another 4 husbands, but all died through accidents. She was very young, full of dreams and never had time to look after her son.

From a very wealthy family, Torres was brought up in an institution for boys without love from his mother or father.

Still very young, Torres ran away from the institution and hid here and there, eating fruit from trees that he could reach.

Torres used to stalk his mother and the men who were passing by in her life. He threw stones at them and then ran.

Torres used to help poor people with small children by buying them food, especially one woman with five children that was struggling to get food on the table almost every single day for her family; he had a better heart for others than for his own family.

The previous year, he had married a good woman called Rosa, Jonny's mother and on the same day, in the afternoon he hit her so badly that she was bleeding and bruised.

"Torres, we have visitors. Sara is the daughter of my older sister who lived in the north, she came to meet your son and she is in the room with him. She looks decent," Maria said, with a deep look into her son-in-law.

After a while Torres, went to the room with Maria and he introduced himself, he was a very polite man, and all dressed in black with dark eyes and a very sad look.

"I'm sorry Torres, about not having sent a letter before. I wanted to let you know about my visit, but an opportunity came along, and I couldn't miss it," said Sara, looking at him very deeply. He then looked to his son.

"You should have" he said, "because I don't like surprises, but...now you are here! By the way, if you want to stay here, we have a spare room. If not, we have a lady friend with a very big house and you can stay there, it is up to you. This friend normally has people renting rooms, it's a way of living, and she gives breakfast every morning to her guests."

Sara, still holding Jonny in her arms, said that if he and Maria don't mind she could stay in their house and in Jonny's room. "I can look after your baby while I'm here Torres, if you don't mind!"

"I don't mind, but I think you don't know what you are getting in to, because he cries too much sometimes, I'm surprised that he is so quiet now!"

That night, Sara prepared everything, and she slept with Jonny, not really sleeping because she was just so happy to have him in her arms.

To everyone's surprise, Jonny did not cry that night, or during the day; Jonny was a completely new baby! Sara started to take him outside, giving him a bath every day, always at the same time and keeping him clean and fed.

The days passed very calmly; no one could say that there was a baby in the house.

Chapter 3

After a few days, Sara was with Jonny in the kitchen when Torres came in.

"Jonny looks happy with you; I don't know what you have done but for sure he likes you!"

"I love him so much too, I don't think I can be away from him, ever!" said Sara.

After a bit of hesitation, Sara asked Torres.

"Can I have him, do you want to give me your son, Torres?"

"Are you crazy? I would never give my son to anyone! He's mine!"

Sara continued:

"But you are always busy, and your mother-in-law doesn't know how to take care of Jonny! Please Torres, let me keep the boy, please!

I will stay here in this city, but I will raise him!"

"No! End of conversation!" said Torres and he started to leave the kitchen. When he got close to the door, he turned his face back to Sara and he said,

"If you want to keep my son, you have to marry me; that's the only way."

When he said that, Sara froze for the first few seconds, and after a while her mind started to think all sorts of things: 'Marry him! Oh my God, I wasn't expecting that, I wasn't even looking for a husband!'

In the middle of these painful thoughts, she looked at the baby and, as he smiled at her, her heart immediately melted.

'How can I marry him? He is much crazier than I thought.'

For the next day or two, she could not take his proposal out of her mind, what a decision. When Sara went to see them, she wasn't expecting to fall in love with this adorable and sweet little creature.

Every time she thought about when she saw the boy for the first time, she felt sick about the way his grandmother kept him so unclean.

'Oh my God!!!

I must do this!

I must, there is no other way, the boy needs me.'

That night, when Sara went to bed, she couldn't sleep very well, and all her thoughts were travelling very fast. It was a very big deal for her to get married, because it was the kind of thing that she had never thought about before.

When she spent her early years in the convent, she was busy all the time, several times her sister asked her about what she wanted to do one day, but marriage was never on her mind.

This was not very common in young women, normally girls from a very early age started to think about which kind of man they are going to marry with, one day, but in Sara's mind she didn't need a male presence in her life.

Since she met Torres, she thought he was a very nice-looking man, very charming but no other thoughts entered her mind. Lots of times she used to say she could live by her own and work, because she was not afraid of life.

Finally, she fell asleep but soon she woke up because Jonny started to cry.

"Hello, my little man, no need to cry I'm just here sweetheart."

Sara lifted him out of the crib and then kissed his head and held him against her chest. "You are so sweet my little man."

After she changed his nappy and fed him, she laid him again in his crib, and, because it was still very early to go and wash the nappies, she went to her own bed and laid there with her eyes open and just staring at the ceiling.

It was 6 am when she got up and looked at Jonny who was asleep. She picked up the nappies and some other clothes and she went to the patio to wash them. She then hung them in the little back garden.

Just after 7am, she heard the front door slam. Sara went to the window to get a glimpse of who it was, and she saw Torres going up the road. She went to check on Jonny and after she went to make a coffee for herself, and when she had just filtered the coffee, she heard another noise on the front door and it was the baker delivering the bread. People who want fresh bread straight from the wooden oven normally leave a bag hanging outside of the door, and the next day, very early, the baker passes by and leaves it, and depending on the costumer, some pay by the end of the week, others by the end of the month.

Sara was enjoying a breakfast when Maria came to join her. "Good morning Sara, did you make enough coffee for me too?"

"Good morning, I did. You know me, always make enough for us all", said Sara.

After they both had breakfast, Sara went to check on Jonny.

Later that day, Sara cooked a nice dinner for the three of them, but both women had to wait till 8.30 pm for Torres. They ate and after dinner Torres picked up the local newspaper and started to read, while both women cleaned up the kitchen.

Maria went to the patio to chat with a neighbour and Sara took the opportunity to talk to Torres.

"Can I have a word, Torres, if you have 10 minutes to spare?"

He put the newspaper on the coffee table and turned to her. His eyes were very dark and looking very deeply into hers, that in some ways intimidated her, but she tried not to give much attention to that.

Jonny had caused a very deep sentiment in Sara's heart, and the love she had for him was worth every sacrifice she could make. Every child needs a Mum, Jonny doesn't have a real one, but...he can have me, she thought.

"So, you do not want to give me Jonny, isn't it? So, I thought about what you asked me, and my answer is yes. I will marry you but just because of the boy."

Torres kept looking at her and after a few seconds he told Sara:

"You are young with all your life ahead of you...are you sure about this?"

Hearing that, she looked at him and she shook her head saying yes with pure confidence.

After a few moments, he put his right hand in his trousers pocket turned around, and once again looked deep into her eyes and said:

"I do not want a big wedding, just the bride, groom and 2 witnesses," which Sara agreed with. It was not a traditional wedding, but a contract.

Sara was a different girl, she never had the normal thoughts of a young woman, of having a big wedding with a white dress. She never even thought before about being in that position at all.

This occasion was not a dream wedding for either of them, in fact, it was like a contract especially for Sara, a woman who never thought about getting married.

She informed her sister by letter about the wedding, and when she replied, the notice about the wedding was already on show outside at the local court.

Normally this practice has always been in place in case someone has something to say to prevent the wedding.

When the wedding day arrived, it was just an ordinary day like any other day. Torres was dressed in a black suit like always and Sara was wearing her green outfit, the one she was wearing when she first came to Santarém.

At 11 o'clock in the morning, Torres, Sara and two friends of his entered the civil office and 45 minutes later they came out as husband and wife. Torres turned to his new wife and spoke.

"I will see you later at home," and he left.

Sara went straight home, but on her way back one of the neighbours approached her.

"Congratulations Miss, just a pity that; he is crazy."

Sara immediately answered back.

"Did I ask for your opinion? Just mind your own business. When I want people's opinion, I will ask for it." The woman stuck her tongue out at Sara. Sara went to clutch the cuffs of the woman's top.

The neighbour was not expecting this reaction from Sara and ran away to continue her journey home.

The first week after the wedding passed without any problems; Sara hardly laid her eyes on Torres. They had not spent a single night in the same bedroom, which she was happy about.

But during the second week things started to change quite a bit.

Maria had moved out for good; thank God because Sara always thought of her as a pain in the neck, a real pain.

At the end of the day, after Sara gave the boy a bath and a feed, she prepared dinner for herself and her husband. She set the table like always and put the food on the table, when suddenly Torres came in puffing like a bull. The meal was quiet and tense, and as soon as he had finished, he got up and went straight to the main door, and just before he slammed the door behind him, turned his face to Sara and said:

"When I get back, I want you to be in my bed." and he left.

Sara started to talk to herself.

'I'm not going to ask for God's help, because I knew this would happen eventually, but it's for a good reason. My boy deserves it.

Sara prepared herself that evening, went to his room and she laid on the bed. Torres came very late, about midnight, something that happened very often because of his profession.

Sometimes his customers want the books ready very quick, and he tries to organise himself to read them first and bind them after.

When he went into the bedroom, he got close to her and for a few seconds, he stared at her. Sara looked like she was fast asleep. But she was not, she pretending.

Torres prepared himself and got into bed, but she did not move.

About 3 am, she heard Jonny cry. She got up to change the nappy and feed him, after which she went straight to bed. Torres was awake and as soon as she was in bed, he turned to her and consummated the marriage.

Chapter 4

Life for Sara was pretty much normal for the first 6 months after she got married, but one day, like any other one she prepared dinner, set the table, put Jonny in a baby basket and while she was talking to Jonny, Torres came him, washed his hands, and sat to have dinner. Sara – like always - served his plate first and after she did, he asked her:

"What's that? What sort of food is this?"

Sara replied:

"It's a fish stew like I have made before, and you never complained before!"

"It looks disgusting." Torres said.

Sara was surprised by what he was saying, and she added

"Torres, you have had it so many times before and you always loved it!"

"Who do you think you are to answer me like that?"

He got up from the table, pulled her by the hair and gave her two strong slaps, so hard on her face that she started bleeding from her nose and lips. He pulled her by the hair to the floor.

She never hit him back because a woman was supposed to be hit but not hit her husband back. He hit her so much because he knew she was not going to hit him back. Compared to Torres, Sara was much taller and stronger than him and he knew if she wanted, she could hit him harder and if she did, he would kill her.

After this devastating scene, he left her on the floor, with Jonny screaming in the basket. He slammed the door hard. Sara stood up, cleaned her face with a tea towel, and she picked up Jonny.

"Don't cry sweetheart. Mum is here." It was the first time she had said that. Sara had never used the term mum before to Jonny or anybody else. Sara kissed him and comforted him, not like a stepmother but like a real mother. Raquel loved this boy more than she loved anyone in her life, and what just happened shocked her deeply. How could Torres turn out to be so violent?

After a while Jonny was calm, and Sara started to sing for him and dance with him.

Torres didn't come home that evening, neither in the morning, he only came home the next day at dinner time, and behaving normally, and his normal was very quiet most of the time.

Sara had dinner ready on the table like she always did, and when he came through the door, she thought to herself because one thing he cannot do, have access to her thoughts.

'What is this son of a bitch doing here. Big bastard." Yet she behaved naturally.

He had dinner with her, asked about Jonny, and as soon as he finished, he said, 'See you later' and left. Sara was relieved and cleaned the kitchen and she went to take care of Jonny.

The next few days were quiet and normal, and Sara was living her normal life. One day, during dinner, she asked Torres for money because she needed to go to the grocery and to get some new clothes for Jonny. He was really upset but, in the end, he gave her some. It was not enough but she had to manage.

Sara had a little allotment where she worked very hard and there, she always had fresh vegetables. She also had some apple trees and pears.

Since Sara came to live in Santarém, she had made a very good friend called María Adelaide.

Maria had a very big house with a very big garden. She was the one Torres mentioned who rented rooms when Sara came to Santarém.

Maria was a young, beautiful, and nice woman who married a nice man when she was 20 years old, and when she was 23, she gave birth to a baby boy. At 24 years old, she sadly lost her husband suddenly. Maria had a very hard time, because she could not come to terms with the loss of her beloved husband and the fact that she had to bring up a son on her own. Since her husband died, she could not dress in any other colours apart from black. It was a sorrow; her husband was not there anymore for her to share her life with. Since that time, she felt sad and helpless, because her husband was very close to her and the little time he had as a father, Maria could see that her husband was a dedicated and loving father. When the baby was born, he also helped to take care of him, whenever he could, something that was not very normal at the time for a man.

Very often, Maria gave Sara other vegetables and fruit that she did not have in the allotment. Both women along with Jonny and Maria's son used to spend afternoons together. It was a beautiful friendship.

A few days later Sara was coming down the road when a woman with very poor presentation came to her direction and said:

"Are you Torres's wife?"

Sara said yes, and the woman continued:

"My name is Lucy, and your husband has been paying for food for my kids, and I just want to say thank you to him and to you. He is such a lovely man, God bless him."

Sara smiled and replied: "You're welcome." After a few more words, she said bye to the woman and kept walking.

Sara was not against Torres helping others as long as he helped in his own household.

The money was always short at home, and Sara decided to work, against his will.

Sara started to work in the market every weekday very early. It was a very hard life to get little money, but Jonny was growing, and she needed as much money as she could get.

Every morning at 5 am, she got up, prepared herself and Jonny, put him in the baby basket and off she went to work. One morning, as soon as she got up and put her feet on the floor, she felt so sick that she only had time to get to the toilet and vomit.

"Oh my God, my God, what did I eat last night to cause this!"

All day long she wasn't completely ok, and in the afternoon, she went with Jonny to Maria's house.

Maria sat with Sara in the kitchen and asked her if she wanted a coffee or a tea; Sara said maybe a Melissa tea because she was not that well, and this specific tea helps.

"What happened Sara, I have never seen you so pale!"

"As soon as I got up in the morning, I vomited, and I felt a bit strange! Maybe the dinner I had last night caused that, I don't know."

"Sara, when I was pregnant with my son, I felt exactly the way you do! Are you pregnant? When did you have your last menstruation? You know if you walk in the rain, you might get wet." And saying that, Maria smiled gently.

"God!!! I don't know! I never pay much attention to that. Let me think...."

Sara started to concentrate, and whispering calculations, and after a few moments she turned to her friend with her eyes wide open and after a bit, she exclaimed, "God! If you are right, I could be 2 months pregnant! I'm not sure. No, no I can't be!

 But if I am, I want to get an abortion." Sara said fast without thinking twice.

"Are you sure Sara? Think carefully before you make any decision. Imagine that you are pregnant with a girl!"

A boy and a girl!

It will be good!

"And if it's a girl, you know, you can have help with your tasks. To have a girl is always better for us, because as they grow, they learn house chores, and they can help us."

"Maria it is not like I have a good relationship with Torres! God knows how much I suffer with this man to go and have another child. If only things were different!"

And saying that, Sara looked vague and very sad. It was not like she had a normal marriage, but instead a very unhappy one, just like the many times she had thought about it.

In the beginning, when she met Torres, deep down in her heart she thought that he was a very handsome brunet, and she could easily fall in love with him, but after the very first time that he hit her, she thought to herself that she will never ever love this man as her husband. So far Sara lived for her little boy only, nothing was more important than this little person who had stolen her heart.

Over the time that she had become Torres's wife, she changed a lot; she does not believe in a normal life anymore, she doesn't dream anymore. A life could be a happy one but instead is a miserable one, not knowing what is going to make the next motive to be hit by her husband. A few years ago, every time Sara heard about a women being hit by their husbands, she said that if it was her, she will throw a chair at their head.

"I will never admit that a man could touch me to hit me." she used to say. But now life showed her that sometimes things go around and around, and when we least expect, things just happen, and in her case, there is nothing she can do, because she has her son, and she is married to the man.

The rest of the day Sara couldn't think about anything else except the pregnancy.

That evening Torres noticed that Sara was different.

After they finished dinner, he went out, like most evenings and when he was back, she was sitting in Jonny's bedroom just watching him sleep peacefully. Many thoughts crossed her mind, even about her afternoon with her friend Maria, talking about the possibility her being pregnant with a baby girl. Thinking about it made her smile gently, followed by a serious face. One of her thoughts was:

Do not be stupid Sara, you know this cannot happen!

Don't you have enough on your plate!

And?

If I go ahead with this pregnancy, I will get in much worse problems, that's for sure

I can't! I can't! This man is a super king size pain in the ass that I have to live with!

After all these anguishing thoughts, she looked up to the bedroom celling, and put her hands together, she asked God to help her not to have this baby.

The next morning the same thing happened like the day before. As soon as she got up, she went straight to the toilet and vomited. At the same time Jonny woke up and started to cry so loudly that Torres was annoyed. He got up and went to see why Sara was not taking care of the boy. In the toilet after vomiting, she was a bit weak, and she was sitting on the closed toilet seat.

When she came out of the toilet, he grabbed her by her hair and started to hit her very hard, anywhere he could while Jonny was still screaming in his bedroom. It was like he had an evil inside him. He didn't even think that if Jonny was crying and Sara was not with him, maybe it was because she hadn't heard him or in this case, she was in the toilet unwell, but he chose to see what he wanted too.

Torres once again left Sara bleeding, and after he stopped, she cleaned herself up and went to see the boy, the main reason of all this.

That morning, Sara did not go to work in the market, she was too devastated with everything that happened that day. She had thousands of thoughts about her miserable situation, how could her life turn out to be so messy? How could the world shelter so many bad people? How come a real man could live with himself after doing what this one just did to her? If God exists, why does he never help those in need? So many questions without answers... but she did not want answers she wanted situations like this one not to happen at all. In her mind, she had no doubt that he was crazy, she will never raise her son to be like his father, a man so cruel to her. It does not matter if he is good to his friends, but what does matter is what he does to her. She wanted to be treated with the respect that everyone deserves.

After calming down Jonny, feeding him and changing the nappy, she sat aside just watching him sleep and she started to think about leaving Torres for good and forever. She started to put her clothes and Jonny's in a bag, and she was preparing to leave Torres. After she prepared the bag, she took Jonny from his cot very gently for him not to wake up. She slowly started to come out of the room, but the moment she was going through the front door, Torres appeared and took the boy from her arms, like he was expecting something like this to happen. He exclaimed,

"You can go but the boy stays!"

"Why are you doing this, clearly you hate me, why Torres?!"

"The boy is my son not yours; it's my blood" Torres replied.

"But he is my son too. Have you taken any time to think that this situation is not at all good for the wellbeing of Jonny? I'm not talking about me...I do my best to be a good wife for you, but in your eyes, I'm never good enough."

"You accepted to be my wife, you have a roof above your head, but I'm the man here...do you understand me?! You can go wherever you want, but just make sure my son stays behind, because if you don't, things can get very nasty. I didn't make you accept me or him, you made up your mind, now if you are not satisfied the door is just there." And saying that he pointed to the front door. His brunet hair was sticking up and his face looked like it might explode. You could practically see the rage fuming from his eyes. Sara knew exactly what she thought to do, and what she needed to do. They were two very different things, the first was she felt like giving him a punch and carrying on going away with Jonny for good, but she could never do that because it wasn't in her nature to attack the father of her son. The second option was she needed to let go this idea of getting away from Torres, because by the sound of it, he would never let her take Jonny. So, she decided to stay, but this did not invalidate the fact that she felt devastated about being unable to implement the decision that could change her life for a better familiar environment.

"If one day I come home and my son is not here, I will go around the world and I will find you, and when I do, I will kill you. Never doubt what I just said. Never tempt me, Sara. If you do, you won't even regret it because you won't be around long enough." With his dark and evil eyes, Torres said this, and he seemed to regain some masculine power over her.

After this terrible episode, Sara felt that her husband could be much worse than she initially thought. One thing was very clear to her: he loved his son very much, and she could guess, after what just happened, that he loved his first wife very much. Maybe Torres sees Jonny as the mirror of Rosa. In Torres' eyes, who knows, but at the same time she was thinking, if Torres loved Rosa why had he hit her on the day they got married? What an awful way of showing his love. For a man like him that fed his own brain with reading lots of books and being very clever, it was an appalling way to treat his family. Sara never understood his way of seeing life or her.

Chapter 5

In the beginning, when Sara married Torres, she thought maybe one day she could have a happy life with this man, she had plenty of dreams, like any other person but now she thinks sometimes it is better if we leave the dreams to just fade away for our own good. It's not very reliable to keep dreaming if things are just not meant to be healthy and happier. In her opinion after everything that has being going on in her life, it's just safer to keep her feet on the ground, or probably...one foot just behind just in case something turns up.

The situation was very clear in her mind: she was married to a monster. Torres was highly respected by everyone; he helped so many poor families, but for his own wife he was a completely different person. She felt like the walls were caving in on her; she wanted desperately to leave this demon that was her husband, but she did not want to leave Jonny behind. But that was not an option. She loved Jonny with all her heart. In fact, her heart was so full of love for Jonny that it left no love for Torres. It was quite the opposite. Sara had grown to despise that man. It was a feeling she had never experienced but one she could not get rid of. Try as she might, she was stuck in this cage of emotions and the hormones of having a baby would only make it worse. This -and what had just happened- led her to the conclusion that another baby was just not what she needed in her life right now.

She was more than sure she needed to get an abortion.

Only one week after what happened, things started to not be so tense in their house, but Sara continued to have morning sickness.

One afternoon she asked Maria if she knew anyone that could help her with the abortion.

"There is this woman who normally does these things Sara, but you need money because she is not cheap." said Maria.

"I don't care, I will get the money somehow and I just want this thing done as quick as possible. I will ask Elizabeth if there isn't other way." Elizabeth was Sara's friend; they met up at the market. Elizabeth was a woman working very hard all the time. She had a donkey with a wagon, and she transported all vegetables from the farms to the market. She had her own stall there and she made money like water, that's why Sara thought about asking her for help, and she did.

The next day, Sara and Maria went to see the "midwife" and the woman talked to both and told Sara what to do and that she needed to come back in 2 days to complete the end of the pregnancy. Sara had a mix of feelings; why is life is not much easier?!

Sara did everything the woman told her to do and she ended the pregnancy. It was really painful but there was nothing she could do about it.

The next day after dinner, before Torres went out, he picked up his son and started to talk to him.

"You know Jonny, you were supposed to have a brother or sister, but Sara just got rid of it." Jonny was paying attention to his dad, but he didn't understand; he was too little. Sara didn't understand how he knew about it, it was not like she gave the news to the local newspaper.

"I don't think you should be saying that." Sara mentioned. He turned his face to his wife and whispered for Jonny not to hear.

"You are a killer."

"If you say so... I am not bothered, I just didn't want another innocent life to suffer, and the baby is nothing yet... Killer? Doing what you have been doing to me...you are the one who is going to be one soon."

He turned to her with a deep evil look that she was used to seeing and put his son on the floor. After a few seconds, he left, banging the door behind him.

Sara picked up the boy and sang a song for him and then they both played together, and she was happy to see a little boy enjoying it. The smile on his face compensated for all the pain she was suffering in this awful life.

Sara's life was very difficult, she was still hit by him over the years; very often she went out with lots of bruises on her face. She was not the person that she used to be when she first came to Santarém.

Sara used to be a lady in all aspects, but now she was a tough woman, most of the time she was in her own thoughts. The only thing that kept her going was her intense love for Jonny. Every time Torres hit her, she asked God to help her to calm down, because more than once she felt like grabbing his arms and doing to him what he was doing to her. Without saying anything to anyone, she was ashamed to go out when she had marks on her face, her lips with cuts that she couldn't hide. There was always someone commenting about it, something that made her furious, she hated gossiping no matter what. It was like being back in school; the kids laughing behind your back but pretended to be sympathetic when they saw you. She always liked to live without being noticed by anyone, but now, most of times she is motive for others to talk about.

One day Jonny was very sick, he wasn't breathing properly, so Sara took him to the doctor, and to her surprise, the doctor told her that Jonny had asthmatic bronchitis.

She was very worried about this, and every time the boy had an attack, she used to put some linseed porridge on his chest and kept him on her lap for hours.

Sara had enough on her plate, lots of things to worry about.

One day she was coming home with Jonny from her job, and she thought about going to Torres' office. When she did, she saw her next-door neighbour in his office, and she looked very guilty as soon as she saw Sara. At this very moment, many thoughts came to her mind.

What is that bitch doing here, it couldn't be a good thing!

After the neighbour left Torres asked Sara:

"What are you doing here? Is there anything you need?"

"No, I was just passing by, and I thought about coming with Jonny to show him where daddy works, but I can see we are not very welcome...we are going now." said Sara.

Before she left, he picked up his son and kissed him on the cheek, then he gave the boy back to his mother, and they both left. On her way home, Sara was wondering what her neighbour was doing in her husband's office? It was not the kind of place that a simple housewife goes for distraction! She started to put the pieces together and realised that occasionally Torres knew things that happened when he wasn't there, and she always wondered how he had found out, but now everything makes sense! She was the next-door neighbour, she could easily hear things, because it was not like the walls isolated all the sounds completely.

When Sara got home, she knocked on her neighbour's door very gently. She left Jonny playing with some stones on the ground and turned her attention to the task at hand.

Her neighbour opened the door, and it was like she was expecting Sara's visit at any point today. She knew Sara well and she also knew that she liked things sorted. As soon as she opened the door, she said:

"What you want?"

"What do I want?! You bloody cow, I'll tell you what I want, I will kill you." She was so furious, she looked like she really would kill her. Her neighbour was shaking with fear.

"Wait. Wait, Sara."

She admitted that she was occasionally hearing Sara inside her own house and that sometimes when talking to Torres, she let loose one or two things, but sometimes talk is like olives, you never eat just one.

In that instant, Sara's anger grew like a volcano that starts erupting and explodes. She took a look at the boy, saw him playing with some stones on the ground, looked at the woman and slapped the neighbour a few times till her anger started to shrink, and when she cooled down, she whispered:

"If I, was you, I wouldn't talk about this to anyone, because next time the recipe could be much spicier."

The woman looked at her with a face like a big ripe tomato and slammed the door strongly in Sara's face.

After this she took the boy and went inside her house, and he ran to his room to get his favourite car to play, but her mind was a whirlwind.

"Bloody cow, she doesn't even know who she's messing with! Who does she think she is to put her snout where it is not her business? Life would be better if people minded their own business; all this time she was listening to everything that happens here to talk to him and who knows, maybe she told countless others."

Jonny came from his room with the car. "Mammy, look...pi, pi, pi, pi. Look."

She smiled at her son and in ten minutes everything was forgotten, her son was the most important thing ever in her life, not her husband or the stupid cow next door. Cows should be in the cowshed where they belong, and not mixing with real people.

Chapter 6

In the beginning of December 1938, Sara found out that she was pregnant again. She couldn't believe she was back where she once was. One afternoon, Sara, Maria and other people were helping Elizabeth to harvest the olives; the olive Grove only had 24 olives threes, but Elizabeth was a woman who took all types of jobs as long as she could make money, and after she tried to hire people to do the job but for as little money she could pay. Sara and Maria only helped when Elizabeth was short of helpers and had limited time to finish the job, but in those cases both women made their own prices, Elizabeth had to pay what they asked for because there was no escape; it was either pay up or have no helpers. First, they spread some tarpaulin sheets on the ground around the olive tree. After, a man with a long stick shook the olive tree while the others picked up the olives and separated them from the leaves and small branches and gathered the olives in wicker baskets. After the harvesting, the baskets were all put on the cart pushed by a sad donkey and taken to the oil presser. The last journey from the olive Grove was when Elizabeth was carrying all the workers in her cart back to Santarém.

While Sara was helping, she talked to Maria about the pregnancy without anyone hearing her.

"Again, Sara?" Maria asked.

"Tell me about it...it was just what I needed now..."

"What are you going to do Sara? How did you find out...are you feeling sick again?"

"Just a little the other day, but I know I'm pregnant." Saying that, Sara rolled her eyes.

Maria couldn't believe what was happening again to her friend.

"Have you thought about what you are going to do this time? Maria asked.

"Have you forgotten what my life is like? My life is hell and if I have another child, things will get much worse; I'm always struggling to put food on the table, and Torres doesn't give much. You could go and talk to the midwife; see how much she charges this time."

"Are you sure! Why don't you think twice before you make any decisions?"

"Maria, I will do it again. Jonny is enough, I'm struggling most of the time...I can't have this baby! Can't you help me?! Please Maria?"

"I will see what I can do." Maria replied

"Thanks Maria."

They stayed working in the olive Grove till late that afternoon. Jonny was there too playing with little stones, soil, and a little dog, but he kept asking his mum when they could go home. Sara was always very loving and very present for the boy.

When they all finished, Elizabeth was back with the cart. They put the last two buckets with olives on it, and everyone sat in it, except Sara and Jonny who sat in the front seat with Elizabeth.

When they got home, Sara gave Jonny and herself a bath very quickly, and went to finish the dinner that she had left before half done. She gave dinner to Jonny and let him play on the kitchen floor.

That evening when Torres arrived, he sat at the table with Sara but she didn't eat much.

"You, ok?" He asked.

"Yes, I just don't have an appetite."

When he finished dinner he spent some time with Jonny, while Sara cleaned the dishes. Jonny was making lots of cute faces at his daddy; he never stopped talking to daddy. Daddy was so happy to be playing with the boy that he didn't go to the office that evening.

The next day in the afternoon, Maria went to Sara's house and told her about the meeting she had with the midwife. Sara couldn't believe the midwife had increased the price so much, and she didn't have the whole amount of money to do it.

"Sara, maybe this is a sign for you to change your mind...think about it." Maria was saying, but Sara wasn't paying any attention at all...her mind was just spinning around to think of a way to get the money.

"Why is she charging so much? At the moment, there is no way I can get the money. Can you lend me some Maria?"

"Sara, as much as I want to help you, my friend, I can't. At the moment, things are not great, you know this time of the year is difficult. I wish I could help you, even though I do not agree about your decision."

"Maria, I know your opinion, but I have made up my mind...I will sort it, just let me think how.

The next morning when Sara was at the market, she asked Elizabeth if she could lend her money, but the answer was no.

"Sara, now I can't, I am still waiting to receive money from some customers but when I do I need to pay my bills too; you know my money is always on the move. I wish I could help you, but I can't Sara - last month I got a new cart, and my husband doesn't make much money either, so things are a bit tight."

Sara could not get the money to have the abortion, she tried everything she could. So, by the end of January 1939, she thought that it was too late to have it done anyway, so she decided to have the baby.

When she told Torres, he tried to hide it, but she could see that he was pleased with her decision. Slowly, slowly, she started to tell the little boy that he was going to have a sibling. One good thing she had done was that she saved some baby clothes from when Jonny was a baby.

While she was pregnant, Torres only hit her twice, sometimes just a big slap on the face, but hard enough to bust her lips and make her bleed.

By the end of July Sara was huge, and she thought that it might be twins! That thought left her very concerned.

A few times when she was on her own, she thought that was mother nature's punishment because she wanted to have an abortion before, and now she was at risk of having maybe two!

Once she discussed her concerns with Maria, but her friend told her that the problem was Sara eating for two, that's why she was so big.

In the beginning of Summer, Sara was suffering with the extreme heat. Santarém had quite high temperatures, and she couldn't wait to give birth and get it over with. Sometimes after putting Jonny in bed, she sat in his bedroom watching him sleep peacefully and imagining how it will be with the new baby or babies around. Her mind was really messed up. She tried to be calm, but most of the time it was hard dealing with all these thoughts.

Is the baby going to be calm or is it going to cry all the time? Is it going to be another boy or a girl? Is it going to be healthy? So many questions that she did not have the answers to...not yet... but she will soon.

Sara was very organised, and she wanted to prepare everything before the arrival of her new baby...she washed all the baby clothes that she still had from when Jonny was a baby and put all of them in her big drawer.

She had a few blue clothes, that she left aside in case the baby was a girl, but she did not get anything in pink. Having a baby is a sealed envelope; we never know what is inside. The most important thing in her mind was the baby to be perfect without any diseases.

Touching all these little baby clothes, made Sara smile and remember when Jonny was a baby, and since then, too many situations had happened.

Chapter 7

August in Santarém is always very warm, and people try to be out of the streets after lunch because of the heat. It was normal every day to see low clouds of insects; it means the hot weather will continue for the next few days. Some of the people from Santarém during this time of the year like to go to the beach of Nazaré. Most people call it their beach. Nazaré is situated on the silver cost of Portugal, but the beach is quite dangerous because it's on the open Atlantic Ocean; the waves are very strong and not everyone likes to swim there, most of their visitants just like to lie in the sun and get the fresh air from the sea. This place is very famous because of the very fresh fish, especially sardines, and Sara was missing that. The year before, she had spent one week there with Jonny and Torres, because the seaside is wonderful for everybody. This year it will not be possible for them to go and next year, there will be another member of their family joining.

At Sara's house, she was busy trying to organise the very last things before the baby arrives. Jonny was always close to his mum, starting to feel that something was different, but not even for a minute would Sara leave him out when talking about the new baby or organising things in that matter. It was like he had a feeling that soon he will be the big brother and need to share his mother and father with a little person, and Jonny was too close with Sara. Since he can remember, he has been the only one, even the cot that used to be his has been prepared for his brother or sister. But on this specific day, he had been quiet around Sara. She was always very loving to her little man. So far, he was the love of her life and she explained countless times to him everything she thought he understood about the arrival of the baby.

That evening Sara was preparing dinner for her and Torres. While it was being cooked, she gave her little boy his own dinner.

"Dad, Dad." Jonny screamed when his dad came through the door.

"How is my big boy?" Torres asked his son...and the little boy was quite excited to have Dad's attention and was all smiles.

"Jonny when you finish all your food, I have something for you." The boy was moving around in excitement.

Jonny finished all his food and Sara cleaned his mouth with a cloth. Torres had a little book that he was hiding but he pulled it out from one of his pockets.

"Mum, look!" She stood up to put their own dinner on the table while Torres sat on the same chair. He got close to his son, pointed with his finger to the letters of the title of the little book and spelt it to his son, followed by saying, "Snow White."

"Jonny, after I have had my own dinner, I will read the book for you, ok?"

Both parents were having their dinner and suddenly Sara's water broke. She did not panic, she just looked at her husband in case he noticed what had just happened, but he hadn't.

"What are you looking at?" he asked.

"The baby is on its way." Sara continued.

"Why are you saying that?"

"Because my water's just broke, that's why." Torres pushed his chair backwards and peeked under the table.

"Are you in any kind of pain? "

"No…so far I'm good."

"I'm going to call Maria…she will know what to do." Torres said.

"Before you go, just read the book to Jonny."

"And if things get worse?"

"They won't, this whole thing can take hours."

Sara went to clean and change her clothes while Torres was reading the Snow White book to little Jonny, and just before he left them, she was back in the kitchen cleaning everything up. She then prepared Jonny to go to bed.

Half an hour later, Torres was back home saying Maria was organising her things at home including the care of her own son before she could come.

That evening Torres did not go out just in case he needed to take care of Jonny.

Maria arrived close to 11pm and by then, Sara was starting to have some contractions. Torres went to call a woman that always helped with baby births and that he trusted, and so he felt more confident.

It was just after 11.30 pm when Torres and the woman arrived...Sara was getting the contractions closer to one another.

Torres went to check on Jonny and he stayed in his room in the single spare divan.

The birth was developing a bit slow, but Sara was trying to keep calm as much she could. But every time the contractions started, they turned out to be very long and much more painful. The minutes were like hours, she was desperate for the baby to come out, and this agonising delivery to come to an end.

The two women in the room were very concerned. Maria held Sara's hand a few times, and told her to be strong and patient, because it was not long to go now.

The woman who was helping with the delivery, told Sara that her baby had black hair, but she needed Sara to push hard with the next contraction.

She did it a few times, but the result was not the one they expected, and the future mother-to-be was starting to get stressed.

Finally, after an agonising evening and night, Sara delivered a huge baby girl just after 5 am. She was a very big baby, 7kg 800g. Sara was exhausted after that traumatising experience of having given life to such a huge baby. Even so, the first thing she asked was if her baby was perfect.

As soon as she laid her eyes on her new-born daughter, she fell in love, but she did not have the strength to hold her. She was very tired, and her body was still shaking and in pain after this painful experience.

The woman who had just helped deliver the baby girl, was dealing with Sara while Maria was cleaning the new arrival who had opened her little lungs to cry. It had been a very long and difficult night for Sara and for those responsible for the delivery.

"She has good lungs, I can tell." Said Maria, as the baby was crying loudly.

In Jonny's room was Torres, who kept watching his son sleep, but he did not close his eyes for a minute, he was just waiting for a crying baby and finally he heard a very loud cry; at night, every small noise is loud. Torres was anxious to know if it was a girl or another boy, but just by the cry he could guess. His thoughts were that the baby was born. He was waiting for someone to call him to give him the news, but at the same time he knew after the baby has been delivered there were still a few things to be done. He stood up, after a moment he sat on the divan, still waiting...no one was coming to tell him the news, so he decided to go to the kitchen and wait there. He pulled a chair to sit, but in this instant the woman who he brought earlier to help with the delivery opened the door where Sara, Maria and the new-born were and joined him in the kitchen.

The woman looked very tired but pleased; she came close to Torres and said,

"In fifteen years, you need to protect her because she will be devastating boys' hearts."

Torres did not like the joke, but he could assume that he was a father of a girl. He gave a weird look to the woman, but soon he said thank you for all she had done.

"Torres, do you want to meet your daughter?" she said

"Of course, I do; can I go in?"

He came immediately and he could not believe his eyes, his daughter looked like she was one or two months old; she was a very big baby! She did not look at all like a new-born. Because Sara was so big towards the end of pregnancy, Torres once thought that there could be two babies, like Sara, but when they realised that there was only one, a sense of relief invaded their souls.

"Can I hold her?" Torres asked.

Without saying a word, Maria picked up the girl and gave her for Torres to hold.

"It is very nice to meet you my little heart; Welcome to this world; later I will introduce you to your big brother." Torres was so happy to have his daughter in his arms.

"Are you ok?" he asked Sara.

"I never thought I could survive that...she almost killed me... my daughter, my daughter." and saying that, she closed her eyes because there was a tear rolling down her face. Torres saw it but he just ignored it; he was too obsessed with the girl.

Deep down in Sara's heart, she was disappointed to have a girl, she preferred another boy. In so many ways Torres was against women, and she feared one day her daughter could be another victim of his like Sara was.

She wanted to be positive and think that it would never happen to their daughter.

Now they had a boy and a girl, and the only thing Sara wished was for her husband to start to be less violent towards her but at the same time, she knew he would never change, his background was too painful; it left to many stains in his life. Many times, Sara found herself thinking why an intelligent man who reads so many books and newspapers and talks to so many people is so cruel when he hits her. She is his wife, they have everything to be a happy, a wonderful and healthy family; why damage all this?! She felt lots of times that he simply hates having her around; but, why? He was the one who asked her to marry him!

Later that morning, Torres (who had taken the day off) got his son and took him to meet his baby sister. The baby was sleeping; she had just been fed and had a nappy change, and through the cot's railings, little Jonny could see his sister. From the bed Sara was paying attention to her son to see what he had to say.

"My baby sister is too small!" hearing that, Sara smiled. "Her arms are so tiny...so are her hands! Is she going to be small forever Dad?"

"Jonny, you were like your sister, or maybe smaller, and now you are a big boy."

"Dad, when will she play with me?" Torres ruffled his son's hair and smiled.

"Not so soon, son, but she will. One thing Jonny; Now you are the big brother, you need to help me and mum to take good care of her.

"

"Why?" Asked the little boy. Sara (who was looking from her bed) was so proud of her boy, the polite manners really impressed her.

"She is a baby...she needs to grow a bit son before you two can play. Our baby girl is very precious to us all...don't you think, big brother?" said the proud father.

"Oh... I'm the big brother." Jonny said and giggled at the same time.

"Dad, what's her name? Jonny asked.

"Good question son!" Torres said...looking around very thoughtfully. Moments after, he replied to his son while looking at Sara too.

"I think, because our baby girl is so precious for all of us, the perfect name will be Ana, because it means a very beautiful and important being."

Sara didn't say a word about the name; she just smiled at her two men; she liked the name too. The birth of her daughter was so painful for her, but like any other mother in the world, she fell in love with her baby the very first moment she entered this world.

Since the moment Ana moved inside of Sara's womb for the first time, she felt her own heart with a range of strong and positive feelings. With time, she understood that this little life growing inside of her was a unique experience, and as soon as she met her little

Ana, she thanked God for not having money to pay for the abortion before.

At least no one could ever see what is going on in her mind, because in her heart everyone sees; she never hid the feelings for her kids. She had an awful time giving birth to her baby girl, but it's like she almost forgot about it as soon as she held Ana. Mother Nature prepares mother's heart in a very careful way and Sara is no different from other mothers: for their kids, they will do anything at all to protect them from all sorts of danger in this world.

All her emotions were running high, even the very cloudy thoughts of her parents were in her mind; she wished that they could be around to meet both of her kids...but even if they were still alive, Sara's life would have maybe been different. She was very touched the moment she knew about Rosa who died and left a baby son behind. She was the kind of person that likes to help every single child in the world if she could. Seeing her husband talking so smoothly with their son, she thought that having a second child, could be the ingredient they needed to bring Torres to be more loving towards her.

Of course, she did not believe in a miracle but in the back of her mind there was always a possibility for this to happen; she strongly believed that it is never too late for people to change if they want too. In her husband's case, who knows, the only thing she can do is be positive and give it time to backup these thoughts.

The next day Sara wanted to get on with her life, but things were not quite the way she wanted them to be; she couldn't walk without feeling very sore. She knew things needed to be taken slowly but she had no patience to wait to get better.

Her friend Maria came over with her son in the afternoon. While the two boys were playing, she helped Sara with a few chores at home.

Sara was very independent and did not want to be a burden to anyone; she did not have time to be unwell and never complained about not feeling well despite her situation being related to her labour. Between her two kids, husband, and house, she kept herself busy enough. She was slowly explaining things to Jonny because he was their only child for a while and now, he started to be a bit jealous of his baby sister. Babies take up a lot of mum's time in the first few months after being born. Two or three times he asked mum if they are going to keep the little baby. His mum explained to him endless times that Ana was part of their family, and now it's mum, dad, him, and his sister. Sara caught Jonny sneaking at the new baby and through the cot rails, he was touching her little fingers. Sara was always very loving and caring towards him and the little one. Torres was also very loving with his son, explaining that Ana was their little Jesus. Two weeks later Jonny was calmer about the new arrival and his mother was clearly better. Every morning, the first thing Jonny did when seeing his sister was to ask why she was still small and not big enough to play with him, every time Sara answered that she needs time to grow and she would, smiling at him.

Exactly one month after Sara had her daughter, Torres hit her again because she was defending their sons' belongings, something that should be his.

Sara had found out that Rosa (Jonny's biological mother) had a very expensive gold chain and a beautiful portrait of herself, and that should be Jonny's. Sara went to see Maria, 'Jonny's grandma' and asked for the gold chain and the portrait of Rosa that used to be on the wall at home.

"Maria, I believe Rosa had a gold chain and a portrait of herself and I think those things should be for my boy. He will never know his real mother, but it is very important if at least he has something that was hers."

Maria felt so angry when she was confronted by Sara.

"I haven't, I don't know who told you, but you are wrong. I don't have anything."

Sara did not believe her, but there was nothing she could do. That day at home, she explained to Torres that it wasn't fair that Maria kept some belongings that should be Jonny's. Torres looked at her and said:

"That's true, but I don't think she will give it to Jonny, she is very selfish, and you better forget about it."

"Forget it? No, she needs to give it back to our boy! Don't you think that it is bad enough that he is never going to meet his mum? At least he can have things that were hers." Sara said.

"Keep out, I don't want to hear anything about it anymore." Torres said in an aggressive way.

"You are his father; don't you think that you should interfere to have back what belongs to Jonny? One day, he will want to have what was his mother's; that is why we need to have all those things for his future! Or are you afraid of his grandmother?"

As soon as Torres heard that, he went completely crazy and he pulled the belt from his trousers, and he hit her everywhere. He was behaving like a monster. Jonny was so scared and crying that he went to hide under his bed. The poor child, so small and living in a home where his mother was being constantly hit by his father.

At 3 years old, Jonny started to be afraid of his dad and every time dad hit mum, little Jonny went and hid somewhere and cried softly. In his mind, he was afraid dad could hit him too, because mum was big, bigger than dad, but this didn't stop dad from hitting her.

Torres would only stop hitting her when he had discharged his nerves, like an enraged animal. By then, Sara had blood coming from her face and lots of red marks were left from the belt.

As soon as he finished, he left home, and she stood up, cleaned herself and went to find her son.

"Jonny where are you sweetheart... come, do you want to help me with your sister?"

As soon as she said that, he came from under his bed sobbing and hugged his mother.

"Sweetheart, I don't want to see your beautiful eyes crying...you are a big boy."

Sara took Jonny in her arms and cherished him, while she closed her own eyes, thinking about what just had happened.

Inside her head was this thought...Why doesn't he get lost...we don't need him...we will be so much happier without him. What a bloody life I have here. Why is the answer he always has for everything including me, violence?

There are so many good people who die, and this devil doesn't seem to be any close to disappearing.

Sometimes it was hard for Sara to keep leaving and hiding all her suffering with this monster.

Chapter 8

World War 2 had just started and Portugal managed to stay out of the war in a status of "inactive ally". The Portuguese Government had a 550-year-old Anglo Portuguese Alliance that remained untouched and because the British government did not ask for Portuguese help, Portugal could very well remain a neutral country like it did.

As Hitler swept across Europe, Portugal became one of their escape routes, and only in 1944 was a military agreement signed to give USA the right to establish a military base in the Azores, called "Santa Maria das Lages".

The west end in central Lisbon was the nest of espionage; Germans, English and French all used to meet at some bars in the evenings. At the same time, Portugal was living a dictatorship, and Salazar (the Portuguese president) once told the people,

"I can keep you out of war, but I can't keep you away from hunger."

However, Portugal's contribution to the WW2 was with food, so people in the country had less, but with Salazar they never had enough of anything. His government was called the 'new state' and the safes were full of gold, but the people did not have enough food to eat or the right to education.

The Estado Novo ('New state') Salazar and Marcello Caetano were, together, the longest authoritarian regime in Western Europe during the (XX) 20th century.

During WW2, very often people were smuggling food into the country, and Sara was one of those people. Lots of times, she went in the very early hours in the morning, through the fields of vineyards to get some food to feed her family.

It was hard for everyone, every day it was a struggle to get enough food, but everyone was doing everything they could to keep some food on the table.

Ana loved to eat potatoes, but her mother couldn't find them easily, so she cried. It was hard for everyone. At least they didn't need to worry about the bombs being dropped, people being killed like flies like in the other European countries. They were living hell. So far, this century has been disgraceful, so many people died and suffered just because of the desire of one person. How could just one man cause so much pain between men, women, and children of all ages. So many lives ended before their time, just because of a maniac man who thought about nothing but power.

When the war ended, Jonny was 9 and his sister was 6 years old, they were very close siblings, but Jonny was more shy and Ana was more outgoing, he was always the worrier. When other kids were naughty to him when playing in the street, it was always Ana who came and sorted things out.

Ana always took her brother's side because she knew he was always a peaceful soul and every time other kids saw her bite her own lips, they knew it was going to be a blow.

One day, Jonny was playing football outside with other kids and suddenly one of the older boys got close to Jonny and started to look at him with an intimidating look. Jonny started to feel a bit uncomfortable, but he didn't want to ask the other boy what was going on. But the other boy didn't take long to make his point. He turned to the other kids, laughing...suddenly he turned again to Jonny.

"Why don't you have a mother, Jonny?"

The boy was so desperate to be acknowledged, that even inflicting pain on someone seemed a small victory over his insignificance!

Jonny looked at him laughing and replied,

"Are you stupid or what? Of course, I have a mother and you know her, you silly!"

"Sara is your stepmother not your mother; you are the stupid one. You look like the mummy's baby, but in this case, the stepmother's baby." The boy laughed again.

"You don't know what you're talking about, why are you saying that?!"

"It's true, you are not Sara's son, you never have been!"

Jonny started to have tears in his eyes, and he just left the boys game and went home.

His mind was travelling fast. It was like his world was collapsing; his thoughts were all messed up. Maybe it isn't true, because if it were, mother would have already told me! Maybe my friend is confused, maybe it is Ana who is not my mother's daughter. My mother is always softer to me than to her! Maybe none of us are mother's kids!

There were too many maybes in his little mind, but there was one thing he wanted to do: he needed to ask his mother about it.

There was not long to go now until he found out the truth, but one thing was for sure: If the boy lied, he wouldn't want to be in his shoes, because his sister will sort him out. He will never forget the drubbing she will give to him. Thinking that, he smiled through the tears that were already coming down his face.

As soon as he got home, Ana saw him crying and asked,

"Who made you cry, Jonny? Tell me and I will sort them out! Go on, tell me."

And saying that, Ana made the position of a boxer with her tongue halfway out.

"No one... where is mother?" he was very sad and confused, but deep down inside he thought it was just kids being kids.

"You are banana, no one cries without a reason, unless you are a baby, and that I know you are not. Tell me, go on, I need to know if I still have the strength to give a good beating to someone". And saying that, there she was with the boxer position, again.

"Stop Ana, stop!" He shouted.

Sara was in another room of the house and after she heard him, she approached them in the kitchen. Normally in their house the kitchen was always the meeting room and the living area.

"What is the matter Jonny? What is going on, who made you cry, son?"

"One of the boys told me that you are not my mother, he said you are my stepmother. This is a lie, isn't it mother?" Hearing that Sara, opened her eyes in surprise; she wasn't expecting this question from her son.

"Who told you that son?"

"I was playing with the boys and one of them told me"

"Who was he, son?"

"Salvador."

"Salvador, the deeply stinky one?"

"Yes mother ".

"Come here son, sit here with me." Sara sat with her two kids, and she picked up a cloth and wiped Jonny's face.

"You don't need to cry son, when there is a problem, we solve them and like we used to say, you take the bull by its horns and get things solved."

Ana was looking at her mother with her dark, wild eyes open and with an intriguing face. At only six years old, she had a very strong personality that scared all kids her age and above.

"My darling, I was waiting until you were a little older, but since someone has already hit their tongues with their teeth, I will tell you the truth.

Jonny, my son, you didn't come from the inside of my tummy, but you came from the inside of my heart."

Immediately Jonny asked,

"What does that mean, Mother? Am I your son or not?"

"It means Jonny… that ………that you didn't live inside mum's belly before you were born, but as soon as you were born you started to be a permanent resident of my heart."

"And Ana?" He asked quickly.

"Your sister was in my belly before she was born, and after she was a permanent resident of my heart too sweetheart." After saying everything, Sara cuddled the two children, hugging them and kissing them with the affection and love that only mothers know.

"Mother, are you going to love me forever?" Jonny asked.

"Forever and always, both of you, you silly, you can't get rid of me." And saying that, she laughed.

They all smiled after that, but after Jonny left Ana was a bit grumpy.

"What's the matter Ana?"

"That's why you never get cross with him, because he doesn't have a real mother and you feel sorry for him."

"I'm the mother of both of you, silly! "

"But I was the one who lived in your tummy..."

"Yes, you are right...but what is the problem, Ana; I love you both."

"You are always softer with him than with me."

"You are more...disobedient, Ana."

"I'm not...dad laughs, he likes me being disobedient like you say."

"Ana, go outside and play with your friends."

Ana did what her mother said but clearly, she was upset with it, the fact that Jonny did not have his real mother made Sara much more compassionate with him, and for her daughter this was confusing.

Chapter 9

One day Sara bought a little duck in the market, but the purpose of
the duck was to be fattened and then go to the pan, making a
delicious meal, but her kids spent lots of time playing with the duck,

and they got really attached to him. They used to spend hours playing with the duck and sometimes they used to dress the duck, and they baptised him with a funny name. They put the duck inside a basket, they picked up a mug with water and slowly dropped the water on top of the duck's head while attributing the name Pipes. Every time the animal pooed the floor, Ana and Jonny used to clean it quickly before Sara saw it. The poor animal understood the love both kids had for him. Every time the kids went out to go somewhere, the duck was like a dog following them everywhere. The duck was growing fast, and it was fun for everyone to see him. Sometimes, when going out, he was wearing a head scarf. The kids felt really annoyed when the neighbour's saw them with Pipes and made jokes like 'roast duck is good', or 'duck rice is wonderful'; they picked up Pipes immediately and ran home, afraid of someone stealing him from them. More than once they asked Sara if they could sleep with Pipes in their bed, but she always said 'no, don't you dare'. Pipes had a very loving lifestyle, and he knew when they were calling him.

Jonny and Ana used to have school in the morning, Monday to Friday from 8am to 1pm. They always went and returned together.

As soon as they got home, the first thing they did was to go to see their protégé very briefly before lunch.

The days passed by, and the poor duck grew into a bigger one. It was so lovely to see the children playing with it, but Sara was not quite happy about it. Since she got the duck, she thought it was not a god idea for the kids to get so close to it and treat it like a younger sibling, but at the same time she was enjoying seeing them so dedicated instead of doing naughty stuff.

Sara always struggled for Torres to give her money to do some shopping, and she was furious because he always managed to help others no matter what. One day things got worse, and she did not have anything to cook for her family. One morning after the kids left for school, she decided to kill Pipes and cook it for their lunch. She made roast duck with potatoes, and the smell of it travelled down road. She was really concerned about how the children would take the news about their friend, but she needed to feed her family; that's why she got the duck in the first place and they must understand that they couldn't continue to keep such a big duck at home.

Around 1.20pm, Jonny and Ana were coming home from school when the smell of the food got in through their noses and made them run around to see which one got home first. They wanted to check on Pipes, but their mother made them go and wash their hands and go straight to the table.

"Mother, mother can we have lunch, it smells so nice! Yummy!" Ana said.

"Let's just wait for your father first."

"I think we could see Pipes before father arrives." Ana said.

"No, you two stay where you are."

Torres arrived at 1.25pm, went to wash his hands and finally father and kids sat around the table while Sara opened the oven to bring the food. As soon as she put the food on the table, the kids looked to each other as they realised it was Pipes on the oven tray.

Both kids started to cry.

"Mother, what have you done?" Ana asked through her loud sobs.

Their mother said she was sorry for their friend, but she didn't have anything else to cook, and the duck was a good option, that is why she killed it, but the kids were really upset and would not stop crying.

Torres looked at everyone around the table, but the crying of the children was really upsetting, and he lost his appetite.

He put his elbows on the table with his face between his hands, but less than 15 seconds later, he stood up, went around the table, and grabbed Sara by her hair. He threw her on the floor, kicked her everywhere and slapped her hard on the face. She started bleeding immediately from her lips and nose. Still holding her by her hair, he lifted her from the floor, and threw her back down again. He then left, slamming the front door behind him, leaving Jonny watching his back with terror.

Everywhere in her body ached, not to mention the fact that there was blood everywhere, from her mouth and nose.

The kids became frozen upon such a situation, but after this scene Sara stood up, went to wash her face, and cleaned herself up. Then, she returned to the kitchen, picked up the duck and hit both of her children with the duck till there was no more duck left. When she finished, she said,

"You didn't eat it one way, but you did in another!"

Then she asked Ana to help her clean the kitchen. It was complete silence. Jonny was sat facing the floor looking very sad and completely dirty. Ana was the same. There was roast duck all over the kids.

A while later, Sara felt so bad about it that she caressed both kids, putting each one of them sitting on one of her legs, and in the end, they all sang together. It was her way to make up for hitting her kids with the duck and hurting them psychologically as well. It was hard to feed the family when there was not enough food to do so.

That evening, when the father of the house came, he had brought two books for the kids; when he left earlier on, he felt so sad for his kids that he wanted to make it up for them, that's why he thought the book was a good surprise. Jonny's book was a story about a boy who liked adventures in the woods; Ana's was about a princess, but when Torres gave the book to his daughter, she turned it down. At only six years old, she told her father that she was very sad for what he did to her mother earlier on.

"Dad, me and my brother are very sad for what mum did to our friend, but hitting mum? It was worse. You shouldn't have done it."

"Little heart, this is not a conversation for you to have, ok?"

"Okay, but I won't have the book." The little one said.

The next day, Sara had bruises all over her face, arms and on other parts of her body. She avoided going out, and having neighbours comment about her injuries, not just because of her, but also for her kids' sake. It was already so hard for them to see Torres hitting her, so she wanted to spare her kids the pain of hearing others talking about it. She asked Jonny to go to the shop to get some rice. He did, but when he came home, he told his mother,

"Mother, I know you are ashamed to go out."

"What? "

"You look very..." He was trying to get the right words without hurting mother's feelings. "All these marks on your face, everybody can see that you have been hit by dad again."

"Jonny, this is nothing son, don't worry about it...go and play with your friends."

"You know that I love you mother but...since I am alive, I see father hit you. I used to be scared but not anymore." Sara was paying much attention to her son; she wanted him to talk to her about what was going on in his mind.

"I know he only hits you, not me or Ana...but I want him to stop. Mother, when I grow up, I will take you away from him, I promise."

"Son don't worry about it. When you grow, you will have a very exciting life, full of joy and happiness, just wait and see." Sara said.

She was really surprised the way her son talked to her; he was very young, but this doesn't invalidate him expressing his feelings about the way his father treated his mother. Jonny doesn't remember, but since the very first time he saw his dad hitting his mum, he hides. Time after time, this situation left him with trauma. Occasionally during the night, Jonny has nightmares and wakes up screaming. Both parents know why. Sara tries to help in all ways she can, but she cannot do anything about the only thing that really hurts her son.

Along the way, Torres always finds a way to keep hurting his wife, and she cannot see a way of finishing this suffering. Very often, she thinks maybe one day when both kids grow, she can leave for good and put all the suffering behind her. Not completely as he will always be connected to her because of the children, but they can have separate lives.

Since Sara married Torres, her life had been very hard. She knew marriage was a sealed envelope, but she never thought in a million years that her life would be that crazy. There was nothing she could do; she loved her kids so much and because of that she was still living with her husband. She knew about other women being hit by their husbands but none of them suffered the way she did.

Sometimes at night, just before she went to bed, she used to look up and ask God to help her and give her the strength to keep going. She thought many times if one day Torres got out of her life, she would never again want another man in her life. Her desire was to settle her kids in life and for her to have peace. Often, she thought her husband - like many other men - only wanted to get married to have an employee at home to do all the work without getting paid. Women can do all the house chores, have kids and be available for them to have sex every time their husbands want. Sara knew many women that were only slaves for their husband's needs, nothing else. She had a friend, a very rich lady, who one day confided a secret to her; she had been married for a very long time, but she was still a virgin because her husband did not like women and never touched her, but he needed to keep up appearances to avoid being criticised. Every weekend, he used to go to Lisbon to meet other men with the same taste. Women are always the victims of abuse by their husbands; men have used and abused women in so many ways to suit and cover up for themselves.

One afternoon, Sara was talking to Maria, and she told her that sometimes she wishes that a strong wind come and take Torres away forever to another planet, so she could live in peace with her children.

"I don't know how much more I can take! If it wasn't for respecting my Jonny and Ana, I think I would have already given him a punch in the face till I can empty the anger I have got inside of me. I love my children so much and we could be all so happy!"

Maria noticed the anger in Sara's eyes when she said it, but she also knew that Sara loved her children unconditionally and she would never do anything; this was her anger talking. Her beloved friend has a life as Torres' punch bag just because she felt sorry for poor Jonny when she saw him at three months old. Sometimes it is better to be aware of the situation.

"What the eyes do not see, the heart does not feel".

"Sara, you know if one day you do that, he will kill you. I think you should talk to him and bring your kids here; you can stay as long as you want, and you can help me and my garden is big enough for them and my son to play." When Maria said that, her friend smiled at her.

"You know he will never let me take the children, he is a bull, sometimes God takes good people, and he should really take people like this bastard. What makes me angry is that he is so nice to other people and at home he is always so difficult and bad towards me!"

Maria didn't recognise her friend anymore; she was a completely different person from the one who arrived a few years back in Santarém, a very polite young woman full of dreams to live for, and now a tough angry woman.

Normally Sara is a great woman, and she has lots of friends, she never criticised anyone, she is the kind of person that everyone likes to have as a friend, but the pain she carries in her chest is immense and she deserved to have a peaceful life. She never talked about her husband to anyone else apart from Maria.

Sara was struggling for the freedom of peace, she sometimes felt like a prisoner of love, for her two kids; they are the reason why she keeps on with her monstrous husband. Maria knew her friend very well and she also knew if it weren't for the kids, with just one punch, Sara could give Torres a real lesson. After she had her talk with Maria, Sara, left and in many ways, she was feeling better after venting. It's always good to talk to someone, even if that means going back to her hell of a life after. The question that always strikes in her mind was...When is all this going to end...How many years I do I still have to carry on like this... Will I one day have peace? Or shall I die one day without knowing what peace is? How long could I cope with being beaten?

To many questions without answers, the only question she knew the answer to was that she hated her husband. In Sara's, eyes the only good thing Torres did was his two kids; it was his only good job. She prayed every day for neither of the kids to be like their dad when they grow up. She was afraid all the violence at home caused by her husband could damage Jonny and Ana's personalities. Torres had a nasty childhood. Her own kids have a good childhood apart from the way their dad treats their mum, and they are good kids. Sara always defended the idea that it is very important to have positive thoughts and do our best to keep children happy; happy Children will make good, adults.

That evening, at bedtime, she went to check on her kids just before they went to bed. When she kissed Jonny good night, he looked at his mum with a cosy look and spoke.

"Mother are you going to be, ok?"

"What do you mean son?"

"Is dad going to hit you again?"

"No Jonny, he won't. I don't want you to worry about it. Have a sweet dream...ok?"

"Mother...don't let dad hurt you!"

"Jonny son, do not worry...no one is going to hurt me...you just sleep darling." Saying that, she kissed him good night, turned the light off and headed to the bathroom to prepare herself to go to bed too.

As she entered her bedroom, Torres was already in bed reading. He looked at her over his glasses. She noticed but she didn't care, she only went to bed with him because it was her duty as his wife, but she did not feel happy about it. But there is no other option, than to sleep with him. She preferred to sleep with animals, in a farm than sharing the bed with this bastard.

She always put on a brave face for Ana and Jonny to not notice, showing them a happy life, even when she is feeling sick about her life. She had so much energy to live a full life with the kids. Many times, when at home alone, she had these wonderful daydreams of living in Coimbra where she was brought up by her sister, with Ana and Jonny having a big house with a garden for them to have their friend's over. More than once, she thought about it and even the fact that if her kids want to study, Coimbra had a much wider range of schools and Universities. Coimbra university was the oldest University in Europe. Sara always loved Coimbra: its history, fado and the life of their famous students. All of this was a faraway dream that will never happen.

One Friday evening when all the family was having dinner, Torres invited them to have lunch the next day in Almeirim. Sara asked immediately if there is any special occasion for it, but her husband just said that he wanted to take them to eat the stone soup. Jonny and Ana looked to one another with their eyes wide open and laughed.

"Stone soup?!!! Real stones dad?"

"Not stones, it is just one stone - a real one - in each pan, and no, no one eats the stone".

"Why do they call the soup the 'stone soup' then! I don't think I want to eat that; it sounds gross."

Father explained that there was a very old legend behind the famous soup.

"The stone soup has always been associated with the Legend of a monk, a kind of priest that didn't have much to eat and one morning, he had an idea to make a delicious soup with a stone! After thinking very well, he had a brilliant idea, and without wasting anymore time, he started his journey to some small villages. Every time he tried to convince the villagers to help him make the stone soup, he didn't have much luck; no one believed him, but he never gave up.

One day, he arrives at one locality, "Almeirim", tired and with his belly signalling it was time to eat, he knocks on a farmer's door, showing a stone, saying that he would like to make a soup with it. Incredulous, the owners ask

"With that stone? We want to see that; how is it possible?"

That was what the monk wanted to hear. He washed the stone very well and asked for a cauldron with a little water."

"Dad, what is a cauldron?" asked Ana.

"It is a big iron pan with 3 legs that people used to cook at a fire". Torres explained to his kids.

Torres continued with his story:

"Only with this stone and nothing else?" The villagers asked.

"No, the monk said and to make it better, I should put a little drizzle of olive oil and let me put it there in that fire. The villagers were paying so much attention to this recipe.

Always asking for the necessary condiments, the monk puts his hosts in a constant bustle:

"Now some meat. It could be different ones: pork beef, chicken, a little bit of the different chorizo you have. Please get me some beans, potatoes, coriander, ... etc, etc.

In the meantime, the villagers were concerned because they had never heard before about a mixture of so many different ingredients all in the same cauldron, but within a very short space of time the cauldron starts to boil and let out a delicious aroma.

"Hmmm, smells good! You are a good cook."

"Everybody likes that amazing soup." Saying that, the monk smiled at the villagers, making everybody smile, not telling the real story behind the whole thing.

After the soup was cooked, the monk brought it to the wooden table and all of them ate some. The owners of the house were now looking very happy, but at the same time very suspicious. "What about the stone?"

The monk replies

"The stone will be washed, and I will take it with me again for the next soup!" And saying that, he left happy and full after a delicious meal. The villagers looked to one another, and they spread the news about the stone soup throughout their village neighbourhood, Almeirim. And this soup, children, is the welcome card of the city; all over Portugal when people talked about the stone soup, they all know the place to have it is Almeirim.

"That's why kids, when anyone talks about Almeirim they always associate it with the famous stone soup." Dad explained.

"Dad what a nice story! Is our soup tomorrow going to have the monk stone? Jonny asked.

"You are so silly Jonny; didn't you pay attention? The monk took it with him! Duh!" Ana added waving her hand across her eyes, meaning her brother was nuts.

"Have you got more stories Dad, real ones?" Jonny asked.

"Don't think I remember any, but I can get you a book about this legend son."

"And for me dad, you are not going to give me one?" Ana asked. "

"Do you want one too?"

"Yes, but can it have other stories, because I already know the soup one." Torres looked at his daughter and smiled; she was so spontaneous about it, and there is no need to read about something that she already knew.

Torres always liked to give books to his kids according to their own age. He didn't want them to believe in Father Christmas, his kids were brought up knowing the truth about life. Dreams, in Torres's view, are always good if you are in bed sleeping, not in real life. He believes people need to keep their feet on the ground because if not, when they wake the fall will be tough. He normally answered all the questions that Ana and Jonny asked, even when they are about grown-ups; in this case he tells them. "You need to grow a bit more and then I will explain. He was a very intelligent man and a good father, but as a husband he was a flop.

Ana was little but her own personality was growing to be like her dad. All the kids in the street and her own brother feared her; they even called her a rattle mulatto, because she had dark eyes and long black hair always with two plaits with bows at the ends. More than once, her brother was playing with other boys in the street with tiny marbles, and at certain times all his marbles disappeared.

Seeing her brother crying, Ana started to bite her own lips and ran to the other boys to get the marbles back to her brother. As soon as the other children saw Ana, they panicked, leaving the marbles behind and shouting.

"It's the rattle mulatto, let's run!" And they ran fast, otherwise Ana would bite their ears, as she often does.

The children were very excited about going to eat the famous stone soup the next day; it was something that made them especially excited.

The next day, Sara prepared the clothes for Ana and Jonny to wear (they all had special ones for Sunday, but because it is a special day out, they are allowed to wear them). All of them went to have the famous soup. It was not every day they went to a restaurant, that's why the kids were over the moon; it was something different from the routine of every day.

When they all got to the restaurant, Torres was walking in front followed by Jonny, Ana, and Sara. Ana was walking very smart, looking at other kids in the restaurant and every time they looked at her she stuck out her tongue. Lucky her parents didn't see it - only Jonny did but she made a scary face to him, and he just kept quiet. The waiter showed them a table for four. They all sat, and Torres ordered the soup.

"Dad, are we all just eating soup?" Jonny asked.

"Son, we start with stone soup, after that if you still have space in your stomach, we always can order something else, Ok?"

The kids, especially Jonny, found the soup very strong; it was nothing compared to the soup Sara made at home. The meat they used to make that soup (in Sara's opinion) was enough to feed her family for a week; though she loved it, she was a good fork, meaning a good eater.

"I'm so full, I can't eat more" Jonny said.

"If you do not want to eat more, don't! I think you have had enough son!" Torres said.

But Ana thought quite the opposite:

"But I'm not finished yet, this soup is so delicious; can I have some more, please?

"Yes, Ana, you can have a little more, I can see that you are enjoying it, but don't eat till you get sick, right little heart?

"Yes dad, but don't worry, I still have lots of space in my stomach! Can I have a desert after?" Torres and Sara smiled at her.

"The way you are eating, I'm assuming that you are not going to have dinner this evening, am I right?" Torres said.

"No, you are not dad...this is delicious."

During the lunch, their daughter was the one talking more, but at one point Jonny turned to his dad.

"Dad, I want to learn English." Dad stopped eating, cleaned his mouth with a serviette and replied to Jonny with another answer.

"Where has this idea come from Jonny? "

"I want to learn and when I grow up, I want go to England!"

Ana looked at his brother and said,

"You don't like to live with us?"

"I do...but I want to go and see places, I want to travel."

"What's wrong with Santarém?" she teased.

"Little heart, this is between your brother and me, ok? Just let him talk.

"I know you learnt French by yourself, but English is much more difficult. I would really like to learn it if you let me."

"Of course, son...the other day I made some covers for a few books for an English lady. She is a teacher; she lives near the sun doors. I will ask her if she can help you. I can't promise anything Jonny - you need to wait. If we are not lucky with her, we will find another option. It is very important not to give up on learning... when we educate ourselves, we will never be left out of a conversation, we automatically understand lots of things around us, learning is always the most challenging thing we can achieve. I'm feeling very proud of you son."

When they got home, Torres went to his office like he always did; he liked to be surrounded by books and he loved his job. The kids went to play with their friends and Sara sat outside of her front garden watching them. The rest of the day was nice and peaceful.

Almost two weeks later, Torres had good news for his son regarding the English teacher; he was able to learn the language with a proper teacher. That day when he told Jonny, he was very happy about it.

The only concern Sara had was about the money they were going to pay for each lesson. It was supposed to be one a week, but Torres was the one organising the payments - at least it was one less concern for Sara.

As soon as Jonny started his English lessons, he became a bit snobby, and Ana made fun of him, but they always were like that.

Chapter 10

The years passed, the kids were growing up and Sara continued to be hit by her husband, not so often, but always with the same brutality, leaving her bleeding and with bruises all over.

Ana became a beautiful young lady, not too tall, sometimes a little overweight, with dark eyes like her father, and a great personality. Everyone liked her and admired her because of her way of talking, to people. She always knew how to give advice when someone needed it but at the same time, she was a little bit bossy. She wasn't the mulatto anymore; she had cut a bit off her long hair, and she was not the girl that used to bite others ears. She was young but quite mature, loved her father very much, but did not like it when he hit her mother. More than once, she left him aware that he shouldn't do that because he knew Sara wouldn't react to him in respect for her and her brother, because if Sara did, she will kill him. Torres did not like his daughter talking to him about it, but he respected her.

Jonny had dark hair like his sister, but he was vain. The first time he wore a watch, he was showing off to everybody. When he was walking down the streets, he would just pull his sleeve up a bit, for strangers to see his new watch. He was always wearing a suit and ultra-shiny shoes, but he didn't like to have much responsibility about anything- something that annoyed his sister quite a bit, not just because of him but because Sara always had an excuse for him.

Torres didn't get along with his son much, they always had different views about most of their subjects - Jonny liked to do things his own way, thinking he always knows best, even when (by his own young age) he could not have experienced enough to think he was right and have an opinion the way he has. But he respected his father; he didn't have another choice. Maybe because since he was very young, he saw how hard his father hit his mother, countless times he saw Sara really hurt and bleeding. Jonny always thought about his dad as a communist. That made him really sad, but Jonny never had the guts to stand up to his dad the way his sister did, because he was afraid that he can be hit too, like his mum.

Ana was completely different from her brother, she always had answers for everything, she was very bossy but at the same time she was a very responsible young woman. She always had good taste to dress, not to be overdressed and always with a nice hair style. Very often she asked for her mother's opinion when buying some fabric to make dresses. She learnt (by herself) how to do it because she wanted to be fashionable.

Ana was without doubt daddy's favourite kid, but she liked both parents the same way. She still felt more confident and comfortable talking to her mother rather than her father.

Ana had become Sara's best friend and she felt very proud of her daughter for that.

When Ana left school, she started to work straight away in a shop. Her father asked her if she wouldn't consider studying a bit longer, but she declined his idea.

The shop was a big one that sold everything for the house: bed linen, towels, pans, dishes etc.

Their principal customers were mother's buying trousers for their daughter's. When girls reach their teenage years, mothers get them a kind of wooden baú (chest) to store everything they may need for when they get married. All mothers collect things they keep safe till their daughter's get married. There were some customers that had an open account so every month, they got something different for the baú.

In the beginning, Ana had to learn to deal with customers and negotiate. It was a challenge; she liked to learn new things; she was a quick learner. She started to help more at home too and her responsibilities started to grow. She went to the shoe shop, and she opened an account with them so every time she needed shoes for her or her mother, she went there and bought them. Every month - after she received her wages - she went there and paid the bill. She was never late, and it was a good way to get organised and deal with her own money, making it last till she receives the next salary. Ana's parents always taught her and her brother to be organised with their money, and never leave debts behind because if they do, they cannot control it anymore and things will grow like a snowball. But so far, she learned very well about it, something that can't be said about Jonny.

Jonny was a very different person and every penny he earned he spent with friends. Every month was the same: before the end of the month, he was without money. He also had a job in a hardware store, but he didn't like it, he was just getting experience working and then he wanted to jump to something more interesting.

Sara was lenient; she never criticised her son, but Ana was different - she nagged him. Sara was more tolerant than might be expected. Jonny was three years older than his sister, but it was her who had to pay for him to have nice clothes and shoes.

Ana told her mother lots of times that it was not right that she had to pay for her brother, but Sara always told her that it was nice of her to be helping her brother, because men need women to take care of them the right way.

Since always, Sara had felt sorry for Jonny not to have had his real mother and that is why most of the time she was not hard on him. This worked many years ago, when Ana was little, but not anymore. Both kids were old enough to know what was right or wrong, and Ana had the impression that her brother was taking advantage of the situation. When they were both kids, sometimes Ana was a little jealous of him, but that was not the case now; now she just wanted

.

her brother to take full responsibility for his own actions. The fact of him being a boy was always like a premium because he had the freedom that she will never have. He could go out with his friends at the weekend, no one asked him for details as long he was back in time for meals; with Ana it was a completely different story because she was a girl.

But she did not mind it, the only thing that annoyed her was his lack of control over his money because in the end she was left having to pay for him.

He had become a very handsome young man but a bit snobby too and sometimes when walking through the city, others could see it. He did not always talk with people that saw him grow through the years since he was a baby. In his own view he felt too important to be living in a place like Santarém, maybe if he was living in a big city full of life and excitement, he wouldn't be so snobbish.

Most of times when going out he had the looks of a film star from Hollywood, always immaculately dressed with shiny shoes. All the girls were a bit crazy and nuts for him, he only enjoyed being a star. In the end he had no intention of getting a girlfriend from there; he wanted someone at his own level. Lots of times Ana made fun of him, because of his posture and the way he was so...stuck up. He did not care much about her opinion, so he did not want to change, and his sister laughed so much every time Jonny was walking all very stuck up, and Clementino turned up around the corner and her brother to avoid getting embarrassed took a different way, just not to be seen with him, but Clementino understood, still he always waved to Jonny which made him furious.

Clementino was a very typical and popular figure of the city, and when he was younger, he worked in a famous theatre in Lisbon as a dancer, but after he became older, he moved to Santarém and started working as a cleaner for some very wealthy ladies and they loved his work. Clementino dressed and used makeup like a woman - and he was an extremely polite, caring, and friendly person. At the time there was a lot of prejudice from certain people. Clementino felt he was a woman in a man's body and a lot of people did not understand that and made fun of him, but then these people heard what they didn't want to. Like we say in Portuguese, they heard what the devil doesn't want to hear.

Every time Clementino crossed Ana's way, they always talked very happily and at the end he always sent his love for her family. She never felt embarrassed by him; Ana always found him to be a very polite, intelligent, and pleasant person. More than once, she gave him makeup as a present - something that he loved.

Sara had a good friendship with Clementino too, and many times he opened up to her the way he never did to anyone else, and she was always very supportive of him. Sara never criticised his way of being. She always said, what is important is what is going on in people's hearts and minds. What really matters in life is how people behave towards others, we do not need to agree on how people live their own lives as long as they respect us. These were Sara's words to her kids many times, words that never had a place in her son's mind, but even so, she never gave up on her son to help him be Clementino's friend.

Sara was very different from most of the people in the city; she never took a single minute to talk about anyone's life and she taught her children to do the same. She always said that we should never criticise anyone because we all have glass roofs. It means that we are all started but not finished, and in this life, anything can happen, life is full of surprises, some good, bad, or worse.

Clementino liked Sara very much because she was always straight with him and very honest, and never criticised him.

Once, he went to her house and he knocked on the door. When she answered, he presented her with a little paper box with the most traditional cakes from the city.

"Clementino they are so delicious! You brought so many!" she exclaimed.

"Sara darling, I'm glad you like it! It's for the kids and Torres too... make some tea and we can sit and chat for a bit!"

He brought some pampilhos, arrepiados and celestes.

The pampilho is a traditional and very popular cake from Santarém.

Its filling is made of custard and cinnamon, and its shape was made in honour of the Campinos {a man on horseback} since its name and shape are related to the long stick used by them to lead the cattle. They always wear green hats with a red stripe - this symbolises the Portuguese flag - and red vests with navy knee-length shorts. They also have white socks with black shoes. They always have a spear as this symbolises their role.

Arrepiados were created in the monastery of Almoster, Santarém founded in 1289 by a nun named Bernarda.

Celestes were also created by the nuns, from the "Convent of Santa Clara in Santarém" but the name of the nun or nuns who invented them is unknown.

But an old story originating in Almoster tells us that the rivalry between the nuns from both convents over sweets was so great that one day a nun, upon hearing she was going to be visited by a highly ecclesiastical dignitary, said that she was going to make a pastry so good that they would shiver! That is where the name came from - shiver means "arrepiados" in Portuguese.

The celestes are very small and cylindrical cakes, wrapped in 'obreia' (the bread given out in church) with a toasted yellow top.

Both Celestes and Arrepiados are made with almonds.

"Sara darling, it's so good to spend time with you, and this tea is wonderful!"

"Oh Clementino, you spoil me with all these treats; I'm not used to it."

"Sara I can always go and get some more, darling. If I don't have money, I can always show my upper thigh to them, and I might get them for free!" Both laughed but she continued.

"No need Clementino; there's still plenty - but if you do that, they will shoo you out with a broom, I can tell you."

"Because I'm a fag not a girl, if I were, they would all be melting like hot butter. Men are strange animals; don't you think Sara?"

"Oh yes - I couldn't agree more Clementino, you are absolutely right."

"Men like to prove their macho side, even when we know they haven't got one; I'm happy the way I am - not like some...supposed gentlemen; they look like true machos, but when they drop their trousers..." He smiled. "To others...you know what I mean...they are a volcano. They switch rapidly Sara...but still they need to have poor woman by their side just to show off." While he was talking, Sara was listening without blinking. "I just wish, my friend, one day things can be different, and people can just live and be happy...of course many need to learn not to criticise and mind their own business - then things could be different. What do you say Sara?"

"Clementino, so far the present world belongs to men, but I want to believe one day if I get lucky and have grandchildren, that this planet could be for us all, men and women, with the same rights and obligations." Both smiled and made a toast to their thoughts with their cups of tea.

Clementino was preparing to leave, when Jonny was coming in and as soon as he realised Clementino was in the kitchen with his mother, he turned around to get away as quickly as he could, but Clementino called him.

"Jonny, you can come in darling, I don't bite darling, you will be safe and there are some cakes".

But Jonny had not heard anything Clementino said because he was out as quick as he could to get way. Jonny was afraid that other boys and girls of his age could make fun of him if they saw him with Clementino, something that never happened with his sister. Ana was always a lady of her own nose; she was always herself despite what others thought of her.

"Sara, it was nice spending time with you darling. Don't forget to say hi to the kids and to the old Torres." And saying, that he kissed her on both cheeks accompanied with a hug. "Take care."

"I will Clementino and thanks again for the cakes." But just before he left, she told him,

"My house door is always open for you Clementino."

"I know Sara...you are a true friend...the world needs more people like you, believe me."

Clementino walked very elegantly down the road, while Sara kept herself at the house door to see if she could see Jonny. She waited a bit, but nothing, and when she was turning around to go in, she saw him from the corner of her eye.

"You are silly, why did you run away?"

"You know I don't want to be seen with the guy. Mother, can I have something to eat?"

"You have fruit on the fruit bowl, go and get some."

"I don't want fruit; can I have a sandwich? Can it be a sandwich with some roasted meat leftover from lunch? Don't say you don't have it; I saw you put some away."

"Yes, yes – I will do it.

"Jonny son, today make sure that you will be at home in time for dinner - let's avoid your father getting angry with you, ok? Let's avoid arguments, shall we?"

"Yes mother."

After Jonny ate the sandwich, he left, and Sara did some house chores. After, she started to prepare dinner. A little later Ana came home and asked her mother what was for dinner, and if she needed help. Sara said she could get the table ready.

Torres came home, went to wash his face and hands before dinner, and just before he did, he turned to Sara and asked about Jonny.

"Sara, is Jonny back?"

"No, I'm sure he will be here in no time."

While the old man was washing himself, Jonny came in very slowly and smiling through the door.

"Jonny, are you stupid or what? Are you going to challenge dad?" Ana interfered.

"Don't get angry, sister, I'm here, am I not?"

Both women looked at each other with concern.

After Torres came to the kitchen to have dinner and when he saw his son, he looked at him with the look of trouble like his family knew very well and spoke.

"Jonny, I truly hope that you start to be responsible and be on time for dinner every single day, you have always known that main meals are to be with all of us at the table. Don't you ever forget it, do you understand me?"

"Yes father, but sometimes I'm with my friends and I lose track of time".

"Don't be stupid Jonny, and don't play games with me, I know you are only working a few hours a day, and friends...it's not an excuse! Just be responsible, will you"

"But dad-!"

"Shut up Jonny, there are no excuses! I believe you do not want to try the weight of my hands! Ever..." And saying, that Torres gave a deep and angry look to Jonny.

Sara and Ana started to serve dinner, but worried that something bad might come from all of this. They knew Jonny was a bit late almost every evening for dinner and both women tried to make Jonny realise that was not the way forward. Many times, Ana got upset with her brother because of it, but their mother was always gentler towards him, and that's why Ana got angry with her mother for always finding excuses for the mummy's boy. It was obvious. Since the very first time that Sara met Jonny, she felt so sorry for him because he didn't have his real mother, that over the years she instantly defended her son without thinking twice. In many ways she could be easier going with her son than with her own daughter. She loved them both the same way, but she felt sorry for him, and many times Jonny abused that. If sometimes Sara felt like Jonny needed to learn a lesson, he always came to his mother, grabbed her, kissing and hugging her and in the end, she was all melting and sweet to him again.

The next few days, before Jonny left home, Sara always reminded her son not to be late for meals, and every single time Jonny said that he won't be, but Sara's heart was tight every day, because she knew her own son very well and she knew also that it was very easy for him to forget about it, especially when he was having a good time with his friends; things can get out of hand. Even his new watch didn't help him to be on time, and one evening the expected happened.

Sara had prepared dinner like usual, Ana had set the table and dad was almost home, but no sign of Jonny, and both women started to feel really worried. They kept looking back and forward at the time and to each other with concern.

"Where is he Ana, where is your brother? What is going on in his mind? Your father will be home very soon, Jonny is pushing his luck too far, but your dad is not playing games! Where is he? Oh my God"

"Mother, don't stress, Jonny knows that he shouldn't do what he is doing now. You know what is most likely to happen is that father gets home first and prepares for dinner without Jonny being here. You need to understand, he is pushing dad's buttons too far."

After a while Torres came through the door, said good evening and very discreetly, he looked around trying to see if his son was already there, but his eyes didn't see him.

"Where is Jonny Sara?"

"Not here yet, but he will be soon, just give it a few minutes!"

"Sara, you know what I think about it. You keeping defending him, and one day you are not going to have success with it. Although Jonny is almost a man, but not quite yet, he needs to learn that time is to be respected. He knows at what time we have our dinner, every day...I know he is playing with fire...You both know what happens when someone plays with fire...They get burnt." Saying that, Sara's heart got dark.

Torres like always went to the bathroom washed his hands and face, before returning to the kitchen. Ana was at the door looking to check if she could see her brother, but she hadn't had any luck at all. Both women's hearts were getting tight, there was nothing else they could do to minimise the situation that was about to happen. After a few more minutes Torres came to the kitchen and all three sat at the table, but no one started dinner.

Torres put his elbows on the table with his hands together on his face looking down. No one talked, no one made any noise, only mother and sister looked very worried to one another. The look that both exchanged was of concern. Every day Sara made sure Jonny was aware of the time, be responsible, but it seems Jonny forgot about it.

Minutes were like hours, but no sign of Jonny, and the atmosphere at home was hard. Suddenly Torres took his hands away from his face looked at his watch, then at the mother and daughter and he said:

"I guess we better start our dinner while it's still hot, because Mr Jonny isn't going to have any today!"

Sara felt her heart really tight; Torres was crazy about Jonny's delay. A thousand thoughts were coming and going into to her mind, she always tried to avoid conflicts at home but Jonny, knowing his father the way he knew, he shouldn't have pushed Torres so far, the way he was pushing him, this was not going to end well.

"Oh, my good Lord" Sara thought.

The three of them started to have dinner, but the silence was enormous, not even the cutlery touched the plates to make a noise. No one spoke, and this deadly silence lasted for more than 10 minutes, Sara was trying to eat, but it was like the food didn't want to be swallowed. But suddenly the front door opened, and Jonny came in smiling and saying good evening to everybody, something that revolted his family even more.

The minute he approached the table where his family were having dinner, Torres put down his knife and fork, stood up looked at his son with the deep look that everyone knew well, and asked,

"What time do you call this... how many times did I tell you that I want you on time every evening for dinner?!"

"Dad my watch just stopped working and I lost track of time, you know what is like to be with friends." Jonny looked a bit silly saying that and having all these excuses, again!

"Stop this crap Jonny, stop!" and continuously shouting, Torres said:

"I'm going to give you a lesson that you will never forget for many years that you live, while you live under my roof, it's my call...always."

"Torres, please, just take a break! Just give him one more chance to not repeat this again!"

"Shut up, this is all your fault, it's because of you that he is the way he is!"

And saying that, Torres pulled out his belt and without thinking twice started to hit his son the hardest way he could without caring which parts of Jonny's body he was hitting. Sara stood up screaming for Torres to stop but he didn't hear her, he was like crazy, and she stood in the middle of Torres and Jonny to protect her son from so much whipping. This made Torres even angrier, and he threw Sara hard onto the floor to get her out of the way, but she stood up again to protect her son, and this time the aggressor was much harder on her. Jonny screamed at his dad saying, "Stop hitting her, it's me that you are angry at!". He was really getting hurt, but his mother...oh my God, she was bleeding, the belt buckle left on both some severe marks and cuts.

Ana tried to tell her father that was not the way, but he didn't even hear her. The scene lasted a few minutes, but for all of them that was too long. Ana repeatedly asked her dad to stop but it was like he was deaf; he didn't hear her, and he was completely crazy about it, like a jungle animal that got a prey after a few very long days without food. When the violence finally stopped Torres, was sweating with anger and he left the house, smashing the front door behind him. Ana was crying, Jonny was really hurt and had a terrified look on his face. Sara had blood all over her face and her heart was completely devastated, she never thought her husband could go that far and hurt their son the way he did; she was used to being Torres' punch bag, like she described many times, but their son! Jonny was almost a man, what he did wasn't correct but what Torres did was far worse!

Torres was a monster, and he only hurt people that he knew couldn't turn against him. It's so easy for people to be strong when they are taking advantage of those who can't do anything because of fear. If it weren't for the respect that she had for her husband, she would give him a good beating that he would never forget. During her life, this feeling came to her mind lots of times, but if she did not have the kids, the scenario would be completely different. Well, if there were not any kids, she would not be in Torres' life in the first place, that's for sure. Jonny was the reason Sara's life was so horrible. Many times, she thought that one day when the kids left home, she would probably leave her husband if she were still alive. It's hard to be in this situation, when it doesn't matter, how, when, what you do, you always receive the blame for everything, even when you haven't done anything at all.

Sara took her beloved son in her arms. She did not need to ask how he was; everything was very visible: physically, emotionally and psychologically, Jonny was shattered.

"Mum, how can you live with him? He is a monster Mum, he is selfish. Mum, you can't live with him Mum." Jonny insisted. He was very nervous, and in so many ways he was used to seeing his father angry, but never like today. One thing his father was right about, Jonny would never ever forget that scene; it was too horrible to forget. And from now on, Jonny's love for his father was even less than it used to be.

Ana couldn't stay quiet; she was fuming with anger.

"How could you Jonny?! You know how dad is; you knew this could happen; you have always known what dad is like when he gets mad. All these years we have been watching him hit mum; didn't that mean anything to you? I thought you liked peace, brother, but I guess I was wrong. You know that mum always gets the blame for everything, and you let this happen. I think sometimes your brain is like a crazy chicken, you never think of the consequences of your actions, and I think it's time for you to think like a man because you are not a kid anymore."

"You are right Ana; I really need to think like a man and stop being afraid of our father." Sara turned to her son with real concern and asked:

"Son what is on your mind? What are you going to do? What are you thinking?"

"Don't worry mother, you will be the first to know when I decide what to do."

After some silence, the three of them exchanged a worried look. Jonny went to his bedroom and Ana and her mother cleaned the kitchen. In the beginning, both were very quiet, but a few minutes later Ana started to cry.

"It's all over darling...I know you were frightened Ana but-"

"Stop mother, stop..." sobbing she tried to speak, her voice was scrambled. Sara tried to caress her, but she repelled her mother. She gave her daughter some space till she could calm down. It took a good fifteen minutes before that happened and when it did, she sat close to Ana.

"I'm so sorry darling...I know it's my fault!"

"Mother...it's not, I just...I was so, so scared. I never expected to see the scene that we just saw...my brother and I were brought up seeing dad do to you what we know, and Jonny was warned lots of times, not to be late for meals, but he simply didn't care...like always, he only cares about himself, and that's ok as long he didn't bring anybody else into his mess."

"Ana, I know darling, but violence? I just want to make sure this won't happen again. I will talk to your brother, none of us want this to be repeated."

"Talk? The talk to my brother enters one ear and leaves from the other at a great speed, he only pays attention in the moment, you know that. Mother, I love my family very much, but please do not let this happen again. Please."

"Go wash yourself and go to bed...tomorrow is a new day; you need to be fresh to go to work." Mother and daughter cuddled.

That night Torres didn't come home, he probably slept in his office like on so many occasions throughout the years after problems at home caused by himself. The only difference now is that he stepped over the line in Sara's opinion.

In the beginning, when she met Torres, she found him a very attractive man, very nice looking, but with his personality so bad, she soon couldn't agree with the thoughts she had before. Over many years sometimes Ana used to tell her mother that she knew how she loved her father, and Sara only smiled at her, she did not want to disappoint Ana - that's why she chose just to smile. If Sara at any point told her daughter that she does not love Torres, Ana will feel really sad, and there is no need to bring such a worry to her young mind, maybe one day when she is a grown woman she will understand. Only time can tell; time cures everything - even what we think is incurable, we need to give time to heal, she thought.

That night, after Sara prepared herself to go to sleep, she went and knocked on her son's bedroom door.

"Can I come in son?"

Jonny was in his bed reading.

"Yes mother, come on in, how are you feeling?"

Sara entered his room and sat on the bed. Jonny just moved his legs aside to let his mother sit properly, and them she answered her son's question.

"I'm good son, how are you feeling? Jonny, please son, don't let this happen again, just come on time every day for dinner and after you can go out again and meet your friends! Jonny, you know how your father is, and while you live under his roof, you know that you have to obey him if we want to have peace."

"Mother I will, but this is not a life for me. I am so grateful for what you have been doing for me since I was a baby. Even if you are not my real mother, you have always treated me like a real son. If you weren't in my life, I don't even know if I would be alive today. The only thing that I am grateful to him for is that he has always given me books since I was very little according to my own age, for me to have knowledge, and I have it but apart from that mother…You know that we don't get along - we never have, we never will, he is a person full of bitterness, but that is not our fault. "

While saying that, Sara was looking at her son knowing that everything he was saying was true.

"Jonny, we all know what your father is like, but you know he loves you very much, he always has, and he always will. There is a reason for him to be the way he is - he was a very traumatised boy, and he never overcame his traumas. You know son, I think your father is the first to suffer with himself, I don't think he is too happy about doing what he did tonight."

"I'm not so sure about that mother!"

"Don't be silly, of course I'm right, he loves you, he has a very strong temper, he likes people to obey him, he likes to be in charge, discipline, but he loves his family, son!"

"Mother, I'm sorry but I don't agree with you; everything has to be the way he wants; he always wants to be in charge. Why has he hit you for as long as I remember? Sometimes I have nightmares about him; it is not good to live in fear, fear of what's going to happen next. Ana is always in his heart, he even has a special nickname for her, "little heart", and for me? What nickname does he have for me?" She looked at her son with concern about everything he was saying. She tried to interrupt a few times, but Jonny was determined.

"Mother, he wants me to be like him, a copy of him, but I'm not, never! It is late, go to bed because it's not only me who needs to rest, you must have your body in pain because of him, again."

And saying that he turned his eyes as if he was in pain of the situation.

Sara understood her son's anger very well, but as his mother, she needed to have a different approach to this dilemma, and she can never agree fully with her son for his own sake. Today broke Sara's heart, just to see her husband hit their son with such violent blows.

Jonny was not happy, and he had his reasons. He needs to be more mature, but to be mature is something that comes with time. If he was mature enough, he wouldn't have come late for dinner and all this mess would have been avoided.

That night Torres stayed at his office, and the first thing he did when he got there after the argument was sit behind his worktop and cover his face with his hands, and after a while he sat back in his chair and facing the ceiling, he talked to himself.

"Why son, why? Why did you make me do that?" Torres kept looking at the ceiling and imagining what Rosa would say if she was alive. He was a very clever man, and it was not hard to see that a good mother would never want to see her children being beaten. He was aware of what Sara would be feeling towards him, but he did not care. More than once, she knew Rosa was Torres' true love, but even so he hit her on the day they got married; what kind of love is that? Sara wondered lots of times. In her opinion her husband was a sick man, still there wasn't anything she could do, apart from avoiding weird situations that could lead to more trouble.

In her own bed that night Sara was praying for Torres not to come home, it would have been difficult for her to lay down beside him. She was awake for hours thinking about it; it is very bad when someone is a troublemaker and can't be too long without arguments. She turned the light off, but she couldn't keep still in bed for long. She got up and went to the kitchen to make a cup of tea to see if it would help calm her nerves. To her surprise she found Ana already there, drinking a tea too.

"You can't sleep either mother?"

"No... what are you drinking? "

"Camomile tea, they say it's good to reduce anxiety and help sleep, let's see if it is true. Do you want a cup of it too mum?"

"Yes, that's why I came... I don't think it will help, but let's give it a go, we never know if we don't try. It was Clementino who brought it once, I have been drinking it when he is here, I never noticed that it helps, but when I am with him it's so relaxing, I don't know if it's the tea or him. I guess it must be him."

"We better call him then; we both need a relaxation treatment." Ana said and they both smiled.

"You see darling, Clementino is an example for all of us. He doesn't care what people think about him, as long as he is happy. People who don't respect him are so empty inside. Life should be about happiness and achievements."

"I like him a lot...I think Clementino is a pure soul and I admire him very much."

"And here we are late at night and talking about him." Sara said.

In this instant Jonny joined them in the kitchen too.

"I was reading in my bed, and I couldn't help hearing you two whispers...are you talking about me? I'm sure you are."

"Here we go again! You think everything is about you... you're so selfish."

"You two stop, that's enough problems for one night." Sara did not like to see her kids arguing.

"Son, we are talking about Clementino."

"Don't you have anything more interesting to talk about than this jerk?" Jonny replied.

Hearing this Ana stood up and said,

"Good night mother."

"I don't want you to be upset because of what I have said Ana."

But she turned to her brother, looked at him from head to toe, and spoke.

"Clementino is a wonderful person, but you...go to bed, tonight you choose to be stupid, and I will not tolerate your stupidity."

Ana was not the type of person to leave things untold; she loved her brother, but because of him they all had a terrible evening - she saw once again her mother being hit by her father, because Jonny simply doesn't want to bother to respect the house rules. She did not like to see her father hit Jonny, but at the same time, maybe it was a lesson for him. She never had problems with her father. Ana knows the discipline they all had, they all knew, there was nothing different, only her brother's irresponsibility.

Deep in her heart, she thought this wouldn't happen again, or so she hoped, because Jonny was very unpredictable young boy.

Chapter 11

One week passed since the argument at home. Jonny was always on time for dinner, but never started a conversation. Ana was the one who always had something to talk about; father heard her and smiled at her. Sara kept quiet most of the time, only talking when asking if someone wanted any more food or replying if someone asked her anything.

Days were passing smoothly. In the morning everyone left home for the day, and they got together at night to have a family dinner, when unexpectedly someone knocked on their door.

"Who is it?" Sara asked.

"I'm your Torres' mother!" A woman's voice sounded from outside of the house's main door.

"What is she doing here, I thought she had died already!" Torres said

"What do you want me to do Torres?"

"Do whatever you want."

Sara went and opened the door.

The woman was clearly old but still very nice looking for her age; she was wearing a dark dress and a nice pair of shoes; her hair was combed back in a little bun and her dark eyes had dark circles around them. She looked very tired, and very happy to see her family, something that didn't happen with her own son. He clearly did not like the surprise.

"What brings you to this part of the world; what do you need that makes you come here? You know that I don't want you to be here, just say it and leave, I don't want you here." Torres said

He was not happy at all to see his mother, and she knew that. Her son did not love her, he never did, he never had any real love from her too; she was never his mother. Many times, he wished that she died, but so far, his thoughts never became reality. She never was a mother to him, her priority was always men, she was only his mother to bring him to this world, after that she simply abandoned him, something that was the main cause for his behaviour throughout the years. She was the reason that Torres didn't tolerate women, apart from his beloved daughter.

"I know that you don't like the surprise of me being here, but I just need a place to stay for a few days, I promise that I won't cause problems...I know you have plenty of reasons, it hurts but.... I'm still your mother...Can I son?"

"Why are you here? What happened to your miserable life that made you come to me for help? Don't tell me that you are single?"

"I'm sorry son, I respect you don't want me to stay, but you need to respect me too because I'm not telling you anything, because there isn't anything to tell. I'm sorry!"

"Father let grandma stay here, please! She can stay with me in my bedroom and it's just a few days." Ana asked

Sara also felt so sorry for the poor old woman.

"Torres she is your mother, she is an old and vulnerable lady, I don't mind having her here and it will be good for the kids." Sara said.

"All against one!" She can stay, but I don't like the idea of having her here."

Ana, Jonny, and Sara enjoyed the days that they spent with Torres's mother very much. Every meal they spent together, Torres never said a word. He just looked from the corner of his eyes to the unpleasant visitor and was surprised by the way his kids treated her.

On one of the days, Torres left and the conversation between the kids, Sara and grandma started to be quite interesting.

"So, Sara, where do you come from?"

"I'm from Coimbra...I wasn't born there but I lived there from a very early age."

"Beautiful place I must say... I love Coimbra, the Rock of Longing Garden is my favourite followed by the mermaid one." Said the grandma.

"I can see you know Coimbra." Sara mentioned.

Ana and Jonny were curious about the first garden grandma mentioned, and Sara explained.

Penedo da saudade (Rock of longing) is a historical public garden, on a hill, with various and long pathways and an amazing panoramic view of the city with poems engraved on marble, showing the old great memories of love from students to women, the University, some representing dates of graduation and courses.

"Amazing..." Ana comments.

"My city, like I love to call her, has the oldest University in Portugal and Europe and has so many traditions, that's why so many students like to study there. All the time they spent at the University, studying and graduating leaves a unique experience that lives in their memories forever, and these old traditions have been happening for many, many years."

This romantic spot is connected to the love affair between Lady Inês de Castro and Prince Pedro who came to this place lots of times to mourn her."

All of them were paying so much attention to every single word that Sara said.

"Saudade is a very Portuguese word, like your father explained to you before, there is not an exact translation in any other language; It means to miss someone or something, but still feel it deep inside, like a memory you want to live again, melancholy." She smiled saying that. "Like you're happy that happened, and this very strong feeling lives inside of every single student's heart forever. Saudade is one word that feeds lots of fado music from Coimbra, the city of many loves and the nest of poetry. Every time they sing fado, all students dress in black clothing and a black shawl like the University uniform. Once performing fado, the students are accompanied by the Portuguese guitar.

The Portuguese guitar is round and has twelve strings, all with different tunings, and is a musical instrument full of symbolism and mercy of its very long connections with fado, also filled with the people's way of being where destiny and longing are words that are naturally associated with, and the three are always very present in this kind of music.

Coimbra fado is related to academic traditions in this University city. Fado was created by some groups of students when they started living there to attend the University and they had brought their guitars with them. This beautiful fado is always sung by students from Coimbra University in the small traditional streets, retreats, restaurants, some squares and under some windows but always at night and this way it makes the event very solemn and enchanting. When singing under a window it means it is a serenade "serenata"

A student is in love with a girl and wants to demonstrate his love. All the students who sing the fado are very proud of themselves and they take all these feelings and memories with them, through their lives.

Even now, no one says anything; they are too scared but the fado of Coimbra is used too as a form of "intervention" among some most daring students showing as a way of expression of their political opinions and passing messages without being caught, when people don't have the freedom of speech, and this phase of dictatorship seems eternal and has been going on for a so long, 20 stupid years... These traditions made by the students have been going on for many, many years. Just to finish, the word fado, comes from a Latin word fatum, meaning "destiny and fate".

Her kids and mother-in-law were stunned by what they had just heard. Even Sara had a very happy and relaxed face after talking about something that she loves, something that is very close to her heart deeply. She has lots of "Saudades of her amazing city."

"Mother, why haven't you ever taken us there, I would love to go." Ana asked.

"Ask your dad."

"Sara I can see in your eyes the love you still have for Coimbra; I think my son doesn't stand a chance in competing with that, but if I might... do you sing Coimbra fado too?"

"I used to, when I lived there, not anymore."

Ana and Jonny looked at their mother at the same time.

"Did you?"

Sara smiled at them. "Yes, many times...and there is one in particular that I love the most." She smiled at them, and their face was imploring Sara to continue.

"Samaritana...it is lovely. This fado was created in 1910, if my memory doesn't fail me. The last time I sang it was two or three months before I came to live in Santarém."

Jonny was paying attention to his mother, seeing in her the shiny look of a very special subject, the love she has for Coimbra and all it came with. It was the very first time Jonny noticed his mother entering a different world, one that brings her lots of good memories, fun, happiness, and peace.

He was looking at her eyes when he heard his sister make the request he was about to make himself, but she was faster than him.

"Mother sing for us...please."

"Don't be silly."

"Mother please."

"I haven't sung for a very long time. I don't know - I will make a fool of myself."

"Let me see the fool you are, and let me be the judge of that...I love you and I just feel that I don't know you, how can you hide this important part of your life from us?"

Sara smiled, letting a tear roll down her cheeks and spoke.

"Life is complicated, better to leave good memories stored away because if we don't it will be even harder to carry in life, my life...as it is."

"Please mother, even if it is just once, you have no right to deny us to listen to you sing the fado of Coimbra. This evening has been so full of personal discoveries! It's like we don't know you fully. But you are not just a wife and a mother...you are a person! Someone with a story, and a good one. I would like to hear you sing - please mother..."

"OK... ok but don't you make fun of me afterwards."

Sara stood up and told her audience to wait a second while she went to another room. When returned she had brought a black shawl that she had kept in the bottom of one of her chests drawers.

"Fado from Coimbra is always sung by a man, another stupidity, but I don't care, women have voices and feelings like men." Putting the shawl around her, she straightened her neck and started singing.

Of the loves of the redeemer

Do not say the sacred history

But an enchanted legend says

That the good Jesus suffered from love...

He suffered with himself and shut up

Your divine passion

Just like any mortal

That a day of love throbbed...

Samaritan commoner of Sychar...

Someone lurking saw you kissing Jesus

In the afternoon when you went to find him alone...

Quenched of thirst at Jacob's fountain...

And you laughed welcome

The kiss that enchanted you...

Serena, and pale

And Jesus Christ blushed

Blushed to see how much light...

It radiated from your face

When you said oh my Jesus

What good did I do, Lord to come to the fountain...

Samaritan commoner of Sychar

Someone lurking saw you kissing Jesus

In the afternoon when you went to find him alone

Quenched of thirst at Jacob's fountain....

All of them stood up clapping and feeling so happy for what they had just seen and heard - no doubt Sara still had the timbre in her thick and deep voice. She had tears in her eyes, but she wasn't alone - her daughter did too, she cuddled her mother and thanked her for sharing this moment with them.

"You see, everyone has secrets but mine was just revealed."

"Sara, it means a lot what you did this evening, I will remember this for as long as I live...it would have been even better if my son was here too."

"If he was here, I can tell you, none of this would happen."

"Why?"

"I'd rather not talk about it. I am glad you enjoyed it; for a while I left my soul and travelled to a different place, the kind of one that leaves good scars in you. Saudade, at least all my memories can live inside me without being hurt. I was never a university student, but the beauty of Coimbra is incomparable, when we talk about it, all the memories flying to our mind, and it's a contagious feeling. Coimbra is a city with lots of charm, there is plenty of history about it. We have the botanical garden, beautiful, just in the heart of the city. In the 18th century there was a donation, mostly from some friars, of a piece of land, a big one for its own creation. The botanical garden belongs to the University and apparently it was created with the aim of complementing the study of Natural History and Medicine.

Avelar Brotero was the first Portuguese researcher to start the number one practical school of Botany - that is why he has a statue there. In this garden we can see a vast collection of all sorts of plants from all regions around the world, like a museum alive because there's so much diversity. All those plants fill each little piece of the garden and has the magic touch of making us feel that we are travelling around this amazing planet, without leaving the garden. It's a fantastic feeling I must say."

"Mother, who decided to make the botanical garden?" Jonny asked.

"Marquis of Pombal, the one who decided to make the freedom avenue in Lisbon as well, and before you ask, he was a statesman and a diplomat that ruled the Portuguese Empire from 1750 to 1777, but he was well known for the job he did to recover the country after the devastating earthquake in 1755. He was the kind of person who liked innovation, and new exiting projects. Let's say he was a man who deserved to be in our history for the right reasons."

"Mother, you should have been a teacher!"

"My good Lord, no way Ana. "

"Why not? You have a nice and funny way of explaining everything; it's so easy to understand."

"Ana, a teacher is hard, tough and serious all the time, and all this is my complete opposite. I believe most kids fear their teachers. In my humble opinion, teaching should have a different approach - it's not expensive to smile, to be pleasant or to explain things more than once. I don't agree with the fact that when kids don't know a subject or are failing to do something in school they get hit on their hands with a ruler.

But do you still want to hear more about Coimbra or not?"

All of them said 'yes please!' at the same time.

"Another thing that brings lots of people to Coimbra, in July is the commemorations of the city, which combines, traditions, history and modernity I must say, to simply celebrate Coimbra. The celebrations about Coimbra happen every single year, but we have another one – the celebration of the Holy Queen, (Saint Isabel) is every other year, both events can make the city very crowded.

This amazing Queen used to be known as Elizabeth of Portugal, she was born (if my mind doesn't fail me) in 1271, 13th century in the Royal House of Aragon, and she was the daughter of an Infant, who later came to be King Peter the 3rd, and Constance of Sickly. Queen Isabel had three brothers who became kings too. But this does not matter because what I want is to explain about our Queen.

Since an early age she showed some enthusiasm about her own faith attending at least twice daily mass, fasting herself and other penance.

In 1281, when she was only ten years old, a marriage was arranged for her and King Denis of Portugal, but it was only in 1288 that the wedding was celebrated. Denis was 26 and Isabel 17; the celebrations lasted for a week. He was a poet and statesman, apart from being a son of a bitch too, I believe, and he was also known as the farmer King, due to the planting of a pine forest that he created to prevent the soil from degrading that was at the time threatening the region of Leiria. Queen Elizabeth – more commonly known as Queen Isabel - without a big fuss, pursued her daily and regular religious practice and devoted herself to the poor and sick people. She prayed for those in need, including her husband who she considered sinful. Isabel had lots of patience and tried to convert her husband into being a better person, with her faith's help.

Elizabeth started to take a special and active interest in Portuguese politics and was a decisive conciliator during negotiations of the treaty of Alcanices, between her husband Denis and Fernando IV of Castile in 1297, creating the border between Portugal and Spain. Later she had two children, a girl, and a boy. The girl named Constance later married King Ferdinand IV of Castile and years later, her son became King Afonso IV of Portugal.

The Queen Saint Isabel became very famous because of her good heart, she was spending her time always helping others in every way she could. She was immensely kind, doing good things for people who needed help, visiting and treating the sick, distributing alms to the poor. During the great famine of 1293, she had donated flour from her cellars to the starving people of Coimbra. The Queen was also known for being very modest in her way of dressing and with a humble conversation, for providing lodging for pilgrims and giving people small gifts, educating poor children and many more kinds of help.

But the commemorations in Coimbra are very much loved by everyone, and they have a legend of a miracle related to the Queen Saint Isabel, Patron of the city.

King Denis was very irritated from seeing his wife quite often walking from the Royal gates and joined with the poor and beggars and he had forbidden her from giving more alms to them. But one day, he saw with his own eyes Isabel steal from their Palace, and he went after her. He asked what she was hiding under her cloak. It was the bread that she had stolen before, but she was distressed because she had disobeyed the king. Suddenly she exclaimed, "They are roses my Lord." King Denis' face was suspicious, and he replied that there is no way we could have roses in January - he was doubting her.

Queen Saint Isabel lowered her eyes, uncovered her cloak, and the bread had turned into beautiful roses like no one had ever seen before." Hearing this part, Ana had tears rolling down her cheeks.

King Denis died in 1325, and the Queen retired to the monastery of the poor Claire nuns then, but now it has another name, the Monastery of Saint Clara, that she herself had founded in 1314, in Coimbra, devoting her remaining life to the ones in need. She later died on July 4th, and she earned the title of peacemaker on account of her hard work and efficacy in solving disputes and avoiding conflicts. The Queen was buried in the convent of Saint Clara in a magnificent gothic sarcophagus, but in the 17th century after frequent flooding by the Mondego River, the nuns moved her mortal remains to the Monastery of Saint Clara main chapel in Coimbra where she was buried in a sarcophagus of silver and crystal. There are appropriate times when we can see her hand - after all these years, can you imagine."

"Oh my God mother, I'm shivering." said Ana.

She was beatified in 1526 and canonised by Pope Urban VIII on 25th May 1625.

"After all these years, the city of Coimbra held the commemorations of this religious party for a week to celebrate this incredible Queen. All the celebrations take place in some of the most important cultural heritage sites of the city, and she is usually depicted in Royal garb with a dove or an olive branch. The parties of the Queen Saint Isabel have been celebrated in Coimbra for about four centuries, and to the prestige of it she is the patron Saint of the city. This religious event includes exhibitions, conferences, church services and a big procession in honour of her. The possession of Penance is when the image of Queen Saint Isabel is carried from the church that has her name on it to the church of Saint Cross, but when it gets to the Saint Claire Bridge, a "firework bouquet" is burned and roses are thrown over the image of the Holy Queen. Then the Solemn Procession takes her again from Sé Novation to her own church. The andor - weighing about a ton - is carried by 24 men, travelling through the streets of the city and using the same paths so often used by herself when living in Coimbra.

Those celebrations in July are their way of paying tribute to her life, which left many good examples for the city, Portugal and around the world, because even today the devotion for this Queen remains very active. After the canonization of Queen Saint Isabel, several religious manifestations occurred in her honour, under the Royal patronage. Since the 16th century the streets have been decorated by their own residents, something that even happens in our days, bringing to Coimbra all sorts of people.

"My tongue today won't get rusty." said Sara.

"Mother, I have learned so much about your city tonight...Thank you for sharing all of this treasure with us. From now on I'm going to look at Coimbra with a much different view."

"Ana everything, I told you this evening, about Coimbra, it's beautiful but it's much more about history, traditions, culture and gastronomy, but some of it I forgot. Do you know Coimbra was the first capital of Portugal?" Jonny opened his eyes with surprise and spoke.

"It was? How? I know that Portugal was born in Guimarães, but I have never heard about Coimbra being the capital."

"It was and there are some people who can confirm that it still is." This was too much information for the poor old woman, and she kept moving her head from one side to the other, like watching a tennis game, without saying anything.

"Very quickly...There are still people saying, Coimbra is the official capital of Portugal, and this subject can take us again back in time to the 12th and 13th centuries. Around 1255, the official capital was Coimbra, where the Royal Court presided, but D. Afonso III, wanted to move the entire court to Lisbon because it was becoming a prosperous and big city. The harbour was so big that it could receive all ships with goods. This was something that made plenty of people move nearby. All of it made Coimbra fall behind in the living conditions it offered, still D. Afonso III packed and moved. But neither him nor any other king after him signed any document that made Lisbon official as the capital of Portugal.

And for today that's enough history... now who wants some toast and a cup of coffee or milk before going to bed?"

All of them wanted toast and a hot drink after this very unusual evening. For Sara, she was reliving lots of things that used to be part of her life back all those years in the city that she loved with all her heart. It hurts sometimes, since she left and never went back, but it does not mean the true love for it doesn't still hide in a special corner of her heart.

They all ate, and they were very pleased Only Ana missed her father not being there, but since his mother had arrived, he avoided being around. For Sara it was a relief - it meant less possibility for trouble. She did not like to think this way, but Torres did not give her any other choice. She tried to be happy and conformed for the kids' sake. That evening brought some temporary comfort to her soul - let's see what tomorrow brings.

They all finished their midnight supper and now they could all go to bed. Sara put all the cups and plates in the sink, saying she would wash them in the morning; they were not going anywhere and if they did, they can return already washed. Everyone laughed about her joke.

"Now, bed because it's almost morning."

"Mother!!"

"What Jonny? Go to sleep, you can hardly keep your eyes open."

All of them said good night to one another and they went to their respective rooms, only Ana paid a visit to Sara in her room just before she went to sleep.

"Mother from tonight on, I can see that you are a person with so many other qualities that I didn't know about...Thank you so much for being my mother."

"Go to bed Ana...don't be soft, this is nothing, all the things that I shared with you are back in my storage, a corner right at the end of my brain, for good."

"Don't say that! You have a great voice mother; I want to hear you sing again one day."

"Ana tonight was something unexpected - from the beginning of the evening talking about my city... it made me enter a different place of mind and everything just rolled on, I almost didn't have time to think about it...it's like when we start to eat olives, we can't have only one, we keep eating them and when we realise we have eaten plenty because they are delicious and easily eaten, do you understand?.

"Hmm...Ok, I got it! The secret for you to sing again for us is talking about Coimbra."

"No, I won't. Didn't you pay attention to all the rest that I talked about it?"

"I did mother...and it's annoying that no one ever talked to me or my brother about it. One day I want to go to Coimbra to visit all the places that you talked about earlier and visit the tomb of the Queen Saint Isabel. I want go with time one day to explore."

"Ana, there are plenty more beautiful places to visit...one thing that I forgot to mention earlier is the convent where I grew up - it's very close to the Rock of Longing, that's why I know the place inside out. I used to know by heart most of the poems that are engraved in the stones; I used to sit on the benches with a friend of mine just admiring the view on the summer afternoons. Sometimes both of us took some food and drink and had a picnic under the tree's shadow. Old times that are now gone; Now off to bed." At this moment, Torres entered the room and the first thing he asked was what Ana was doing at that time in his room. Very briefly she explained to him and dashed off to her own room. The next day at breakfast, Ana and Jonny were talking about the night before, but their mother told them a few times to end it there, there was no point keeping on talking about it. Grandma defended the kids a few times saying she did not expect herself to have a lovely evening, like she had the night before.

Grandma had a good time - she enjoyed staying with her family, but it was time for her to go. Her grandchildren were in love with her - they enjoyed every story that she told them, and every moment they spent together. Now it was time for the worst part: her leaving. The kids were inconsolable.

They had never experienced this before, to have a grandmother just by their side, even just for a few days - it was a good experience. Even Sara liked her, she never criticised her mother-in-law for her own choices in life, maybe because she was old, and her life did not look great anymore after all.

While she was young and beautiful, she had lots to offer - that's why she had men at her feet to choose from and for the time she lived in, this was something not normal at all, but now it wasn't the case anymore.

She left very moved, after saying goodbye to her grandchildren and Sara.

They all waved to her, apart from her only son who didn't care about her. Ana was looking sad with the departure of her grandmother, and she asked her mother why her father doesn't like his mother, but she explained that sometimes life is a bit unfair.

"You see Ana, she got married very young and she had a kid straight away, she lost her husband - too many things for a young mind and heart, she wanted to live and be free. Life is not a bunch of roses Ana! Roses have too many thorns in their stems, that's why young people need to live and enjoy life before settling down."

"Mother, you are so different from my friend's mums! Why are you so different with a vision completely different from the people I know?"

"They are not people, they are cows.... I just think people take life too seriously and they forget that this life is just a holiday. We all have our leaving ticket; we just do not know the departure date. We must all live life the best way we possibly can, without hurting others and without letting others hurt us. Some people are too complicated and they just like conflict, and in the end, they are not happy. The world could be a better place if people looked at themselves in the mirror before criticising others."

"Mother, when I grow up, I want to be like you - not singing though because I have a terrible voice. If I sung, everyone would run away fast. I am so proud of you being my mother. You have so many things to teach me, Jonny and others."

"Ana darling, I'm just a normal person...I'm normal...I'm not a troublemaker, I would just like to see humans being kind to one another, instead of just wanting to see people getting hurt, that's what this is all about. Sometimes darling, people are more concerned with others' problems than their own...people just need to be wise, not doing bad things to others that they don't want for themselves – it's just as simple as that.

Chapter 12

It was June of 1954 when the Santarém council held the ribatejo fair for the very first time. This fair came as a replacement for the miracle fair - an old one that had lost interest and suddenly due to lack of visitors, it came to an end.

This event was organised by a man named Celestino Graça. He got some ideas, and he gathered some friends together and started planning everything, and everyone who worked with him enjoyed it so much and never felt afraid of failure because this man was so confident in himself and had a team spirit that all the others felt confident enough to get along on this adventure. All his ideas went from paper to action, he was thinking of something big, that would make people go for it with enthusiasm.

The new fair would have a purely regional character, based on a pure agricultural and animal exhibition. The idea of this new fair was to highlight the region's agricultural and regional wealth side, by showing to their visitors what they can produce, what they have and what they can offer. This new fair would hold some activities that pleased everyone such as bullfights, bulls released into the streets, horse races and farmers processions / walks.

Maintaining its genuine Ribatejo, (the county) area component by the bulls and what they involve in the charming countryside, folklore and local cuisine. 'Folklore' is a traditional and regional Portuguese group dance; men and women characterized by variables and take different forms depending on which region of the country they are presenting. Their way of dressing is based on how people used to, many years ago. Depending on the type of clothes they were wearing, there was the possibility of knowing countless characteristics of it and recognising the region they were representing, and this was very important for our culture, social reasons and professional recognition because each region had different ways of dressing.

They had already started advertising; on each day they would leave one bull hanging around the city streets. It was going to be dangerous but at the same time can bring lots of fun to people especially the young ones that are brave enough to jump in front of the terrifying bull.

Everyone was excited about this new event, in all corners of the city no one talked about anything else, and the most exciting thing was the fair taking place in the city itself, in a large space that was given especially for the purpose of creating something that people could enjoy. All of those involved were working very hard to achieve the best they could with regards to this enormous event.

"Mother, what is for dinner?"

"Jonny, I made the thing you and your sister like most, can you guess?"

"There are so many things that we like!"

"Yes, but something that you and Ana like most!"

"Roasted lamb with potatoes!"

"Yes son, I thought you and your sister would like to have this meal today, and this morning I went to the market, and I saw this leg of lamb so fresh that I couldn't resist... I had to get it - it's a quite big leg and if there are any leftovers, I can keep them for tomorrow and I can make a nice tomato rice with peas, what do you think?" Hearing that made Jonny put his arms around his mother.

"Mother why do you make such good food! I don't want to be fat! "

"Don't worry son, a good girl will pay attention to your personality. Of course, being a balloon doesn't help I must say, but if it happens, I can pop you with a pin and then you deflate."

"Mother it's not funny."

"Yes, it is, but you are not the kind of a boy who gets fat, at least not yet - let's let more years pass by, get old and then son everything that arrives to our body, doesn't go away easily. When I was younger, I used to be much slimmer and now I'm getting like a big bag of beans!"

"You are my big bag of beans!"

"Now it's not funny."

Mother and son looked at one another and laughed about it.

In the meantime, Ana and Torres came home, had their dinner, and just before they finished, Torres invited all of them to go to the fair the next day for lunch.

All of them agreed, and their daughter took the opportunity to ask dad if she could go to a street dance next month.

"When is that little heart?"

"The first Sunday of July dad, it will start at four and all my friends are going, it will be good if you let me go too."

"Take your mother with you. And little heart, I'm going to say something to you that I never want you to forget! Never, ever accept anything that a man wants to give you, because there is no man in this world that gives something to a woman, without wanting something in return. Sara take good care of our daughter, because if something happens to her, I will be here, and you know what I'm capable of doing. And I truly hope that you two think about this, because I don't like to talk twice about the same thing!"

The moment that Torres let these words come through his mouth, Sara shuddered, Jonny felt sick, and Ana looked at her father with a suspicious look.

"Father, I only asked if I could go dancing, nothing else!"

"Ana, I know this all very well, and I also know that man is a kind of animal that doesn't care about which way he takes, as long as he gets what he wants, and a daughter of mine is not fodder for a cannon, like we used to say. Understood?"

"Yes father!"

"Good, so I don't need to repeat myself again, do we understand each other? Ana, I want you to know that you are not like any other girl...you have me as your father, it means that I will be watching you like a hawk. I know you but I know also how girls of your age are, and when they all get together, they can very well do things that they might later regret, not in your case. If any time your mother is not keeping her eyes on you, I will find out, then the music will be very different."

Ana was incredulous at what her father was saying, but one thing for sure was - he will be spying on her and Sara all the time that she spends with her friends. Sara was seeing her husband terrorise their daughter. She didn't agree with him, but she didn't show him. She always talked to her daughter to prepare her for any circumstance and tell her what to avoid, not to get in any sort of trouble, but the way Torres said it was horrendous.

After this lecture, all the family members got up from the dining table. Father went out, Jonny kissed his mother and left too, and Ana helped her mother clean up the kitchen and after they chatted for a while.

"Mother I don't understand father sometimes, he talks in a way that makes me feel..."

"Ana, I trust you, I know you are young, but I also know that you are very mature for your age. I can't keep my eyes on you all the time, but I have trust of 100% in the person that you are. You must respect your father all the time, but I wish you and your brother never give me a grandson with his personality."

"Mother if - just if - I have any kids one day, you will be there to help me, right?"

"Probably not."

"Why? Don't you want to be close to me?"

"Ana, you don't know what man you are going to have as a husband, if he wants me around or even if you move with him to China!"

"Oh, my good lord mother, your imagination is fertile. My future husband has to be a kind and respectable man, if not I will sack him." They laughed at the way she said this.

Chapter 13

Ana was very excited about going to the fair. She spent a while choosing which dress to wear. In the end she looked very pretty -

she was wearing a beautiful dress in white and red, flat shoes, and a handbag matching her dress, her father was very proud of her, as they walked side by side in the front while Sara was with Jonny walking just behind. They took about half an hour to get to the fair because so many friends made them stop just to have a quick chat. They always have something to talk about, but Ana was quite anxious to get to the fair; she was feeling very pretty.

The entrance to the fair was free, and there were lots of people gathering, mother's holding their children's hand's tightly because of the confusion - it wasn't good if they lost them.

There was something very special about this event. There were huge fences with different animals: cows, sheep, goats, oxen, bulls, and halters a kind of crazy small cow, all of them looking very frightened because of the amount of people staring at them, obviously it was a new experience for animals and people - none of them are used to all this fuss. All these animals looked very healthy and big, there were some very cute calves too and they got lots of attention from children. There were birds too, an enormous variety of them, all sorts of chickens, big, small ones (with a funny look that made people laugh) others with a very extravagant look, peacocks, pheasants; there were birds for all types of tastes. Ducks too, lots of different ones. Sara was staring at them because there were a few she never had seen before.

It was a supreme agricultural exhibition of everything that grows in this part of the country.

This was an opportunity to show, buy and sell agricultural products, livestock, and machinery. Even so, in parallel, several activities related to the festival of bulls. For the very first time this initiative was looking very promising, so far it was very successful. Everyone looked very happy and proud about their region, and at the same time people have the opportunity to see friends that they haven't seen for a very long time.

There was tasquinhas (taverns) with barbecue meats, pork, beef, and chicken all very delicious and home-made chips and the wonderful wine of the region and even people who have had lunch before couldn't resist the lovely smell.

It was funny because some groups of people were making plans to go there every day during the week that the fair lasted for, to have these delicious barbecues.

This particular part of the region has very rich gastronomic recipes and a very good and strong wine that people make for their own consumption.

The family of four chose one tavern, from a friend of theirs and had a wonderful meal, braised beef chops, bigger than their plates at home, with chips and lettuce, tomatoes, and onion salad, dressed with virgin olive oil and vinegar - everything was from the region. The wine was red and strong, and Sara loved it. She tasted the meal and wine; there was not one day as long she can remember that she didn't do this; today it tasted different. No one could understand that, but she didn't bother to explain it, she was there to enjoy. She had the opportunity to eat a few slices of three different kinds of chouriço and she loved it; she appreciates good and rich food.

Torres and his family spent a good five hours hanging around in the fair, but Sara was starting to complain about her feet - she was starting to feel very tired, and her husband agreed with her, that was time for them to head home.

Jonny had found some friends and asked his dad if he could stay, and he was surprised when his father replied saying that Jonny was a man and that he could stay. Jonny looked his father in his eyes and asked if he could miss dinner that day. The father told him, just today. Without Torres seeing, Sara winked her eye to Jonny and Jonny replied with a wink too.

Torres, Sara, and Ana went home, but once again friends were coming and going to the fair and always stopping for a chat.

After a while Sara was quite fed up with this walking and stopping, she thought that people were annoying. How could people have so much to talk about, and most of this cheap conversation doesn't even matter to the fleas. But still they can't be rude to others without a reason, but even so in her opinion all these people were surprised seeing them all together; it was not a usual thing.

That evening Jonny came home a bit late but very happy. When he opened the front door of his house, his mother was having a cup of camomile tea.

"Mother are you ok?"

"Yes, Jonny I'm ok, and you son? Is it just me or are you a bit too happy? Did you have too much to drink?"

"Just a bit mother, but the reason that I'm really happy is because I had a job offer in Lisbon from a car company!"

"Wait, what are you saying Jonny?"

"That's what you just heard mother. It looks like I have got myself a good job in the capital, and I'm really looking forward to it, to tell you the truth I can hardly wait, I just hope father doesn't get in my way."

"Jonny, how was this job offer presented to you son? Do you think it's serious? What are going to do at your job?"

"Mother, calm down, take it easy, don't get over excited! I was walking around with my friends, and Joe just asked if any of us were interested in a job in Lisbon at Fiat. He is responsible for the place, and immediately my ears were on alert. I asked for all the details about it, and everything sounded good. I will be working in the spare parts warehouse and mother, it will be a good challenge for me, something that will bring me a good opportunity to get away from this house!"

"What is wrong with this house Jonny?"

"Mother, my lovely mother, what's the matter with you? I love you so much, but I can't wait to get away from here, to get away from him. You know that he doesn't like me, and I don't really get along with him. If we don't live together the possibility for us to get along is greater, even so I don't think that I will miss him."

"Jonny, your father loves you very much, and if sometimes he is rude to you, it's because he wants you to be a good man. I know sometimes you don't understand, but he wants what is best for you."

"He has a stupid way of showing it, but mother let's stop talking about my father. Mother I will be living in Lisbon, isn't it amazing?"

After mother and son talked for a bit more, both went to their respective rooms, and in his bed, Jonny was looking at the ceiling and dreaming about the exciting idea of moving away from home. Sara was also looking to the ceiling above her bed but with the fear of losing her son. She knew that one day both her kids will fly away from home, but she never thought that day was coming so soon, and if Torres agreed with this decision, it means that soon Jonny wouldn't be living with them anymore. Her little bird is about to go and fly away with his own wings. And the day will come for Ana to leave too, however she will need to get married first, and so far, there is no future husband, yet something made Sara smile just thinking about it. But knowing Torres the way she did, she knew that when a man came along to date Ana, her father was going to observe him bit by bit, and only after that Torres can give his blessings or his punishment. It has to be a very special man, for Torres to let his daughter date, and even after that it will be a daily nightmare to be watching Ana very carefully to avert any temptation.

The next day (Sunday) Jonny asked his father if he could have a minute to have a word, and Torres sat and said,

"Go on son, what happened?"

Jonny explained everything to his father, and after he heard his son, Torres looked a bit surprised at his son. At the time so many thoughts came to his mind, like 'my son is growing, and he is not a child anymore, but a young man and the time has come for me to let him go'. Jonny was starting to fly with his own wings and there is nothing anyone could do, apart from support him in this life changing situation, and that is exactly what Torres was planning to do for his son.

"Is that what you want son? Do you think it's a wise move?"

"Yes father, and if everything goes ok, I can start at the beginning of the month."

"Jonny it looks like you have everything sorted about the job, but what about the accommodation, have you thought about that too?

"In the beginning, my friend Joe offered for me to stay at his place, and after with time I can rent a room, and I will see how it goes from there, I just need some time to figure things out Dad. I'm very positive about this job and everything that it can bring me. I know in the beginning things will be a bit...different because I don't have you all with me! I don't have mother to cook every day the delicious meals she does, but for me it will be a challenge - one day I need to learn how to do things myself and I believe this chance is just around the corner, that's why I want to take it. Everything has a start everyone wants to work hard to get a better life, and I'm very positive."

"Very well son, I will not get in your way, it seems to me that you have already made up your mind but let me tell you something. You were brought up in this city, and so far, you have never lived in any other place. Lisbon is a much bigger place, with many more people and a night life. You will be noticed in the beginning as the boy from the countryside, and it means that you need to always be alerted to not let anyone take advantage of you, that will happen Jonny. I know that because of my job, I travel very often to the capital, and the things I see every time I go there, it's unbelievable. I believe every other big city and capitals are more or less the same. Be careful with night women, most of them have been having a tough life and want a port to dock...You are a man Jonny, be careful not to make children with random women. Before you commit yourself to a woman, see all aspects, all sides, and never put the cows in front of the cars. The day will come when you feel like settling down but with no hurry son...everything in life should take its own course...another and the most important thing, that I want to warn you about. Jonny, please be careful when talking to others, we never know who is around the corner, the informants are everywhere, and I don't want my son to be arrested or simply disappear because of something he shouldn't have said. I helped you to escape the military service, but I can't help you if you get in trouble with the government."

"I know dad, but thanks for warning me, it's not like we can forget the lake of freedom we have been living in, sometimes I wonder until when we are going to stay like this."

"The only thing we should do is not get in trouble, people need to show respect and have discipline." Torres saying that made Jonny think, this was not respect or discipline, it was people being afraid all the time and getting suspicious even of their own shadow. Of course, he would never say anything to his father, he knew how his father defended Salazar, and the last thing he needed was arguments to make his father forbid him to go and work in Lisbon. For Jonny, his father's political ideas had been obvious for a very long time even without talking about it, it was clear.

"I'm sure you already talked to your mother about it!"

"Yes Dad, last night when I came home, mother was having a cup of tea in the kitchen, and she noticed that I was happy, and I told her everything about it."

"Well then, I think there is nothing else to talk about, everything seems to be explained, I just want to wish you luck, and I'm sure now your mother will organise everything you need for you to take to Lisbon, but if you are going to stay at your friends' home, there are not many things to take.

What can I say...just want to wish you all the best for your new life. Jonny, just in case things don't work out for you, you know where your home is, right?"

"Thanks Dad, I know."

Jonny was quite surprised with his dad and the way he talked to him, but Torres had always been the kind of father that worries about his kids.

That evening Jonny sat down with his mother and sister, and he told them about the conversation earlier with his father.

Sara tried to be strong but deep inside she knew that her son was hungry for freedom.

Jonny was very young, but he did like to have fun with his friends without thinking about what time he should be back home. He didn't like to be controlled by his father or anyone. His mother was a bit afraid because Jonny wasn't very good with money, sometimes he got overwhelmed and spent more than needed, afterwards the money is never enough for things he should really get. Since his sister Ana started to work, Jonny got to have free clothing and shoes, because she was the one always paying for them, something that she always complained about - he had work too doing bits and pieces here and there- if he had wages too, why rely on his sister to pay?

Sara always made excuses for him, no matter what, forgetting that he is not a child anymore, and part of being an adult is assuming responsibility for all the things you do, good or bad.

When Ana found out about Jonny's new job and him leaving, the first thing she thought about was she could save money at the end of each month if she didn't have to pay for him in any way, but at the same time she was sad too about her brother's decision. She loved her brother very much, but she didn't always agree with him, especially when she was very clear about something and Jonny was always indecisive - she didn't like doing things by half and she always knew very well what she wanted from life for herself and it definitely wasn't living for others to pay for their expenses. She was very happy to have her own money, without needing to ask others to pay for her own things. Every month when receiving her wages, she gave some of the money to Sara, to help with the daily expenses. But it was clear to anyone that Jonny thought of his sister as very bossy. He always respected her and sometimes he avoided telling her things just so he would not be criticised by her, and she knew that very well. She always thought Jonny was a mummy's boy, and it never bothered her too much, as long as she wasn't left behind.

Sara and her children talked for a long time, and she had some ideas about what to get ready for Jonny to take with him to Lisbon.

"Son, in my opinion as soon you get set with your new job, I think you should get your own place to live. You don't need a house, you can rent just a room, and you can have privacy, and son, when you have your own place, you don't need to justify to yourself what time you get home.

Jonny when we stay at another's place, after three days we are not visitors anymore, and we start invading their privacy, which is not very good."

"Mother, my friend is a really good friend and he told me that I can stay at his house as long as I want to."

"Jonny son, your friend was just being polite, but with time you will understand that everyone needs their own place. Life Jonny, it's not always fun, it's not always being surrounded with people, sometimes we all need peace and quiet away from everything and everyone, but son in due course you will get what I'm saying.

Changing the subject son, I was thinking that I will prepare some meals on the weekends that you can take with you every Sunday evening to Lisbon and this way I know that you will eat well and save money because in the capital everything is expensive."

As soon as Sara said that her daughter looked at her mother with a very critical look.

"Mother you are joking, how can you get meals for each day of the week for him?"

"Ana if it was you, wouldn't you like to have good homemade food every day? My food?"

"Of course, I would, but him... as soon as he gets to Lisbon, he will start to discover all the restaurants, bars...mother you know Jonny, he likes adventures, new things and he will not stop till he knows

Lisbon inside out, and you are going to work even harder to prepare food for him."

"Hello, I am still here! You are talking about me like I wasn't! You know mother...Ana is right. I have always dreamt about going to Lisbon for good, and I guess this is it." Sara knew very well what that meant - she needed to be strong and just let her boy go, and in case he needs her, she will be there, always. She was the kind of mother who was like a lioness, always prepared to be there for her kids, no matter what, and her kids knew that well too. Their mother was their friend, bodyguard, private organiser and more.

Sara was not the fine girl who once came to Santarém anymore - through the years she learnt many things, she suffered a lot and she became a tough person, but very loving and caring towards the ones she loved. She was the kind of person capable of changing the world for her kids, and always very caring for all the children she met throughout her life. Maria was still close to her, but not as close as in the first years when she arrived in Santarém. Since Ana became a young woman, Sara found in her daughter a very good friend, and mother and daughter were very close. Some of their neighbours and friends made some comments about Sara and her daughter, because they had never seen a friendship between mother and daughter like that, always a very honest, and dedicated friendship and even on weekends they both went for walks around the city, always talking, laughing, and having a good time; they were inseparable.

The next few days, Sara was organising everything she thought Jonny would need to take to Lisbon, but like always there was still some stuff for Ana to help with. She used to have an account with a very special shoe shop, a little book, and every time she got a pair of shoes for herself or her family, the price was registered and at the end of every month she paid the amount of money that was agreed with the shop's owner.

"Ana, what is the bill at the shoe shop? I would like to get a new pair of shoes for your brother to take with him, but only if you can manage."

"Mother don't you think that it is time for my brother be responsible and manage his money in a better way, getting his own things without me paying for it?"

"I know you are right Ana, but your brother is not very good at it, and I know how much you have been giving to him, but I'm quite sure that this will be the last time you are going to pay for him. You know darling, this is just the first step for Jonny, I have the feeling that Jonny will go on to discover the world if given the opportunity. You know as well as I do that your brother loves travelling, food and fado, and he is a boy! He is going to have a little sip of freedom, and who knows when he will stop, if he will stop. That's why I'm asking you for this favour darling!"

"Ok mother, tomorrow I will ask my boss if I can meet you at 11 am at the shoe shop. Ok?"

"Thanks...I wish I didn't have to ask you for this...but..."

"I get it, don't worry, but you treat him like a baby, and you need to let him grow. Mother, I have told you this time and time again. I'm not saying it's right, but lots of the times my father hits you, it's because of Jonny... don't you get it? My brother is stupid as a bat, and he doesn't learn because you don't let him. I'm sorry mother..."

Finally, the day for Jonny to leave came and his parents and his sister were a bit sad, but on the other hand Jonny was a very happy and confident young man.

Jonny had a little suitcase and a big bag with red and white squares with a zipper. It contained lots of things that his mother had prepared for him.

Jonny was very amused when he started saying goodbye to his mother and sister. But he then saw his father ready to go with him.

"Father you didn't say anything before about going with me to Lisbon, how come this decision now?"

"Son, I never explain myself to anyone, you included. I just want to see where you are going to stay, see your conditions there and what kind of people are going to have you in their home! I'm your father Jonny and I know that we don't always agree on lots of things, but this doesn't mean that I don't care, that I don't worry about you, you are my son, my blood." Sara didn't even dare to ask Torres when he was coming back.

After this lecture both men left, and Sara had tears rolling down her cheeks, but Ana quickly put her arms around her mother and said:

"Don't worry about him, he will be fine... I'm here to give you headaches every time you miss him Mother."

"Don't be silly Ana."

"If it was me going away, you wouldn't be so sad... but I'm not jealous don't worry!"

"You will only leave home if you get married, if not, there is not a chance of it."

"Mother why are women treated differently from men? I never understood!"

"Because men are so ignorant and stupid, and they don't want women to show them that they can do things the same way they do, most of them want to get married just to have a slave to do all the jobs for them. It's like having a maid without having to pay her. The first person in the world that invented the idea that women are less than men should have been a meal for crocodiles."

"Mother!"

"What? I'm right! Man is a cruel animal, most of them treat women badly but on the other hand they can't live without us. In the end I never understood why because they are sons of a women."

"Mother I think the reason most men treat their wives badly is because they are jealous, don't you think?"

"The only thing I know Ana is that women can live happily without men, we don't need them… they just need us to have headaches and chores to do at home, nothing else."

Both women laughed about what she just said. They cuddled and went inside.

Chapter 14

The flat in Lisbon where Jonny was going to live for the time being, was on the fifth floor. The flat was quite big and very cosy, it had four bedrooms, one for Joe's parents, one for Joe himself and another for his sister and Jonny was going to stay in the spare one. The kitchen had lots of space, and it had a rectangular wooden table with six chairs. They had another big room that they divided in half, to have one living room and dining room. The dining room was normally used on Sundays and when there were visitors.

Joe's parents made Jonny very welcome, and Torres liked the people that were about to have his son as a guest, and this was a good thing. Jonny really got along with everybody.

The family used to live in Santarém too, but a few years back, Joe's father got an opportunity for a new job in Lisbon and the family decided to move to the capital. It was a big change for them, but it was also a smart move. All their lives changed for the better, and they did and still do a great job with their kids. They still go to Santarém occasionally, never missing the famous fair and the spectacular barbecues, not to mention the opportunity to see family and old friends. It was always good for them to go home, and every time they did, Joe's grandparents never let them leave for the capital without giving them some bags with potatoes, carrots, onions, garlic, beans, cabbage, fruit, and a chicken or two. In Lisbon, normally they never spent any money on this kind of food, and even in October when back home the family had one or two pigs killed, there was always a big piece of meat and ribs reserved for them, apart from the chouriço and black pudding they always made.

Normally in the countryside, it was a tradition in October to slaughter a pig, make a very nice and rich meal and start to drink the new wine that was made previously privately by people. This time of the year is always very special and touching because they can bring families and friends together, however the true Portuguese people never needed an excuse to have everyone around a table. It has always been a tradition for centuries in this part of the world to have extra food at meals in case someone knocks on the front door; it's the way of making people welcome. The real Portuguese people like to have a good and rich meal, with a good glass of wine and fado. Lisbon Fado is different from the Coimbra one, it's more music played with the same type of guitars, (Portuguese guitar) and the other one with a normal guitar, usually with just one singer for the interpretation.

Apparently, the Lisbon fado was born on slave ships or 'by the sailors', in the notorious alleys of Lisbon, where it evolved to be performed in the restaurants and bars and eventually concert venues. Fado of Lisbon is the popular music of Portugal, that appears in the rich broth of cultures that present in Lisbon, being therefore an urban song, and the Portuguese people adopted fado as an expression of their own nationality and not just the vast world of the Portuguese people but their language itself, fado travelled around the world and made itself known. Fado is like a very special stamp for Portugal and Portuguese culture.

Fado is the musical genre that mostly evokes the Portuguese people's spirit. It encompasses several styles and themes, but it is mainly characterized by sadness and melancholic songs, and in its essence, we can say that it sings the people's feelings, after a heartbreak of love, the longing for someone who left and the daily life of people in Lisbon. Fado music is a form of Portuguese singing that is often associated with bars and restaurants. After all, life's encounters and mismatches are an endless theme of inspiration for this kind of music. They say when fado is being sung that it truly comes from within the Portuguese deep soul, and the singers, "fadistas" often sing with their eyes closed to feel it deep in their hearts too.

There has been fado sung by people who made it their way of living and others that sing as amateurs, just when they get together with families or friends to have a good Portuguese get together.

There are people saying the true fado singer is never invited ... he or she invite themselves and have no established repertoire.

Amália Rodrigues is the most charismatic singer "fadista" and who internationalized fado, taking it to the greatest and most chic places around Europe. With a powerful presence on stage and a natural sense of the performance herself, we owe her the spread of this marvellous music and the image of the always classic black dress with shawl.

There are some Lisbon neighbourhoods always connected with fado bars and restaurants that attract many people, and Amália Rodrigues lives in one of them called "Madragoua".

Apart from Lisbon and Coimbra, Porto has a kind of fado too, but nothing compared with the two previous ones.

The fado from Lisbon is more musical, but the one from Coimbra is always more emotional, they sing the love, deep love and are sung by the University students and always dressed in traditional costumes.

Since the coup in 1926, fado underwent mutations from its original form, after being through censure; but also, with everything evolving, the performers and performance spaces suffered. The regime was on top of everything and everyone, controlling every little detail and punishing people with tough measures in case of disobedience.

Chapter 15

The first week at home was very difficult for everyone without Jonny. Even Torres the very tough man was slightly sad. His only son had left and especially at dinner time was when he missed him most. He never talked about it, but his family knew him very well and noticed him hiding his feelings. there was nothing for him to be ashamed of, but men are created to be strong, masculine, hard and not to cry in any circumstances.

Down throughout the centuries, people were too hard on themselves, they cultivated the culture about all the rights for men and even to be always ahead of women on almost everything. But men can't demonstrate their feelings, because if they do, it means they are weak. On the other hand, women (regardless of what age they are) need to obey their father and husbands after getting married. It is like women are always someone else's property. It was a subject that always made Sara angry.

Sara deeply felt her son's absence - her boy who was the cause of her life changing was not there anymore, but she always put on a strong face to not let anyone notice her sadness. In a way she was relieved - Jonny not being there meant less of a chance to get in trouble with his father, but Sara knew her son - it was just a matter of time before he would forget what had happened before.

Ana was missing her brother too, but she was happy because she thought she could save money now that he wasn't there anymore. She knew Jonny was happy for his new life, he had everything he wished for. Now it was just giving time to see if he could adapt to it, but she was sure he would. His new job was related to cars – something he really liked- and in the city he wanted to discover the freedom he was looking for.

At the end of this first week away from home, Jonny came back for the weekend, and everyone was pleased. Sara cooked nice meals, but she hardly laid her eyes on her son because he spent most of the weekend out.

Jonny kept coming home most weekends and his family was getting used to it, but especially his parents were preparing themselves for change. Jonny was young, full of life and starting to discover Lisbon in it's full, and those days were very close to starting.

After a few months of working at Fiat in Lisbon, Jonny started to avoid coming home so often - he had made new friends in the Capital, and he was completely in love with the city. Almost every night he went to seafood restaurants and fado house's and it started to be normal to go home for weekends towards the end of each month. Every end of the month started to be an extra expense for Sara and Ana. Jonny was not afraid to ask his mother to lend him some money till next month, and his sister to buy some things he needed, like shoes, shirts, suits etc. Ana was furious and she complained every time to her mother about it, but Sara always defended Jonny saying that this was a phase, and because he was discovering a new world in Lisbon, soon, he will settle his feet on the ground and things will change.

"You know Ana, men can't survive without us women! If your brother now that he is still single does all the things that he wants to, one day when he is married, he won't do bad things to his wife because he's done it before. It's like an investment I must call it."

"Mother I don't care about what my brother does or not, I'm not his wife, he can live and waste, as long as it doesn't cost me any money, I will be happy with it. You just have to let him grow and be responsible for his actions - come on Mother he is my big brother, and he needs to behave like one, just let him."

"Like I told you Ana, it's just a phase."

Their mother was pretty sure this would happen, but her daughter didn't believe it. For her, Jonny was a spoilt stupid boy and Sara was to blame for his behaviour. She needed to be harder with him - it was not ok to let him waste all his wages and come home to get extra money, and whatever he was doing, he needed to slow down and take control of his own money and make it last till the next wages come in.

Ana was starting to be really upset every time Jonny was coming home, and one day she was talking with her friend Carla about it, and her friend was quite supportive.

"Ana, I know your mother wants to help him, but I think giving him money just because he can't control his own is not the way to do it - he needs to learn from his own mistakes. We would like to have an easy life too, but for us this has to work in a different way..."

Both girls rolled their eyes in discontent, but not everything was bad. After a while talking, Ana's friend invited her to go to a prom in two weeks' time.

"Ana we can have a good time, I have another 4 friends to come with me and it will be awesome if you come too. We will have lots of fun and we can be home around 11pm, and because we are all together our mothers don't need to go, and we can have more freedom and it's just down the road. What do you say my friend?

We will have an excuse to buy new dresses, and probably new shoes."

"I say... you have everything well planned... I would like to go too, but...I need to convince my father to let me go, and I know for sure that it isn't going to be easy."

"But it's not impossible - you're the one that says that you're the daddy's girl, it means you are halfway there. Just trust me, this is going to be fine."

Now Ana needed to ask her father, and this was going to be hard because he was so protective of her, but she was going to ask her mother for help.

Just imagining dancing and having a good time with friends made her very excited, she normally spends her free time with her mother, and she loves it, but at her age she liked to have some excitement too - going to a party was everything she needed now.

That evening after dinner, Ana was helping Sara clean up the kitchen after Torres went out, when she put her arms around her mother's neck.

"Oh, what's up... what is that you want?"

"What makes you think that I want something mother?"

"Because I know you like the palm of my hand, and the way you put your arms around my neck - that's for sure that there is something you really want. Am I right Ana?"

Ana took her arms off her mother's neck and with her very dark eyes she looked at her mother and spoke.

"You are right mother, there is something that I want to ask you, but I don't know where to start!

"Normally people start from the beginning - I don't think it's much fun if you start from the end, don't you think?

"Why are you always right mother? I was going to start from a different beginning but since you made me see things differently, I will give it a go starting from the beginning."

"Stop small talk and get it over with. What do you want?"

"I'll try..."

Mother and daughter laughed.

"Mother I was invited to go to a prom... and apparently a few of my friends are going too, and I really want to go too, if you agree... and if you do, can you help me ask my father to let me go. OK, it's just that. What do you think?"

"Ana, for me there is not a problem, I think it's perfectly normal at your age to enjoy yourself, you know that you need to take care of yourself and have your brain always in place. Life is full of temptations at your age, that's why you need to be careful. Sometimes when a girl is on her own, she behaves calm and weighted but when she is with other girls, she can be very different, that's why I'm asking darling, do not ever be the cause of others' gossip ok?"

"Mother come on, you know me... if I can go, it will be fun, you know I like to dance, and you can go with me, ok? I know if dad lets me go, he will give me another lecture."

"When did you say will be?"

"Two weeks from now. "

"Tomorrow after lunch ask your dad, you don't need me for that Ana...ok? But before you do it just pay attention, if his mood is good or not. In all aspects of life, you need to analyse people and situations. Most of the time darling, depending how people are feeling they can make things easier or not, and tomorrow if your father is not in a great mood, it's worth waiting a day or two and just giving it a little time."

The next day after lunch, Ana exchanged a look with her mother and after a positive reply she got courage and asked her dad.

"Dad, there is going to be a prom, not next weekend but the one after and one of my friends asked me if I want to go." And saying that, she made a pause and looked at her dad.

"And..." said Dad

"I would like to go too; I spend most weekends here with mother, but it will be fun if you let me go. Quite a few of my friends are going too and it is here in Santarém."

"Ana, I don't care if one or twenty of your friends go or not - I know all these prom things very well, and I know there are always smart guys trying to have fun with girls. You are a very pretty young lady, and I want to be completely sure that nothing of this kind of situation happens to a daughter of mine. Understood young lady? You can go but only if your mother goes too!... just be careful, remember what I have told you in the past, and everything will be ok."

Ana was so excited that she got up from her chair and cuddled her father and gave him a big kiss. Sara just looked up to the ceiling like the ceiling was the sky and thought... Thank God.

However, Sara and Torres knew their daughter very well and they trusted her, but it was better to be safe than sorry regarding having a daughter in the first place. A boy - no matter how silly he was – always had all the freedom in the world, just because he was a man. If you were a girl, it was a different story, something that Sara never understood. In Sara's opinion girls and boys should have the same values and the same obligations, people just need to be educated to respect one another and take responsibility for their behaviour. Why do parents defend the idea that only boys should study, only boys can choose what they want to do in life... girls have opinions too about themselves, they are clever and just need opportunities and not have others complaining about them.

Girls aren't dolls, they are human beings with desires, tastes, opinions, and capacities. If they learn, they can do everything a boy does.

Sara never understood why most people defended the idea that women don't need to study because they were born to marry, have kids and to be there for their husbands like employees. If it wasn't for Jonny, she would never have had a man by her side because she simply doesn't believe all these crap opinions that most people have about women.

Once Sara was coming home from shopping at the market, when a neighbour called her to have a bit of gossip, something that she didn't have patience for. The news was about a girl from the neighbourhood that was going to marry soon...but the problem was the girl was pregnant, and the problem was when a girl marries normally in the bride's flower bouquet there must be some orange tree flowers too, as proof of her virginity, like a kind of stamp again in women. When this neighbour criticised the bride to be, Sara (as a joke) said for her not to worry because instead of her orange tree flower she could take the whole orange tree on her shoulder. The most annoying thing for Sara was the fact most of times women are their own worst enemies and this is bigoted. How could a woman be the first in line to criticise another woman? They should be together to fight all these petty ideas.

Just before the prom day, Jonny came home to everyone's surprise, when he had told his family before, he wouldn't.

It was just before lunch time when he came through the main door. He still had the house keys. He knew that there were going to be questions about this unplanned visit, but Sara happily put another plate on the table for him. She was always very pleased to see Jonny, but she could feel that there was something wrong. The moment she laid eyes on him; she could see that was something not quite ok. She didn't want to be unpleasant or give Torres a reason to object, but why did he come so early when they were all waiting for him the following weekend?

In the beginning Jonny used to come home every weekend – after which things changed a bit and he was coming home before the end of each month, but this was an unexpected visit, in the middle of the month. Sara knew her son very well, but the thing was, Torres was there, so she had to wait till the coast was clear from Father Torres. At the same time, she could see Torres looking with a suspicious stare towards their son. Her heart just froze for a second, she was really scared of Jonny's visit turning into a conflict.

She was praying for Torres to go out, but things didn't go the way she wanted.

"Son, why are you here when you were supposed to be in Lisbon working, did you lose your job, or get yourself in some kind of trouble?"

Jonny looked at his dad and spoke.

"No father, I didn't, why are you assuming the worse about me? I just miss you guys!"

Torres put down his knife and fork, put his elbows on the table with his hands together and looked his son in the eyes.

"Are you sure it is just that? You are not the type of person to miss us; I think I can put my hands on the fire, and I won't get burnt. You will probably wait till I get out of here to implore your mother for help."

"Dad I have been working extra time and I got a promotion... they like me, there are people who like me."

"Don't be stupid Jonny. As your father, I would like to know why you came home when it was not planned for you to come. I like to have you here, but you decide this way. Still, you don't want to talk but you don't fool me son."

They all finished their lunch and before Torres left for his office he turned to Ana and said,

"I will see you later before you go, ok?"

"Yes Dad."

As soon as Torres left, Sara told Ana to go to her room to prepare her dress for later and check if it needed to be ironed. Her daughter understood immediately what her mother was up too; she knew Jonny well enough to know he had some kind of problem - she didn't feel sorry for him.

"Mother shall I help you clean up the kitchen first?"

"No need, go and prepare your clothes for later - you want to look beautiful, don't you?"

Jonny stood up, but his mother turned to him.

"Where do you think you're going young man? Sit down and start to talk." She sat as well.

"Mother... I don't have anything to talk about..." but she told him to start again. "Mother why are you convinced that I'm not ok?"

"I know my children well enough to know when they have a problem, you don't fool me, neither your father nor your sister. I'm waiting.... and I know you want to talk to me, alone, that's why I asked your sister to go. And you better start talking Jonny - I know you, and I guess that you might be in some kind of big trouble. Am I right?"

"You know me so well mother!" and saying that Jonny smiled at his mother, but it was kind of a very pale smile that confirmed to Sara that something was up.

"Is it money Jonny! What sort of trouble are you in?"

"There is this guy that I met at work that has been trying to convince me to go to this place for gambling..."

"Gambling! Oh, my dear God, Jonny what have you done? How much did you lose? Are they coming after you?"

"Mother... Stop... it's nothing like that, let me talk please! If you don't let me explain you will not understand!"

"Jonny son, I have been around for many years, and I have seen the worst when men enter those paths and they lose everything, can you hear me? EVERYTHING Jonny. You have to stop now."

"Mother it was just a one off!"

"A one off? Are you stupid Jonny? I don't think you are... are you in debt?"

"I lost all my money and... I need you to help me because I don't have any, till my next wages. I'm sorry mother! It won't happen again I promise."

"It was nothing? It doesn't look like nothing to me! You didn't want to tell me, but you came here to ask me for money...I should have guessed...the thing that impressed me is the fact that you look like a man but when spinning out you behave like a kid...when are you going to grow up? When are you going to start to be a man? You have the life that you choose, living in a place that you like, stop being stupid and grow." There was silence for a minute.

"Jonny you are a very bright young man with a brilliant future ahead of you, don't mess that up son." After a pause Sara continued.

"I will lend you some money till you receive your next wages, but I have to deal with your father... and after you pay me back and from now on Jonny your sister won't pay anything for you anymore. Your sister has been spending money on you when you don't need her help at all because you have your salary too, every month. You must learn how to organise yourself and do not spend money on stupid things and for sure, not creating a stupid habit. I thought I was helping you but now I realise that this situation is my fault too. Lisbon is another world, and very different from Santarém, with lots of temptations but... you must control yourself if you don't want to end up being miserable.

I think you are becoming a bohemian like plenty in the capital. I can say to you son that I'm feeling very sad about you. As a mother, I tried to raise you and your sister the best way I possibly could, to be very decent people, but now I'm not so sure about it. I'm not very proud about the way you are going...you need to stop now!"

"Mother wait up! It was just a one off, I promise you that it won't happen again, but I need you to continue to trust me! Please mother!"

After a moment of silence Sara covered her own face with her hands, took a deep breath and looked at her son, she said:

"Jonny, I trust you son, but only you can change the way your own life's going! You have two ways ahead of you, one of disgrace and another of honesty and everything that comes with it. You were brought up by your dad and I with dignity and I truly hope that you continue to choose the road of honesty, going forward in your life."

"Ana did you get the clothes you are going to wear this evening ready darling?"

"Yes mother, just my new dress, the one I picked up from the dress maker last week, the pink and white one, and my beautiful shoes and my handbag matching the dress... you will see me later. And what are you going to wear mother?"

"Just a normal skirt and blouse. You are the one who needs to go pretty because you are young and want to enjoy the proms, I'm just an old goat who goes to keep an eye on you... nothing else, you are my sheep and I'm your shepherd. I just need to feel ok myself."

That evening all of the family had dinner a bit early and just after it Ana ran to her room to prepare herself while Sara cleaned up the kitchen.

Torres normally went out after dinner, but today he stayed just to see his daughter before she left. It didn't take long for him to be amazed the minute she joined him in the kitchen.

"Wow little heart! You look absolutely gorgeous! What a beautiful woman you turned out to be! I'm very proud of you... you know that right?"

"Dad stop...I feel embarrassed!"

"You shouldn't because I'm telling the truth! And embarrassed? Don't be silly, lots of girls would give anything just to look like you."

The minute he was saying that Sara entered the kitchen and without making a big deal said that her daughter looked very pretty. Sara was never vain - she always liked to be well dressed and clean. Torres never told her if she looked good or not, not that she ever expected it from him.

Mother and daughter were just about to leave home when Torres turned to his daughter and said,

"Have fun, don't do anything stupid and don't come home after 11.00 pm." He turned to Sara with his finger and pointed to her. "And you look after her! Understood?"

Every time Torres said that Sara, felt very cross inside. Ana is her daughter too and Sara doesn't need to be reminded by anyone to take care of her own daughter. Conversations like that made her feel sick, it's like an erupting volcano of emotions against him but in a way, no one can see it, but she couldn't say anything to him because if she did, he wouldn't let them go to the prom and she would never do this to her lovely daughter. Most of the times when Torres annoyed her, Sara (in her own mind) called him empty plonker.

The prom was held in a big salon not far from their home, and when both women entered the place the young girls that were already there looked at Ana and a few of them felt a bit jealous. Ana acted like she didn't notice because the purpose of being there was to have a good time and it was not her fault if the other girls didn't have the taste to dress beautifully. Sometimes it's not the clothes they are wearing but the combination of colours they choose. One of her friends had a dress with a cardigan in pink and yellow and without saying anything, Sara and Ana looked at one another and exchanged a funny look. Both thought that it was like eating pasta and rice all together.

The truth was Ana always liked fashion - she was learning how to make her own clothes; she had great taste in combining colours and she loved shoes. She always took care of all her clothes and shoes, and they lasted years always in good condition.

The prom started and Carla who invited Ana talked animatedly about a guy who was coming to the prom too.

"Ana, he has been in the military in Gôa, India for 18 months and he just came back - I'm so excited! He is a gorgeous looking guy."

And saying that Carla was all agitated like she had flees all over her body, without stopping talking and moving, giggling like a kid that had a thrilling present.

Carla was so enraptured, but in Ana's opinion this was silliness because there were a few boys there and very nice looking too - why be wasting time talking about some guy just because he has been away for a long time?

"Ok, ok let's dance... mother do you want to dance with me?"

"Ana, you know that I don't like to dance, go and dance with one of your friends."

Ana turned close to her mother and whispered in her mother's ear.

"Mother please save me, I'm so fed up with this stupid talk about this guy that is going to come here, and I have been paying attention to the girls - they all look a bit crazy, every time someone comes through the door, they all turn at the same time to see if it is the boy! What's wrong with them?"

Sara looked at her daughter, lifted her eyebrow, took a deep breath and then she went to dance with her daughter. They danced to two beautiful songs. At first, Sara stepped on her daughter's feet a few times - she was starting to become annoyed and when they were dancing the third one more perfectly, Ana was facing the main door and she saw this tall, blond guy with blue eyes coming in. This very precise moment she had a very deep feeling in her heart. She stopped dancing with her mother but kept her mother close.

"Why did you stop? The music hasn't finished yet!"

"Mother it's him!"

Sara (with no vision whatsoever about what was happening) looked at Ana.

"What are you talking about?"

"Mother, very slowly face the main entrance without people noticing. Look at the guy who just came in."

Sara did exactly what her daughter asked her to do.

"Wow gosh, it's a gorgeous boy...God bless a mother that gave birth to this gorgeous piece of gold! But... he doesn't look Portuguese...maybe English?"

As soon as the boy entered the room, lots of girls gathered close to him like chicken when being feed corn.

"Mother he is the one! He must be! Stupid girls, they don't give him space!"

"The one? What are you talking about?"

"Mother...he is the one!"

"You girls are so strange...What do you mean 'the one'? Am I missing something here or what?"

"Mother, Carla was talking about him before!"

"Oh, ok and so? They don't have good teeth for him."

"What?"

Sara looked at Ana and explained.

"It means the boy is too bloody gorgeous for those flipping crazy girls!"

"Mother it's stupid of me but I have a strong feeling about him, I feel like I have met him before."

"Now I know that you are giving too much freedom to your imagination - it might be, who knows, but he just came to the party, you have never even talked with him before ...Ana just let your feet be on the ground, will you." Saying that, mother and daughter went to sit, but Ana's eyes were following the boy everywhere, and she felt sorry for the girls who were fussing about him. This time it was Sara who asked Ana to dance, to distract her, but she refused - there wasn't anything that would make her take her eyes off this guy.

Sara was talking to her daughter, but Ana couldn't hear anything – her mind was miles away, only her body was there. There were quite a few girls still making a big fuss around him, asking him to dance but for some reason that didn't bother Ana, and she refused to dance with other boys, telling them her mother didn't let her and Sara at first looked at her daughter in surprise but after they turned around, she made jokes with Ana.

Mother and daughter were sitting and talking - it was almost time to go home when someone got close to them without them noticing. When they looked up, they saw the gorgeous boy that Ana was curious about - he was wearing a grey suit, white shirt, and a burgundy tie; he looked very elegant. He held out his hand to Ana and asked,

"Would you like to grant me the next dance?" Sara thought her daughter would decline it. But she was obviously wrong.

Ana stood up and immediately looked at her mother as if she was asking permission, and Sara nodded her head. Mother and daughter were very close and didn't need to talk to know what the other was thinking. But just before the two of them went dancing, the guy said,

"Let me introduce myself, my name is Peter, I'm the son of Joseph Ross, and that girl over there," he pointed at a girl in the crowd "is my sister."

Sara looked very seriously at him as if her memory was searching for a quick answer and in a fraction of a second, she said,

"I know your father, but I didn't know he had a son. I know he has three daughters; grown women I must say. By the way I'm Sara and my daughter is Ana. Nice to meet you, Peter."

"Good to meet you too, and your daughter... wow what a beautiful name for such a beautiful girl."

Ana blushed – she was as red as a ripe tomato, but she said thank you.

The other boys were not very happy to see her dancing with someone else when she refused to dance with them and they looked to Sara with a questioning look, but she pointed a finger saying no. Sara was always very respected in the city and because she was a big woman no one tried to confront her in any way.

While dancing, Ana felt very flattered because all the other girls were acting with jealously, some of them were complaining like Peter was kind of their property.

He told Ana that he had been in Gôa in military service for the last 18 months guarding the tomb of St. Francis Xavier. Ana was very religious, and she was very impressed by what she just heard. She asked many questions about it to Peter, and he answered all of them.

In the meantime, Jonny got there too and as soon as he saw his sister dancing with Peter, he didn't look very happy about it and tried to locate his mother with his eyes through the many people that were there. Finally, he found his mother and walked towards her like he was a leading man with some girls just staring at him.

"Mother, why my sister is dancing with Peter?"

"Good evening to you too son."

"I'm sorry mother... Good evening...But why is my sister dancing with that guy?"

Jonny was looking very handsome himself. He was wearing a navy-blue suit with a white shirt and a blue tie. Jonny was normally very vain, as he has always been since he started to look like a young man.

"Do you know him?"

"I do and I can tell you that Ana shouldn't have been dancing with him!"

"May I ask why son, what have you got against Peter?"

"Mother he thinks he can have all the girl's attention... I want to keep my sister away from him."

"I beg your pardon?"

"Mother, my sister deserves better...this guy sucks..."

"Jonny stop right there... I know his father and he is a good man, and I know his sisters too, they are good people and besides your sister is just dancing with him nothing else."

"Mother he thinks that he is God's gift to women."

"Maybe he his!" Sara laughed saying that. "Jonny go and find yourself a girl and enjoy yourself. Son, would you like others to say the same thing about you? I don't think so Jonny. We should never criticise others just because of their outside looks... right son? By the way Jonny, if I was one of those girls, you would never escape me, because I simply wouldn't let you. Go on gorgeous, go and enjoy yourself."

Jonny went to the bar, and he had a drink, but his eyes were following his sister and Peter everywhere.

Ana and Peter looked happy because they were enjoying each other's company always hitting the dance moves and never stepping on each other's feet – it was like they had been dancing for years.

Just before their last dance, Peter asked Ana when he was going to see her again, but she said she didn't know. She added to their conversation the place where she works, but she warned him that her father was very strict. Peter suggested that she went to another party in three weeks at Baron's square so that they could meet again. Ana was very excited, and she told him that she would try.

The dance finished and he walked with Ana towards Sara. They both looked very happy - Sara and everyone else could see it.

"Sara, thank you very much for letting me dance with your daughter."

"At your age you need to enjoy yourselves without causing problems. Now if you will excuse us, we must put an end to this evening and head home. Shall we go young lady? Peter give my regards to your family, will you?"

"Of course...I won't stay long either." He looked at Ana and continued. "I am still a bit tired because of the difference of hours between India and Portugal, but I'm glad that I came here. It's always good to meet new people, and although this party was really well organised, there are some quite new faces that I don't remember!"

On their way home Ana wouldn't stop taking about Peter, and she told her mother that Peter had invited her to go to the next party in three weeks. Sara was quite worried because of how Torres would take this news about his daughter being invited by a boy to go to a party?

What a worry for her...she told Ana to be careful and tell the truth and not to make any decisions without talking to her parents first. Parents are always too protective of their daughters, and they don't want their daughters to be in people's mouths for the worst reasons.

When they got home Torres was sitting in the kitchen reading while waiting for them to arrive.

"Did you have fun little heart?"

"I did father, it was really amazing, thank you for letting me go."

"Did you dance with someone?"

In this very moment Ana had the feeling that maybe, just maybe her father went to the proms just to check on her... and like her mother said before, the truth, always, and she wanted to be straight from the beginning with everybody.

"Yes father, I danced a few times with mother," and saying that she put one arm around Sara and smiled at her "and after I refused to dance with one or two boys, and I accepted to dance with one."

"Why did you accept to dance with him little heart?"

Ana was very calm, and for her father to call her little heart - it was because he was not mad at her, and that was good news.

"I know that you don't believe me father, but when Peter entered the prom, I had a strange feeling deep in my heart, it was like I already knew him. I have never felt that way, and when we danced, I felt very happy because he had so many girls he could choose from to dance, but he found me with mother in a corner talking and asked me to dance with him."

"Did he ask you to meet again little heart?"

"Yes father, he asked me if I would like to go to a party in Baron's square in three weeks, but I didn't say yes."

Torres turned to Sara and asked her who he was.

"Do you remember Joseph Ross the carpenter who did some work for Antonio at his home just before Easter last year, if my memory doesn't fail me."

"You mean the Abitureiras guy?"

"Yes, that's the one. He lost his wife when their kids were very young, but I never noticed that he had a boy too - I know his sisters. Peter has been away in Gôa the last 18 months in military service, and he just got back, they are a good family." Sara answered all the questions her husband wanted to know; she had a feeling Torres had been at the Prom too, and now was just checking if they were telling the truth or not. It was very hard to share your life with someone who doesn't trust you and is always trying to catch you around the corner. He wasn't the one who carried Ana for nine months in his belly - Sara put her kids first in all circumstances no matter what. Her husband was clever in many subjects but in this one, she believed he just liked to hurt her as hard as he could...but for what? She always put her family above all else.

"Little heart do you want to meet him again?"

"Yes Father, I do."

"OK... you tell him to come and talk to me first."

"But I don't know when I'm going to see him again!"

"Don't worry, when he turns up you will give him my message, understood? I'm sure he will turn up during the week."

"OK Father, I will."

"Now I can go to bed. Good night."

After making sure her father had gone to bed, Ana had a question for her mother. "Mother why does Father want to talk to Peter? We are not dating!"

"Precisely Ana, when you told us that he invited you to the party, your father and I realised that he wants to date you, and you know the rules. No girl should be dating without the boy asking her father for permission. Ana if Peter has good intentions with you, he will understand! Just relax darling, everything is going to be alright and remember an old saying. Whatever is kept for you, the mice won't gnaw."

That night Ana was so happy, and she felt very special, and after turning the light off, she relived the time she was dancing with Peter. She was so excited that she couldn't sleep. She started to imagine Peter kissing her, with his strong arms around her, keeping her close to his chest, but she felt this strange feeling in her tummy. She covered her head under the blankets, and she smiled, at least no one could see her or imagine her thoughts - she would be ashamed if they could.

In the morning she was in a very good mood and even her father thought something was changing about his daughter. She was becoming a woman, she was developing feelings for a man, and he respected Ana when she told him that she felt a deep feeling in her heart the moment she laid her eyes on Peter.

Torres already knew that sometimes his daughter had premonitions about things, but he never believed them. However, he always respected her, and occasionally he had asked her to pray to her saints to help him achieve something. More than once she had asked him, if he doesn't believe in it why does he ask her to pray, and he always says that he doesn't, but she does, and there is no harm in him asking because it's always a possibility. Ana understood her father and for what it was worth, she felt flattered.

She was a young woman with very strong faith. At night she never fell asleep without praying first. In her room, she had the image of the virgin Mary and Jesus, and every Monday evening she had a little candle lit in her bedroom. She was very devoted to her religion, and every year, she simply loved Christmas, preparing everything very carefully.

Chapter 16

It was a lovely Autumn morning, the sun was shining, and the first leaves were starting to fall. The streets in Santarém started to have this amazing mixed colour of yellow, red, and brown, like a natural work of art and a lovely picture of the city. Slowly the city started to have a blanket, a very different one from the previous season, when the sun used to shine for very long hours making the day be longer and making everything and everyone warm. Autumn days start to bring the first breeze, the beginning of the changing weather. The wind sometimes blew strongly, and all these lovely colours flew very high, some of them disappeared in a whirlwind and others landed everywhere causing a simple natural beauty.

Ana was a bit sad when she went to work, because a few days had passed and no sign of Peter. She was concerned - not because she didn't trust him, but maybe because someone could try to interfere. Her mother had told her to be patient because sometimes people can have other things to do, things do not always happen the way we like.

Ana was kind to the customers, she worked in a shop that sold all the accessories for homes. From bed linen to lamps, kitchenware etc. But on this particular day she didn't have the shine that she normally had. Some customers (mostly ladies) were bold and asked Ana if she was ok. She replied with a smile saying that everything was ok, but everyone who knew her, could see something was up.

It was around 10.30 in the morning and Ana was writing a list of stuff the boss needed to get for the shop to restock their storage, and she was so concentrated that she didn't see or hear a customer come in. She was behind the counter when she heard a familiar male voice.

"Good morning, Ana."

She recognised that voice straight away and when she lifted her head, she already knew who he was, and she couldn't hide her happiness. He was looking very elegant in a brown suit, cream skirt and a red tie. All her colleagues at work clearly saw her reaction and discovered why she had been a bit sad before.

"What time is your lunch break Ana?"

"Peter it's not appropriate for you to be here if you are not going to buy anything - my boss is very strict, and I don't want to be embarrassed."

"Who said I'm not going to buy anything?"

"You are?... very well, what can I get you?"

"I would like to by two mugs for coffee, in red if you have them, please."

She looked at him and smiled - she understood this was an excuse, but she went to get what this special customer asked for. After a few minutes she came with four sets of different mugs for him to see if they were what he was looking for.

"Oh, they all look nice!" and he picked up two and he looked at her with a very intense look deep in her eyes, something that made her feel wanted.

"Can I wrap up those two?"

"Hmmm, let me think... only if you promise to spare me five minutes outside before you go home to have your lunch, ok?"

Ana looked at him with only her very naughty smile.

"I could do that...but ...it has to be only five minutes."

"Lovely, now you can wrap up the mugs, thank you."

Ana prepared the things that Peter had just bought and told him how much it was. He gave her the money, and when she gave him the change, he just grabbed her hand and smiled at her, but she took her hand away immediately before her colleagues or boss saw it. Peter winked at her, smiled, and left just to wait outside till it was time for her to have her lunch break. As soon as he left her colleagues started teasing her in a good way about Peter, but she smiled, and never said a thing. She didn't need to because it was very clear from her attitude before his visit and after; it was like a winter day, compared to a hot summer one. Love can bring out the best in humans. True love can make all sorts of miracles, and any rainy day could turn out to be a very pleasant one. It was love which caused her mother to have an unexpected journey in life. She had so much to live for, but because she fell in love with her brother, everything took a different path in her life. Love can have a big impact, good or bad. For love her mother had suffered for so many years because she couldn't turn her back on her kids. Ana knows a lot about this extraordinary feeling, it has been present in her life since always.

It was half past midday when Ana stepped outside from the shop, and there was Peter trying to smoke a cigarette without the wind blowing it off, even her hair was all over the place because of it.

She was a bit nervous because she wanted to tell Peter that her father wanted to talk to him, but she didn't know how he would react. In the end it was just the second time they are meeting but Ana was afraid that Peter might feel pressure, and see things in a different way, and wanted to leave - on the other hand she must tell him what her father asked her to do, if not, there would be consequences.

"Ana you must be wondering why I wanted to talk to you...you know I'm the kind of guy who likes to do everything by the book...Ana," he took a moment. "Since the day at the prom, I think I fell in love with you..."

She was looking at him with her dark eyes in a tender way.

"But I can see that you are feeling something for me too... Am I right Ana?"

Ana smiled at Peter.

"Is it that obvious Peter?"

"What do you think?"

"Yes, I'm in love with you Peter since the very moment that I first saw you, but..."

"Before you say what you are going to say I want to tell you that I want to talk to your father first. I know how things work, and I want to do what is right from the beginning." Ana was relieved after she heard what he just said. Since he came in the shop before, she was wondering the best way to tell him, but now she didn't need to.

Peter told Ana that the next day at the same time he would be waiting for her, and he hopes that she can have arranged a time for him to talk with her father. The two of them went away in separate directions.

When Ana got home, her mother noticed that her daughter was in much more of a good mood than when she left for work a few hours earlier, and in her heart, she simply knew what must have been the reason for that. Ana looked at her mother with very happy, sweet, soft, and tender eyes.

"I think there is someone who just saw a little bird!" Sara said. Her daughter smiled, got closer to her mother's ear, and whispered.

"Mother, Peter came to see me at work!" Saying that Sara was a bit worried.

Torres came into the kitchen and all three sat around the table to have lunch.

"Father...Today I saw Peter outside my work." Sara was so surprised by the calm and cool way that her daughter said that to her father that she choked up.

"Mother are you ok?"

"...Yes, I am." Sara answered while trying to compose herself, while Torres put his knife and fork down.

"You know little heart, your mother just choked up because she was impressed by the way you talk about Peter. Now Ana, have you asked him to come and talk to me?"

"No, I did not, because before I said anything at all, he told me himself that he wants to talk to you."

"I'm impressed...I like that...it's a good start I must say." Torres picked up his knife and fork again and started to eat. There was a silence while the family were having their lunch. Ana was worried because she was waiting for her father to set up a date and time for both men to meet. As soon as Torres finished his lunch, he said that he could come one day in the afternoon of his convenience to his office, and they can talk peacefully.

Hearing that Sara was more relaxed, and Ana looked pleased.

After mother and daughter had finished their lunch Torres went to his office, Ana went back to work, and Sara stayed at home cleaning up the kitchen.

All afternoon Ana was in good spirits performing her duties perfectly as always, just continuously looking at her watch, but each hour was a week. She couldn't wait for the day to end and for it to be the next day to see Peter. At one point her boss asked her if everything was ok.

That day when she finished work, she went home but her eyes were looking around very discreetly in case of spotting Peter, but she didn't. Instead, she saw Clementino and like always they spent a few minutes talking. He asked about the family if they were all well, but he noticed that Ana was happy. She didn't say anything about Peter, but Clementino did. He told Ana that such a beautiful smile must be the result of love. She laughed, but he knew; he had enough experience to guess that a girl at her age so happy must be love. He cuddled and kissed her and said he was really pleased for her. Ana knew he was a genuine person; someone she could trust.

That night in bed she was having a myriad of thoughts about what the talk between her father and Peter was going to be like. She felt very anxious about it when her mother came through the door and asked her if she was ok.

"I think I'm a bit nervous, I'm scared if something happens, and my father doesn't let me be with Peter."

"I think you must be positive, nothing in this world comes easy...but think, if everything was easy, people would never give value to anything. When humans work hard to achieve whatever they want, they can have a better taste of things when they happen. People who just click their fingers and things come easy never value things. I know you darling, and I know that Peter must have started playing a very important role in your life."

"He has...I just feel like..." She covered her face with her hands. "Like we are meant to be together, mother. I feel like... I'm sorry to be sharing this with you mother, but you are my best friend forever." She smiled. "Peter is something that was missing from me, and finally turned up, and the two of us are one thing, our souls meant to be together; you will see. Do you understand mother?"

"I do...better than you think Ana. I'm really happy that you embrace me as your best friend. I'm very privileged and blessed to have you as my daughter. "

"You?... I'm the lucky one to have you as my mother. All my friend's mothers only know how to criticise their daughter's without even thinking that they can hurt them with their stupidity."

"Tomorrow is another day that you need to be fresh and beautiful for work."

When Sara left her room, Ana switched the bedside light off. Her imagination was travelling fast. Every time she thought about the first time they would kiss, she had this strange but good chill in her belly, then she covered her head with the sheet. The excitement didn't let her sleep till after midnight - even so she woke up much earlier than usual, quite normal.

Ana got up to prepare herself, made her bed and even had time to have a little chat with Sara before going to work, and along the way she was walking with lots of confidence in herself and looking at her watch she was thinking about how many hours she had ahead of her to meet up with Peter.

At home her mother was getting ready to go to Maria's house, because she had promised her friend to help whitewash the walls in her house. Before she left, Sara organised the lunch for later in case she came back later...she didn't want to give reasons for Torres to be angry at her.

When she was on her way to Maria's place, one of her gossiping neighbours asked her,

"Sara yesterday I saw your daughter outside of the shop talking to a boy...is he her boyfriend?"

"And what is that to do with you? If it is not it's none of your business..., don't you have better things to do than talking about someone else's life? Get a life."

The woman knew Sara for so many years, she knew Sara was like a lion defending her cubs from this gossip. Sara never had a good relationship with people that spent their days interfering in others' lives.

Ana kept looking outside to see if she could spot Peter, but she didn't, and her thoughts were maybe he had something to do. Once, she got to the door and looked to both sides of the street but there was no sign of him. She was slightly worried, but there was nothing she could do apart from wait till he turned up.

By the time she was coming out of the door to go for lunch, there he was smoking and waiting for her - she was all smiles when she saw him. Anyone could see the effect Peter had on this very young lady. Her smile was like a coloured flower garden on a lovely summer day.

"How are you since yesterday?"

"Much better since, I can see that you didn't forget me."

"I could never forget you – you are the brunette of my heart." He smiled at her. "Have you asked your father about meeting me, Ana?"

"I did."

"And?"

"He doesn't want to see you!" Peter believed it, and hearing this he put the cigarette on the floor and with his foot he rubbed on it to put it out. Suddenly Ana started to laugh.

"You are silly, of course he wants to see you, I was pranking you. He told me you can choose the day, but it needs to be one afternoon and in his office."

"OK...He didn't choose the day! From what I heard about his personality; he might be   trying to see how serious I am about you." Ana looked at Peter for an explanation, and he continued.

"Old people Ana are like old foxes, tricky, if I go and meet him soon, I will be with good intentions about you, but if for some reason I delay the visit, he will assume that I'm here with you just to have a good time and nothing else. They never think we can have important things to do as well, no, they always assume the worst."

"No, he didn't, he said it's up to you; it just needs to be in the afternoon and at his office, don't let your imagination take over. He was clear as water."

"Where is it?"

"My father's office is just next to Mr Paulo's grocery shop, around the corner from the hardware store, on the first floor. There is one door on the right and one on the left as you get to the top of the stairs, my father's office is on the left. You don't need to knock on the door because it's always open by just a bit, and that's it."

"Very well, you go home to have lunch and I'm going to do the same thing. Tomorrow I won't see you...I must go to Lisbon to the military headquarters. If possible, I will catch the last train back home at night, if not I will be back the next day."

"I will miss you...don't get involved with any Lisbon women, they are bohemian."

"Ana it's very important to have trust, ok?"

"I know Peter, I was just teasing you."

While the couple of lovebirds exchanged animated words and naughty looks, they did not even realize that Clementino was coming up the street. Without realizing it, he stopped, put his hand on his own waist and spoke. "What beautiful babes, wow it's so good to see people in love."

"Clementino!"

"Ana...I was right...I can smell love, such a sweet look for this handsome guy." Saying that he took advantage and looked over Peter from top to bottom. "Ana even I am jealous." And she laughed.

"Clementino, don't be perverse."

"Me?... he put his hand on his chest while saying this. "Miss Ana, you need to keep him well guarded, so nobody can steal him from you. And now what is this fine specimen of a man called?

"Peter." He extended his hand to handshake to introduce himself, but Clementino pulled him in and kissed Peter on both cheeks. The young couple wasn't expecting this, and they laughed so much.

"Of course, you are...And Peter have you got a twin brother out there, who likes other snacks?"

"Clementino?" Peter's eyes were wide open about what he had just heard, but they all laughed.

"What Ana? Ha, ha, it was a joke!... By the way how are your parents and brother, is everything okay? Ana tell your mother that on Friday I will pop in, and I will bring some cakes." And saying that Clementino turned to Peter, and added "Make sure you treat her well, otherwise her father will give you the rice. Bye bye!"

As soon as Clementino left, Peter asked who that fun person was, and Ana, explained that Clementino, although different, was one of the people with the best heart, and sense of humour that she had ever met.

"Not everyone likes him because he is always very sincere with everybody, honest, truthful and a very good friend. My brother doesn't like him, but the problem is my brother not Clementino. My brother thinks if other people see them together, they might think other things. I'm quite sure he was born into a body that he doesn't identify with himself."

"Ana, you have to go and so do I."

"I know, I can't be late, we'll meet in a day or two, right?"

"See you gorgeous." He smiled at her after saying that.

After saying goodbye to each other, she went home for lunch. During lunch Ana told her parents that she had seen Peter outside her work and given him her father's message.

"Ana, before I talk to the young man, I would prefer you to avoid being in his company for long. I don't want people speculating about my own daughter for any reason especially about something like that. Did he tell you when it will be more convenient for him to meet me? By your look I can say he didn't. Ana we should never put the carriage ahead of the horses, what I want to say is while he is not coming to talk to me, I forbid you to meet with him again. Do I make myself clear?"

"Yes father, but he will, Peter was the one who wanted to talk to you."

"I think there is nothing else to talk about...shall we finish lunch?"

By the way Torres was talking, Sara could see he was again in one of those phases that could mean trouble for her. Torres left after lunch and so did Ana, but just before she left, Sara advised her daughter to be cautious because if her father for some reason gets Peter on the wrong end of the stick, there won't be any relationship at all. Ana's father was very tough, and regarding women, he was even worse. Sara was never afraid of him, she just liked to avoid trouble as much as she could. All her life she hated every time he got crazy, it wasn't a good atmosphere to bring up kids. Now her daughter is much older and understands more, but Sara knows how much Ana is in love with Peter and she simply doesn't want anything bad to happen that could ruin that. Since always, Sara knew women had to depend on men, something that she never understood, because man is the one who needs women for everything not the other way around. One thing was certain, they need to be positive about this new love that has flooded her daughter's heart. Ana was a very special girl - she had never felt this way about anyone, she was always there for her family, but now it was her turn to be looking at her future.

That same afternoon, Peter decided to meet and talk to Ana's father, he already knew Torres was a very difficult man, and he didn't want to give him motive to put any obstacles between them. Following the instructions given by Ana he went straight to the building where her father had the office. The building had ground and first floors; the walls were white but a bit degraded - they could do with a bit of repair. There were two windows on the ground and first floor but all of them needed to be substituted for a good pair of new ones. The door was open, and Peter started to go up the stairs, but his thoughts were about a few things that he had been hearing about the man he was just about to meet. In his mind he wanted to get it over with, that's why he wanted to solve this before his trip to Lisbon the next morning.

When he got up the stairs, he headed towards the door that Ana had told him to, and like she said the door was half open and he just knocked very gently to announce his presence.

Torres was very concentrated on a book, and without saying a word he waved Peter in. Ten seconds later, Torres removed his glasses, leaned back in the chair, and took a look at his visitor.

"Mr. Torres, I'm Peter, thank you very much for being able to receive me during your working day."

"You are very welcome... I have been waiting to meet you... finally. Torres was an old fox who liked to observe people. Torres wanted to let Peter talk first because it was his way to examine the boy. Torres already defended the thesis that we can learn more when we keep quiet and listen to others and that's what he was planning to do.

"Mr Torres, I think you are aware that your daughter and I met at the prom." Torres was paying attention but with an intimidating look at the boy. "Back then we got along very well." Torres kept looking at Peter, but slowly he was showing a very authoritarian look that started to freak Peter out. Suddenly Peter stopped.

"Mr Torres, I'm sure Ana told you everything since we meet. I want to ask your permission to date your daughter. I have very strong feelings about her, and I know she has them too. I also know how things work because I have three sisters, and I only want for them what I want for Ana. I know you don't know me, but- "

Torres interrupted.

"My dear Peter, I have been doing my homework... I must admire your courage for being so honest about my daughter but let me tell you something. I know you and your family more than you know..." Peter understood that man had made some investigations about him and his family, but in a way, he was relieved, because he had nothing to hide and now, he didn't need to explain anything because he already knows a lot.

"My daughter has never had a boyfriend and you will be the first - and last. If you two get along it will be good, if not, I won't let her have another chance. I want you to respect her always, do you know what I mean? And think with your head, the top one, because I know how man works. Do we understand each other? I don't like to talk more than once about the same thing, and I hope you make my daughter happy because she is the best."

"Mr Torres, I will respect your daughter like I respect myself and like I want for my own sisters too. You will never regret letting me date Ana... she is too important for me, and one thing that I have been learning over the years is, what I feel for your daughter is unique, not like moonlight kisses that cool in the heat of the sun.

I will do whatever it takes to make her happy."

"I won't expect anything less. I know that you have been away in military service... are you happy to be back home?"

"Definitely... I spent eighteen months away, I saw lots of poverty that really touched me, but there was nothing that I could do to help. I learned many things too; I think all of us learned. But I'm really pleased to be back."

"What are your plans for the future?"

"Tomorrow morning, I need to be at the headquarters in Lisbon, I did my duty for our country, but from now on I want to get on with my life without military time. Next week I will start to look for a job."

"Fair enough, I think we talked about the most important things, I hope all goes smoothly."

Peter left Torres's office much more relaxed than when he came in, now he could go to the capital the next day without worrying about Ana's father. For Ana that evening she could escape without having another lecture from him, and after dinner Torres didn't let mother and daughter out of the table without marking his posture once again. He turned to his daughter and said:

"From now on you are officially Peter's girlfriend." Ana interrupted her father.

"Did Peter go to meet you?"

"Yes, we talked, and he asked permission to date you. Now... I will want your mother with you every single time you are with him... under no circumstances do I want you alone with him, I want to leave one thing very clear Ana." Every time he calls her by her name, and not little heart, it means he is being very serious and is not to be messed about. "I told you once and I'm telling you for the last time...if anything happens that shouldn't, I will kill you and your mother...I hope you and Peter have a future together because if you don't, you will never have another boyfriend - I won't let you. Do you have anything to say?"

"Thank you for letting me date Peter." In that precise moment she feared her dad and didn't know what else to say. For Sara all this talk was just another one; he always wanted to stamp his authority as a father. She understood his concerns but didn't agree with all the threatening behaviour. In her mind she knew all her responsibilities had just increased but she trusted her daughter, although she knew the temptation that could happen at young ages, when one thing could lead to another; she would have to be alert.

Peter didn't meet Ana when he said he would, but she wasn't worried, trust was a feeling that started living in both young hearts.

On Friday evening the family had Jonny to join them for dinner. He had just arrived from Lisbon, all around the table like in the old times sharing conversations, opinions, and thoughts. Sara was so tranquil seeing her children so relaxed. This was something that didn't last long when he discovered Ana was officially dating Peter. He stopped eating and wondered why Father had agreed with it. Torres very calmly explained to his son that he understands his concerns, but he knows Peter's background, and he liked him and what they had talked about when they met, there is no perfect man, but there are men with their fate and success, depends upon which path they choose to walk in their lives.

A good man's reputation is based on his own decisions about how to handle hard situations, we need to give time and opportunities for young men to develop.

Still, all of them could see the expression on Jonny's face about the possibility of Peter in the future becoming a part of their family. Ana only told her brother that she was the one who needs to like her boyfriend, not Jonny, he needed to mind his own business. The meal had finished in a very different atmosphere from where it had started. Torres left, Jonny followed, and mother and daughter were concerned about Jonny not wanting to let go of his opinion about her boyfriend.

On the next day, Ana prepared herself and went to work. Halfway through, Peter appeared and walked with her. She was very pleased about the way her day had started - the only thing she was not at all happy about was when Peter told her that the evening before, Jonny saw him in the tavern and ordered Peter to leave Ana alone.

"I'm sorry but I was concerned about your father...not your brother...you should have seen the way he was talking to me, like you were his property. In the end I had to be quite rude to him. I was there with my father to have some fun, but it turned out to be a stupid evening."

"I'm sorry, last night he started to argue when he found out about us, but I thought he had forgotten already - now I'm not so sure."

"Ana, we need to ignore him for our sake." They had just reached Ana's workplace, and just before they went their separate ways, he asked her to meet the next day after lunch at the main entrance of portas do sol, (sun doors).

Chapter 17

Saturday's shops were only open till 1 pm. Ana had a hard half day at work; how come her brother was interfering in her relationship with Peter, how could he? She got home very furious like an ox smoking through the nose.

"What happened Ana, you look like you saw a monster!"

"Mother, Jonny is touching a very sensitive spot, he has to stop, or I don't know what I'm capable of!" Torres and Jonny were coming in for lunch, something that left Sara speechless, but Torres wasn't deaf, and he knew.

"Little heart what did your brother do?!"

"Last night he saw Peter and told him to leave me alone." In this instant Torres turned to his son with the look that everyone knew so well.

"What did you do young man?"

"Last night I saw Peter at the tavern, and I asked him to leave Ana alone. I don't like him dad, I'm sure my sister could find a better boyfriend." The two women were watching them argue, but in suspense, because they didn't know what could happen.

"Since when Is this your problem, I don't remember asking you to interfere in this matter?"

"Dad I don't like Peter."

"Of course, not...as far as I know you like girls... Jonny, I forbid you from interfering between your sister and Peter, this is their life not yours, do I make myself clear? I like him too, because if I didn't think he was a good boy, I would be the first to stop this from happing."

The family had lunch and Ana told them the next day she was meeting Peter at the sun doors. Torres looked at his wife, lifted his eyebrows and Sara got the message.

The day after it was Sunday. Ana chose a beautiful navy-blue skirt with a red blouse, a black coat, and shoes to go with Sara to mass. They went to the ten o'clock one. After the communion, she was coming back to her seat when she saw Peter from the corner of her eye. Her heart bounced with happiness. After the Eucharist melted in her mouth, Ana looked at her mother, waited a bit and very discreetly told her about Peter. Sara whispered that she knew.

The mass finished and the priest was outside of the main door complimenting the people. It was just about to start raining. Mother and daughter came through the door, and they didn't need much time to find out where he was, because he was standing next to the priest with his father and young sister organising a meeting. Peter looked at Ana and winked at her and said, "See you later."

On their way home Sara opened her umbrella. The rain was starting to fall, and Ana was concerned about what it was going to be like in the afternoon at the garden. Sara told Ana Peter was a family boy, and didn't understand why Jonny didn't like him, but her daughter asked to not talk anymore about Jonny - she had better things to worry about.

After lunch mother and daughter headed to the sun doors, in heavy rain. Each of them had an umbrella but it was not enough. When they got there, Peter was already waiting. The love birds started to walk holding hands, while Sara was a few metres behind wiping the rain from her coat. They all got under a canopy from a shop that sold ice cream in the summer until the rain eased. It didn't take long until it stopped, but it was quite windy and not pleasant at all to be out. The view was amazing, nice to be in a post card and the trees were almost naked, and the birds didn't have much shelter, the grounds had a coloured look, different yellows, like an embroidered cloak.

Down the hill of Santarém, the panoramic view was poor because of the fog, not even the Tagus River was clear to see. It was a very miserable day. Sara was watching the love birds and thinking about all the winter days ahead of her for the next few months, to be keeping her eyes on then, instead of being indoors, warm and enjoying a hot drink. Despite the weather, the young couple were very happy. At one moment Sara, was not paying much attention to them and he kissed Ana in a flash of a second. They couldn't be caught kissing on the first day, because everything could be ruined, and that was the last thing they both wanted. The rain started to fall again and all of them opened their umbrellas, with her mother walking behind, and the umbrellas covered them. They checked to see if it was safe, without stopping, and again they kissed, this time for longer. It was enough to taste one another's lips. At this very moment they could have been in a different situation to enjoy better their first touch, but this was what was possible. Their hearts were full of dreams and happiness, not promises, but honesty, integrity, and love. Since Ana fell in love, she looked even prettier and happier than before, because love always has a especial effect on most people. Love can melt the hardest heart on earth.

Peter took his girlfriend home, but there was no kiss. They wanted to but they couldn't, they needed to behave.

That evening in bed Ana was letting her imagination once again travel in dangerous ways, but there it was safe, no one could see it, her first kiss. She smiled and covered her head with the bed covers to not make noise. She imagined how it would be like if Peter was there in bed with her. As soon as she had this thought her mind tricked her. Her father entered her room with a rifle and killed them both, Sara, and himself. She shivered. She knew, to have Peter in bed by her side, would only happen if they got married, and she was very certain that would happen in some years to come. She had this feeling inside of her that Peter and her belong together, and no matter how long it takes he would be her husband.

It was not the first time she saw girl's hysterics when seeing Peter, but she wasn't jealous, she knew he belongs to her in all senses of the word.

Jonny hadn't given up about what he thinks of Peter. Sara had to put him in his place more than once. Since his sister started to date Peter, Jonny never missed one weekend without being home. He was like a secret annoying agent always wanting to know everything. One evening Ana was really mad at him. She avoided confronting him while their father was around, but as soon as he left one day after dinner, Ana was like a lion defending Peter with all her strength.

"You should be ashamed of yourself. Why are you still being so annoying? Peter has plenty more qualities than you, why don't you find something useful to do."

"I told you time and time again that I don't think Peter is the right boyfriend for you Ana and I'm sorry I don't like him, I have my reasons."

"Again! Jonny get lost...You don't like him, but I do a lot and that is very important, and he did more for this country than you, he didn't have an important father to free him from the military service like you did."

"Ana you are so cruel."

"Shut up Jonny." She was really furious with her brother - she didn't understand why this situation existed at all; she believes Jonny does not like to see her happy because if he did he wouldn't behave like that.

The first week after they had their first date, Peter needed to go to Lisbon again for two days. He told Ana when he is back, he will start to look for a job. She asked him if she can ask her boss, maybe he knows of job opportunities through his professional connections.

Her boss, António, was a man of medium height, his hair was a bit grey, eyebrows very bushy and grey too and he was fat, typical of the region, with a huge belly. He was a man with forced sympathy, but he was a good businessman, and teaching all his staff to do everything they can, but never letting customers leave the store empty handed. His only interest was in the amount of money that costumers could leave at his store. With a pencil always behind his right ear, always walking from side to side, checking the performance of his employees, sometimes a little intimidating. This was something that rarely happened with Ana, because she was able to have confidence in herself and mostly perform successfully.

Peter said no - it wasn't a good Idea for both to be working side by side. In everything they talk about, he seems to be so mature for his age, it was one of the reasons both Ana's parents felt more confident about their daughter and boyfriend's relationship. Friday after she finished work, he was waiting for her, and accompanied Ana home. They agreed to meet up every Sunday after lunch just outside her front door, because he was not allowed to go in. Three weeks later he found a job in the best shoe shop in the city. It wasn't the best job but for now it worked. The surprise appearances to Ana during the week at lunchtime ended, and only sometimes occasionally they met up during the week after work because there wasn't enough time, but they managed to see each other on Saturdays and Sundays.

The winter had gone, and the spring was physically arriving, the most important season of the year for nature. Spring symbolises the revitalization, the start of a new circle, it is the explosion of natural new life when we can see flowers blossoming in all different colours and shapes, birds start singing and being more active, their reproduction starts too and many more other birds migrate to this country for a time, like swallows, who always visit this country at this time of year. They are so elegant in their black and white costumes; they are always making or reconstructing the old nests under the roofs, with mud and straws where sometimes they were born if not occupied. They make a resistant nest with love till they know it's perfect, so they can receive the new generation of birds. Swallows only have one partner during their lifetime, that's why they symbolise fidelity, family, home, and love. These adorable birds are very small but despite their size, they can travel as far as North Africa, there they can join other swallows, and then covering two hundred miles per day, till reaching Namibia and South Africa. Following an inherent instinct, with great resistance and an extraordinary ability of orientation. Swallows have great agility while flying, even when they are low, without putting in danger its physical integrity causing a spectacular exhibition. The female can lay between 4 and 5 eggs, then they are in incubation for 2 weeks, followed by the new arrival, and after with the Summer coming to an end, and the temperatures starting to drop, they gather in large flocks and start the journey back to where they came from, looking for warmer temperatures, and to return to Portugal the following year. These beautiful flying creatures are the first ones to welcome this season and bring people happiness because of their passion, and they are the most appreciated birds in the country. Frequently houses have a replica of them on the walls just outside of the front door as a symbol of calm, love, and family. They can also announce the arrival of dating for young love birds.

Spring is for some people the most pleasant season of the four due to its mild temperatures and all the characteristics making it more joyful, cheerful, contemplative with longer days. It is a season of inspiration and new plans, for all sorts of interests, still a little chilly but the sun shines better and longer bringing extra activities for children to play outside, meeting friends, parties start to be planned and a few weddings happen as well at this time of the year.

After the few months of Ana and Peter dating, Torres started to be a little more confident in her daughter's boyfriend. Jonny wasn't too picky either, but Sara was still being very attentive.

One Sunday during their date in the garden of the Republic near the convent of Saint Clara, the young couple sat on a bench while Sara had just met one friend and both women were talking about food. Her son was getting married, and she needed to organise the menu for after the ceremony, and Sara's opinion about it was always like a treasure, people trusted her.

For the very first time since they started dating, Ana asked Peter about his mother. In the beginning she was not too sure about how he would react. Her idea was to find out, she needed to ask. If he didn't feel ok to talk about it they could stop.

"Ana I rarely talk about my mother...it hurts too much...For me going away to Goa was a way of getting liberation from pain."

"I'm so sorry Peter..."

"Don't be... life can sometimes be really nasty. One day my mother was having a shower and she discovered a little lump on her breast." Hearing that, Ana's eye's minimised suddenly.

"She didn't think the worst, though she started to feel unwell, and after she talked to my eldest sister, and they went to see the doctor. It was a tumour."

"Oh my God Peter!"

"The doctor set a date for an operation, but my mother was deteriorating day by day, right in front of our eyes. We were accompanying her slow dying process, and it is very hurtful to see your loved one like we saw her. Two days before she died, I went to see her. She was sitting on the bed with lots of pillows around her to make her comfortable and I was so impressed when I heard her asking the doctor to open a hole in her chest so she could breathe." Ana had tears in her eyes.

"She was struggling for air...I kept this image in my mind for a very long time, but I realised that I needed to do everything I could to stop that...at least now she is not suffering anymore. We all were very sad with her death, but her suffering was gone. Not because she was my mother, but she was a wonderful woman, brilliant mother, and wife. I never saw my father hitting her, she always put family first, and when she needed help, no one could give it to her, even the doctors. For us it was terrible. We all knew by the law of nature that our parents die before us...but my mother was still young with so much ahead of her to live for, if it wasn't for the stupid lump she found on her breast."

"Peter I'm so sorry...My mother remembers the day of your mother's funeral...it was so much grief and lots of people crying."

"My mother was a kind of person to help the ones in need, food, clothes and other things, but when disease strikes followed by death there wasn't anything we could do."

They were talking for another hour till Sara said it was time to get home and end their date day.

That evening after dinner, Ana asked her father if she could meet up with Peter sometime at Maria's house's garden while Sara was talking to her. Torres was intrigued and asked why, but she told him people had started to see them always at the garden and started to be annoyed. He agreed, but the look he transmitted to Sara was well defined.

The first Sunday they met up at Maria's Garden was funny. Both grown women stayed in the kitchen talking and drinking tea with the door facing the garden open so Sara could keep her eyes on the love birds. The garden was big, with a tall white wall around, so no one could see it from outside, apart from flowers close to the house walls. The garden had three cabbage plots. One of them was tall with lots of big leaves to give to the chickens. There were also onions, tomatoes, lettuce, and garlic. Peter enjoyed it very much because with caution they could sneak a kiss without being seen. Once Sara went to the toilet and for a few seconds they noticed they weren't being watched and their lips got together in very desperate desire. Peter took his lover in his arms and with a feeling of possession kissed her like there was no tomorrow. For very long seconds they both forgot about mother, friend, and father. It was like they were the only people in the world, in their world.

When they finished, they looked immediately to the place where Sara was supposed to be, but she wasn't. Smiling, they went and sat on a bench close to the kitchen door. In the meanwhile, Sara came looking for them but when she saw them seated, she had a deep sigh of relief.

Maria was like family and to have all of them there on Sundays was fun, something thing that became normal because she could spend time talking with her friend and sometimes have help with organising a room for new students who were going to arrive. Santarém had the superior school of agriculture that was the heir to a secular tradition of agrarian education making it one of the oldest and more prestigious institutions in the country, and it was founded under the name Practical Elementary School of Agriculture and fruit in 1889, remaining for forty years, then in 1931 it changed to School of Agriculture Regents of Santarém. With that Maria always had a full house, it was her way of having an income for many years already. She provided bed, breakfast, and laundry for the students, and occasionally if they wanted an extra meal the price would increase. She had a very comfortable economic situation for a single mother.

Ana and Peter liked to watch the snails in their very calm environment when meeting up at Maria's Garden. Going up the cabbage very slowly, while there was a very moment between the vegetables and tomatoes that were attached on sticks to grow, to have a kiss happen. They were taking lots of risk, but it was worth it. Every time her mother looked at them, she never caught them kissing, that's why she assumed everything was good. Maria was having a pleasant distraction with them there and she started to make a delicious cake for them all, for teatime. Ana had a sweet tooth and always had more than one slice. During the week there was never a chance to kiss, they had to wait till the following Sunday, but with care, because if someone sees it, they can go and tell Torres, but no one wants this to happen. In the summer the young couple never missed a party, and they became the most amazing dancing pair. Of course, with a thousand eyes watching them, but that wasn't a problem, she felt always very proud of her boyfriend. Sara knew the true love there was between them, and she prayed every day for everything to go smoothly and they can get married one day and give her grandchildren. Sara imagined more than once if one day the marriage happens how the children were going to look. Ana is very pretty but Peter is awesome too and tall. As long as they do not have Torres' personality, that's fine. She didn't think Jonny would find a girl soon, he was only thinking about enjoying life and discovering all of Lisbon's secrets, he truly loved the place. Every time Torres needed to go to the capital for work, he would meet up with his son for lunch. Jonny knew all the best and cheapest places to have a meal, that's why he always surprised his father with different ones. But Torres also surprised his son. As soon as he started to live in Lisbon, he took Jonny to where pasteis de nata were first born. Until then Jonny used to have it from the normal pastry shop, but as soon as his father introduced him to Pasteis de Belém, the original name and recipe, he simply fell in love with it. Back then Torres explained the history about these wonderful cakes. One day at the end of an afternoon when siting inside for a coffee and cake with his son he explained like he always did to his kids. In the beginning of the 19th century on the Lisbon coast (Belém), next to the Jerónimos Monastery there was a working sugar cane refinery, that was associated with a few and varied small commercial shops. In 1820 the Liberal revolution took place. 14 years later all monasteries and Convents were closed, expelling all their workers and clergy. The misery was a devastating problem back then, so someone from the Monastery that was trying to do anything he could to survive this appalling situation, started to sell some sweet pastries called "Pasteis de Belém. After that, they started to be popular, and the production increased because people were coming to the area to visit the Monastery and the Belém tower who very quickly got used to these delicious cakes. (The secret office), as they called it, was the name they gave to the place attached to the refinery, where the secret recipe originally from the monastery was born. Torres explained to his son that this old recipe remains the same today, without sharing the secret with anyone, but still many bakeries from around the country are doing it, they are good, but not close to the Pasteis Belém. They are unique.

After that explanation, Jonny felt his brain more enriched, he defended the idea that knowledge does not occupy.

Chapter 18

That Summer there was very hot weather. After lunch during the week on the streets there were only people who needed to go to work, after their lunch break, shoppers were out very early to get everything they needed before the sun got too strong. Even very early people are watering pots of plants on balconies, terraces, main entrances of their houses and gardens, before the soil gets too hot, to not damage it because of the thermic shock. Between midday and four in the afternoon was the hottest part of the day, so people were rarely out during these times. Days are longer and nights are shorter in this season. Children are having their longest holidays from school, and it's time to have a few days at the seaside, and one of the beaches close to Santarém is the one at Nazaré. Frequently the people from Santarém call it their beach. Even so most of them go there just to get the marine breeze that is very important for children's development.

Every evening after dinner it is very common to see residents sitting on a bench just outside their front door, while boys play football, girls play hide and seek but all enjoying the very fresh time of day, and a very relaxing time before going to bed. This scenario is daily during the season that brings the highest temperatures of the year. Sara likes summer because when hanging the laundry on the rope, it can dry in no time, and every time she heard someone complaining about it, she always says that people are never pleased, they are used to complaining about something and the weather can take the blame. She understood weather can have a huge impact on motivation, how people live their lives, how they dress. It's feeds our soul. When days are sunny and longer, it can create miracles. It's the season when frequently the birds are bathing themselves in every fountain, tank, anywhere they can find water and to the back gardens of houses and restaurants to get some breadcrumbs after housewives shake the tablecloth after meals to see if they are lucky enough to pick up some food as well. Summer is the time for weddings, but Sara didn't agree with that. In her opinion this time of the year is too hot to be close to another body in bed, winter was better because the love birds can be closer without sweating and enjoying their new relationship in full.

One of this summer's Sundays after lunch, Sara and her daughter were heading to Maria's house, but for some reason they went a different way.

"Ana why did we come this way, it takes longer...and with this heat only you to make me come out."

Her daughter looked at her mother and smiled, and she didn't say a word, but when they got into a square, not too far from their friend's house she looked around to make sure no one was around, stopped, turned to her mother, and said,

"Mother, I'm pregnant." In this instant Sara screamed so loudly that even the trees trembled. Ana was scared...she knew her mother would be devastated but never expected to have her scream the way she did so loudly. Ana was frozen facing the reaction her mother had.

"Oh, my dear God Ana, what have you done...your father will kill us both!"

"I'm sorry mother...I'm so ashamed." Ana was crying, her tears were falling down her face, they had a huge situation to deal with. Sara took her daughter in her arms and brought her close to her own heart. After a few minutes Sara recovered her composure.

"Does Peter know?"

"No, he doesn't mother."

"OK, you are going to stay here, sit on this wall." She pointed to a little wall that skirted part of the square under a tree shadow. "You are not going to Maria's house today...I will, you know no one must know about this. I will bring Peter here and we will talk. Ana avoid talking to anyone, your eyes are red, and we don't need bad attention, I will come back as soon as possible, just wait." Ana could see in her mother, a saviour, a problem solver, her bodyguard, now she needs Sara to adjust to the reality of having her only daughter pregnant.

Sara had a very big problem on her hands, Torres mustn't find out.

When she got to Maria's place, she was talking to Peter outside her front door, under a shadow waiting for them. As soon as Peter saw her girlfriend's mother alone, he asked if Ana was ok. She said she was, but today she wanted to sit in the square instead, and before Maria insisted them coming to her house, Sara continued that Ana hadn't come, so that Maria couldn't change her mind.

On their way to meet Ana, they talked about how hot the day was. As soon as he saw his girlfriend, he understood something was up. The three of them sat. Peter was looking very concerned, but Ana told Peter the same way she told her mother. Peter wasn't expecting that. He turned to Sara and apologised. She told them both that they needed solutions because Torres mustn't find out or anybody else. Peter took Ana's hand and told her he didn't want her to have an abortion, he wanted to go and talk to Torres and ask his permission to marry his daughter. Both women told Peter that couldn't happen because Torres would kill them all. Sara believed he could that's for sure, but Peter insisted on marrying Ana because they loved each other, and they wanted to spend their lives together as a family with their new arrival.

Ana told him she wanted that too, but this time for their own sake she needed to have a termination. He was quite upset, he wanted this baby, he was very confident in talking to Torres, but mother and daughter made him promise not to. In the end after he knew there was not an alternative, he said he would ask his younger sister for help. Joana was very close to her brother. They were used to one another. When she got married, days before he went to Goa, he told her new husband shortly after leaving the church, to always be good for her, if not he will make him be.

When going home, Sara asked Ana to act normal, she needs to be as normal as possible. Both knew how suspicious he was when he smelt something was not right. Both women needed to be the same as always, not even talking in the bedroom. They couldn't risk it under any circumstances.

That day, Peter talked to Joana in secret. She understood the weight of such a problem, but at the same time she felt sorry for him. He wanted this baby so much with Ana. They agreed the next day Joana will meet Ana at the end of the working day, to discuss the pregnancy. "No one should hear you talking. The last thing I need is having gossip about Ana, her name indicates everything she means for me, I don't want her hurt in any way." They understood the gravity of the situation. It was not the first time they saw other girls from their city carry on their shoulders the heavy weight of being the centre of news in others mouths for the wrong reasons. Every time this happens most parents' interpretation is that the family name has been tarnished. It never occurs to them that this is part of life, no one is perfect, in this situation parents must be the ones to support their daughters, and not to make them feel like rubbish. They need to be respected not judged, most young couples take responsibility, but it's very hard if everyone is against you.

Sara had a different point of view about life. The only reason she didn't agree with her daughter's boyfriend about keeping the baby was because of her own husband. She knew how far Torres could go when he didn't like something, and she couldn't cope if he knew about their daughter. She had been hurt countless times by him, but watching Ana being punished was something she wasn't prepared to accept, so they needed to work hard to not let ends loose that might make him suspicious of this tremendous situation. Not even Jonny could know, the less people knew, the better.

It was ten minutes before the shop closed and a woman went inside heading to Ana's position and asking her if they sold kitchen towels. She got three and talking softly to her brother's girlfriend, said she would be outside waiting for her. António asked if everything was ok, Ana only nodded her head in a positive affirmation. It was very hard to act like all was good when it wasn't, but there was other way. Outside of the shop Joana put her arm on Ana's shoulders and started walking. When they were alone next to a little way, she whispered that everything was sorted. In two days, she would pick up Ana from home after dinner. They organised everything - supposedly Joana asked Ana to help her choose a fabric for a dress, at the dress maker. It was the way of not having Torres asking questions, two women together wasn't a problem to him.

The day before while having dinner, Ana had the guts to ask both parents if everything was ok for her to go the next day after dinner with Peter's sister to help her choose some fabric for a new dress. Before Torres even said something, Sara anticipated herself.

"I can see...you girls when it is fashion time, they lose control of time, just hope Ana you don't spend too much money, because I know Joana loves having a new dress when possible." Torres was observing and got his time to comment too.

"Little heart where are you going to meet?"

"She will come here father; we will meet up just outside if that's ok."

"Peter?"

"He won't be with us, tomorrow is just girls time...Joana was going to go in the afternoon, but the dress maker will be coming back from the retailer in Lisbon, so she asked Joana to go in the evening after dinner to give her time too, for her it will be amazing, I can have a look at the new fabrics, who knows if I will like any."

"Little heart I want you home before 11."

"OK Father, but you know sometimes it can take a little longer." Torres gave her the look of a big no.

Like most days, Torres left after dinner, then mother and daughter alone in the house went to Ana's room to talk. Her mother was very concerned about what her daughter was about to do. She told her to be careful. In the end they were both sad about not being able to keep this little person that was growing inside her belly. At some point, Sara asked her daughter how she became pregnant, when she kept her eyes on them the whole time, but smiling Ana answered with "Not all the time."

"I have heard before girls getting pregnant just while the church bells rings, but I never thought of you! Are you not afraid of your dad? Ana this time we will see how this goes, but I'm not looking forward to another episode like the one we are living. Promise me it won't happen again.

In bed, later that day, Ana cried under the sheet. She was confused, hurt and sad. In the room next to hers, the scenario wasn't much different. Her mother was in her own in bed, sad about everything. She prayed for God to help her daughter the next day when having the abortion. She wanted to go too, but she couldn't in case Torres made a fuss about it. Sara and Ana were inseparable, but this time they needed to be cautious.

The next morning Ana's eyes were looking very tired, she hadn't slept enough and neither had Sara. They both wanted this over and, for all this matter be resolved so things can go back to normal.

That evening as agreed, Joana picked Ana up and went to the dress maker. They spent half an hour there. After they left very discreetly, Joana opened her handbag and she pulled out a big scarf and put it on Ana's head. They kept walking by the back streets. When they got to the place, there were two other women waiting, but Joana had the priority to go in, because it was what had been agreed. No one could notice who the woman with the head covered was. They both went inside to have something done that will live forever inside of their hearts and minds and that will change the lives of the young couple in love forever.

Ana got home just before 11. Her father wasn't at home yet. Sara was nervous, who knows if he had been lurking on their daughter, just time would tell if he had been. Without a big deal, Sara helped Ana get ready for bed. It was close to midnight when Torres came in, prepared himself and went straight to bed. Sara was still awake. She didn't want him to ask questions, but she assumed that night was a success, he didn't notice a thing.

Since the remarkable time that took away his baby, Peter was making plans for a future with the love of his life. They continued to sneak a quickie, without being caught, but with extra caution to avoid pregnancy. The one before was painful, and no one was looking forward to having the same problem. Sara kept her eyes open, but it hadn't helped before, she could never see anything then or now.

She was still being the third wheel for them, but she knew how much they wanted to be together, but she also knew that there was tradition, a stupid one, to be dating for as long as they could before officialising the relationship with a marriage ceremony. She had lots of concerns on her mind, including with Jonny. She hadn't heard from him the last 4 four weeks, and it was a new chapter in their life too. The kids weren't kids anymore, they were grown people giving others headaches. The concerns now were different and much more serious, to control them now is out of the question, and when sharing with Torres a concern about their son's lack of news, it was motive for him to slap Sara hard on the face, bursting her whole mouth, leaving it bleeding, just to make her believe Jonny is a man not a mummy's boy. She had a true mother's heart and wanted to know that her kids were well and safe. One Friday evening after dinner, they heard a knock on the front door. When Ana went to see who it was, she was stunned when she came across her brother, all torn, blood all over him and a bandage on his forehead.

"Jesus Christ, what happened to you Jonny?!" Sara joined them in panic.

"What happened son?" She noticed he was smelling of alcohol.

"Oh, let me go in first." They were waiting, but he just asked his mother to get him a towel and pyjamas, went straight to the shower and then to his old room and in no time, he was fast asleep. Mother and daughter did not have the chance to learn what happened till the morning after. Whatever had happened didn't look too good for Sara, and she was worried; what if her son was in trouble with someone and was hit on purpose. Only speculation. She checked on him overnight, but he was ok. In the morning he came to the kitchen to have breakfast with the rest of the family. When Torres saw the bandage on his forehead, he asked Jonny what that was. Jonny was very relaxed, and without making a big deal he explained to his family that he was coming from Lisbon, with friends and Joe was driving. He was asleep on the back seat and when he woke up, he was in the Hospital. When they discharged me, I saw

Tó, he was one of our friends, and he told me Joe crashed the car into a house, close to the street, just very close to Santarém - he doesn't know the area very well. He smiled saying that he thought it was funny, but no one was laughing. Jonny thought he was being clever saying that, but his parents understood immediately what had happened.

Sara was surprised why he didn't wake up with the crash, but Torres, the old fox hade something different to say.

"You all were very drunk."

"No dad."

"Shut up. I let you talk now it's my turn without interruption. You were all very drunk, and you... to not feel anything? You could be dead. Is that the kind of life you want for you? Is that what you are learning in the capital Jonny? I expected better from you...and how is Joe?"

"Last night he wasn't that good!"

"You are a good friend...no doubt about that!" Torres was shaking his head. How can you be so relaxed, and stupid? You have the duty of checking if he and the others are ok. Do their parents know what happened?"

"I don't know dad."

"You better finish your breakfast and go sort things out."

The atmosphere was tense as they finished their breakfast in silence.

Before Torres left the house, he advised his son that drinking till you fell over was not a good option of life. It is very important to know when to stop before any harm can be done.

After he saw his dad leaving, he turned to his mother and with a sarcastic look told her that now it was her turn for a lecture, but Sara just said she would agree with what his father said. However, in the end she had the feeling she had failed Jonny, the way he was brought up. Ana was present but she didn't say a word - her opinion about her brother wasn't secret to anyone.

The dating between Ana and Peter became stronger by the day, and they started making plans, and the first step for those plans was marriage. One afternoon while talking, and walking on the square of the Seminar, Peter told his girlfriend that he had had enough of dating. He wanted to move on, to start a life, and they made the biggest decision of their lives. Five years was plenty of time to know one another, to see each other's bad and good side, and they both knew for sure what they wanted. Peter and Ana decided they wanted to get married, to wake up every morning by each other's side, to have their incomes together, and to get their own place to live. To construct their lives together on all sides. They were old enough to go forward with the new life they wanted for themselves. They loved each other so much, and they wanted to enjoy each other's body and live without challenging the tradition even more than they already had. Peter and his girlfriend always agreed that traditions and people sometimes damaged the good that was in people's hearts, but this time they needed to do everything by the book, for Torres to give his permission and blessing for their union. They knew it was a delicate situation, but the best things always start from the beginning. Both Ana's parents knew this day would come eventually. First it was Jonny and now it was her turn to have her life changing. She was a woman, beautiful and intelligent, earning her own money. She knew the difference between right and wrong.

Peter was a bit concerned about talking to his future father-in-law, but his girl was very optimistic about it. She thought her father might be waiting for this to happen, because he never was against her dating, he never mentioned anything he shouldn't about her relationship with Peter, she believes her own father gets along better with Peter than Jonny, for the very few times they had been together. Peter relied on Ana to organise the best time and day for him to ask Torres for permission to marry his daughter.

Torres was the sort of man, who likes to do everything by Portuguese tradition, and they both knew that.

This walk was one of the few they had on their own since they started dating. She was having a little more freedom with him, of course always being careful of no one to hear them. Peter had something else to talk to Ana about, but he was concerned. He didn't know how she would understand what he was about to say to her. He knew she was very close to her mother, but what he was about to say to her could very well have a big impact on her life, changing her daily habits of having a best friend, mother, supporter, her everything just there for her. But still life is full of surprises, change, opportunities, challenges, and clarity. If Ana agreed with what her lover was about to say, it means she is mature enough to start this long journey that will be their life together from the very moment she would say, Yes.

When they found a place to sit, Peter lit a cigarette, looked around very discretely, looked at Ana, put the cigarette on the ground and with his foot he terminated its short life.

"Ana there is another thing that I want to talk to you about, but I want you to think properly before considering giving me an answer. I know what I'm about to ask you is huge, but I'm prepared to wait as longs it takes, ok?"

"You are making me nervous Peter."

"Ana, believing your father gives me your hand in marriage. Would you after that want to go and live with me in England?"

"What...what are you saying Perter? England? Isn't that where your older sister is living?"

"Yep...What do you think?"

"How long have you had this idea on your mind?"

"Since a while ago...you don't need to give me, the answer now, but if we stay here, our lives will be very limited, both our salaries are ok if we are living with our parents, but I want us to be independent without always having to count our money to check if it's going to be enough till the end of the month. Ana, I want us to have good money, to have a good house and money in the bank. I don't care if I need to work hard, as long as we can put money aside for a better life. One thing I can tell you, I can work hard, save money but I want to enjoy life with you, I don't want to be my own slave and neither do you, I just want to take the opportunity if I can step on board on this adventure with you."

"You want to do too many things Peter."

"Ana, I just want to be honest with you, I want you to know what my plans are. If things are going to be, ok? Only time can tell, it's very important to give time to time. I'm not saying everything is going to be ok, believe me. When I went to Goa, it was very difficult...but I survived. If we are going to England, in the beginning we will stay with my sister and family, but as soon as possible, I want to have my own place with you. But... There is always a but." He smiled facing her. "If God helps us, I don't want to end my days away from my home, when it's time to watch ourselves getting old I want us to be here."

"Wow Peter I wasn't expecting all this!"

"Just think about it, but don't say anything yet to anyone, please."

"My mother isn't anyone, and I would be lying if I said I wouldn't, you know my mother; my mother Peter, is my everything always and forever. She's a very special mother, a mother with a big M.

In the end of this dating and full of surprises afternoon, Peter accompanied his girl home. They gave a quick kiss after checking no one was watching, then he left. Ana was watching him go down the street, then very calmly thinking about everything that had been said by Peter. She took the house keys from her bag and opened the door. As soon as she got in, her father was hitting her mother by grabbing her hair. The poor woman was in the corner of the kitchen floor with her hands covering her face. Torres was a beast not caring where he hit her.

"Father stop!" Ana asked loudly." He stopped, and headed towards his daughter, but she wasn't afraid of him, she was being very brave.

"You don't talk to me this way Ana!"

"You can ask me for respect father but not to be afraid of you!" He was going to walk away, but she continued.

"I'm sorry father, but you are a coward."

"Ana!" He screamed.

"You hit my mother because you know she will not hit you back, in respect, because if she wanted, she could finish you off, you know that I think I already told you that once."

"Ana be careful about what are you going to say next."

"Why? Are you going to hit me too?" Torres looked at his daughter, turned his back and left. Ana helped her mother get up, cuddled her, kissed her and helped her clean up. She never thought she could confront her father the way she did, but she couldn't keep watching her father do to her mother what he has been doing for years, since she started to understand things. Her father hitting her mother was part of her and Jonny growing up, and it shouldn't be this way. Sara was a lovely person, mother, woman, and friend. Ana never understood why her father treated her mother the way she did.

That day he didn't come home for dinner, or the next day or the next one. Sara wasn't concerned, but Ana was - she had to organise a meeting for him and Peter, but now it wasn't a good time, but she wasn't worried about what she had told him, he deserved every single word. She never understood why he behaved like that towards her mother, she feared what he could do to her. She loved both but she needed to protect her mother, and every time this scenario happens, she feels confused about what's going on in her father's mind. During the week, one evening in her own bedroom she told her mother everything she and Peter talked about.

Sara was very pleased for her daughter. She passed her hand on her daughter's hair, smiling and remembering her daughter's childhood.

"You and your brother have grown up so quickly. Jonny left and now it's your turn."

"Mother, but... I don't know if I want to go to England, it's so far away, I can't leave you here."

"Don't be stupid Ana, if you are going to marry you will follow your husband everywhere. He loves you, and you will have an amazing life by his side. I will stay behind, all parents do, and I'm not different."

"Of course, you are, very different, you are my mother the one who knows all my secrets, the person who is always there for me. I wish I could have you by my side."

"But you can't. You must concentrate on your life with Peter, and never let anything interfere in your relationship with him. You need to be prepared for everything in life, if you are not too sure, talk to him, never let gossip get in the way of you and him. Everybody has arguments but the main thing is the way you deal with them, remember Ana; We only argue with people we like, because with the ones we don't, we just put them aside. Another thing: a mother's love never ends, not even after the end."

"This is your way of saying that father loves you. What a funny way of showing it." Ana added.

"Life is not only roses, roses have thorns on the stem. Each pain makes you stronger, each betrayal makes you feel clever;

disillusionment makes you more skilled; each experience makes you wiser. Always pay attention to everything and everyone, never be too generous to anyone."

Her mother always knew how to give good advice to her children. Her daughter was getting closer to changing her simple life from being a girlfriend to being a wife, her kid was a woman that was probably going to have kids of her own. Sara needed to be prepared to let her much-loved daughter go.

Lots of people in this world are living below their own capacities of expansion, and Sara was one of those. She was a very intelligent woman that was stuck in a life in which apart from her kids, she only experienced pain. Every single day when she gets up, the first thing she does is to ask God to help her have strength to carry on her life with Torres, but so far God hasn't done a good job. She asks herself many times till when this violence was going to last, how many years would she still have ahead of her to put up with this son of a bitch. One thing was right when Ana told him - if Sara wanted to, she could finish him off.

That week Sara had bruises all over, so she avoided going out. She felt ashamed by her appearance like a kid who is being hit by Its parents.

That weekend Jonny came over, and again he was so furious about seeing his mother the way he did, but he never had the guts to confront his father the way his sister did. He criticised his father but always behind his back.

When Ana and Peter met up, he asked her if she had the opportunity to organise the meeting with her father, but she explained to him everything that had happened the Sunday before, when he left her outside her door. Peter felt sick after what Ana told him about how her mother was. They decided to wait a little till the dust settled down, if Torres did not do anything stupid, again.

Two weeks later, the air at home was clear and Ana was thinking it was time to talk to her father, and she did, one day at lunch time.

"Dad, Peter and I want to talk to you and mother when possible."

"Talk to me and your mother? Should I be concerned?"

"I don't think so, Peter and I just want you to tell us a date to meet up."

Torres finished his meal, keeping the suspense, leaving both women wondering what the answer would be. Just before he left, he told Ana, the next day around 4.30 pm it would be ok. She was relieved and now she only needed to tell Peter. She must ask her boss to give her a 30-minute break. That's the time she would need to go and tell Peter. Her boss agreed so she ran to the shop where Peter was working to tell him the news. When Ana got there, Peter saw her and he asked permission to go outside to talk to her and he was very pleased when she told him about the meeting, then they both agreed they needed to ask their bosses permission to have a break the next day, for a family meeting in the afternoon. There was no need to tell them anything else, it was none of their business.

The next day came fast, Ana met up with her mother and Peter and the three of them headed to Torres's office. Ana was anxious about what her father was going to say, she was not sure anymore if he would agree, but it was not long till they found out what the outcome was going to be.

Many years passed by since Sara went to her husband's office the last time, and she only went now because of the situation involving their daughter. When they got to the office door, Peter knocked on the door that this time was closed. A few seconds later Torres opened the door, he already had enough chairs for all of them to sit. Torres went straight to asking Peter what's the purpose of this gathering.

Peter stood up very politely before starting to talk.

"Mr Torres, I will be very brief because all of us have things to do so...me and your daughter have being dating for five years, I work and so does she, but we have been talking about what we want from this relationship, and what we want is to go forward and spend the rest of our day's together, so Mr Torres and Sara, I would like to have your permission and blessing to marry your daughter." Sara already knew, but Torres didn't have a clue, so he turned to his daughter.

"Is that what you want as well little heart?"

"It's what I want most in my life dad; Peter is the love of my life, he's my other half, we belong together." Saying what she just said, her dad could see in his daughter's eyes the truth about everything.

"Very well, it looks like we are going to have a wedding then." He took a moment just looking at them without saying anything, and it was a bit intimidating.

"I will give you my daughter's hand, but I want you to make her happy, do you understand me?"

"Mr Torres, you have my word." After this reply from Peter, Torres turned to his daughter with a very serious look.

"Ana, the society we live in likes to applaud those who marry, breed, work and die with dignity, so you better make this marriage work because if you don't, I will never ever let you have another man, do you understand?"

"Father, you know how much I love Peter, of course I will make my marriage work, if God helps us, we will be together for many years to come till we get to be really old, we will be together for ever." While all this happening, Sara was very sickened by all her husband said. He was asking his future son in law to be good for his daughter; who does he think he is? How can he ask something that he himself doesn't know anything about? After she heard

Torres, she felt more disgusted than ever about the bullshit he was letting out his mouth.

The young couple were congratulated by the bride-to-be's parents, followed by Torres asking Peter what his plans for the future where, if he was going to keep working in the shoe shop. Peter felt a bit embarrassed with his question, and he looked at Ana and she shook her head positively, so Peter explained his and his bride's plans to go to England, leaving Torres with his mouth open. Peter said that he has been thinking about this for a very long time.

"Me and Ana have dreams, but we don't think we can achieve them here in Portugal; we have an amazing country but not for everyone...day after day I just hear people complaining about the lack of the most important daily needs. While I'm young with your daughter, we will try to have a better life, we know in the beginning it will be hard, not much for me but for your daughter." Peter looked to both parents while saying that. "Ana is very close to Sara, we know she will suffer till she gets used to it, but the point is, it will be worth it. You must be wondering what job we are going to be able to do; My brother-in-law is a waiter in a very posh restaurant in London, my sister works for a rich guy doing ladies coats, called vision. They just bought a house in South London and apparently, they have a few floors, they live on the ground floor, renting the rooms on the others above. They work hard but it pays off. The other day she explained to me that Ana and I need to have a letter from someone there who is going to employ us, (letter of invitation), a passport, a place to stay and after we get there we need to go to a police station and register ourselves, then they will give us a little green book, like identification, and every month we need to go back to have a stamp on it. But the very first step will be our marriage, every journey starts with small steps, I believe we are just starting to enter the tunnel that leads us to the new life we want for us."

"I can see you have thought about everything. I'm very impressed...just one question Peter... have you thought about dates for the big day?" Peter and Ana looked to one another, and she proceeded.

"I think we first need to find out how long it takes to organise a wedding then we can go from there, don't you think mother?"

"It's a start. You need to talk to the priest, go to the registry Office, have the dress made, the guest list, children to give the rings and the menu." Sara was always organised, and Torres jumbled. No doubt all of them had plenty ahead to do. So, it was decided: Sara would get the requisite legal information, and after she would go with her daughter to talk with the priest, then depending on availability they would settle a date.

Two weeks after the meeting, they started to have a clue about it all including the date for the big day. They had eight months ahead, making the event happen in the following year, 1961 in order to prepare everything. Ana started to be very excited about it, and she went with Sara to talk to the dress maker about her dress. The first step was choosing the right dress from the pile of magazines, then the fabric, and the bride's veil.

Both families, from the bride to be and Peter, met several times to discuss the arrangements for the occasion. Sara was going to prepare all the food for 80 people, with some help, and they were going to rent a big room where many other weddings and parties take place too. It was a very exciting time, too much work to be done and money to be spent. All expenses were being divided by both families; even so, because Peter's father and stepmother cultivated a piece of land, they contributed with all sorts of vegetables, fruit, eggs, and wine. They have a vineyard too, like most people who are living in the countryside, and every year they made their own. Their wine was not enough, so Torres was going to get much more from local farmers. Ana was very organised making choices and always thinking cautiously not to get too expensive options. Torres as the bride's father, wanted a very traditional wedding for his daughter based on the most important of traditional Portuguese delicacies. She was his own daughter, and he would be walking her down the aisle, giving away his little heart, his most precious person in the world. It would be a unique ceremony that would live in his heart forever. Torres was a big admirer of his daughter, he loved her sense of responsibility, personality and caring. He was starting to educate himself to the idea losing her, but the time to let her go was approaching.

Now the only dilemma was telling Jonny.

Everyone could anticipate how he would react, and everyone was 100% correct. The second they told Jonny during his next visit; he was hysterical. He was adamant that his sister could find a better man and that Peter was a good-for-nothing waste of space. He never really understood his sister's love for Peter, but Ana didn't care. Nothing and no one could stop this wedding and her future with Peter.

Jonny came home a few times, but each time his mother wanted to talk to him about what he was going to wear at his sister's wedding, he avoided the subject leaving her very concerned. It was very clear his disappointment in this wedding. Peter was far from his ideal brother-in-law, he never understood but that was nothing to do with him. This was his sister's choice; she was the one who was going to spend the rest of her life with Peter.

One day Ana asked her bosses to have one day off, so she went with her mother to buy the lingerie, shoes, and the tiara, and they went to the flower shop to choose her bridal flower bouquet. They went to the court as well just to check the papers that were on show here announcing the wedding. It's the law in case there is anyone with a motive to stop the wedding.

Chapter 19

Since the beginning of 1960, Salazar's regime started to enter a time of decadence. There was a great wear and tear on the regime due to economic reasons. Portugal was clearly an economically backward nation compared to others in Europe.

On the 9th of January, the Portuguese ship, Santa Maria, with 612 passengers on bord, most of them Americans, and 350 crew members, left Lisbon port, for a regular trip to USA, more precisely Miami, making a stopover at the Venezuelan port of la Guairá, planned for the 20th. But a man, (Henrique Galvão), and another three men had embarked in Curacao illegally on board, joining another 20 members of the Iberian Liberation Revolutionary leadership, a group that would organise an assault of hijack on the ship.

On the 22nd of January 1961, the assault on the Portuguese transatlantic ship, Santa Maria happened, led by captain Henrique Galvão. It would mark the challenge to the Salazar government and introduce the hijacking of ships and airplanes as a means of political pressure.

The operation began at dawn, with the occupation of the ship by 24 men, only one of the board crew offered resistance, but he was immediately shot. All the others surrendered; the ship changed its course heading for Africa.

On the 23rd of the same month, the transatlantic approached the Island of Saint Lucia, and placed in motorboats two seriously injured people and five crew members, which compromised the possibility of reaching the African Coast, without being detected by the authorities. Two days later, on the 25th, they came across a Danish freighter, who alerted the authorities, and a few hours later, an American plane located the transatlantic. On the 2nd of February it docked on the port of Recife, Brazil, and all its remaining passengers and crew were disembarked. The following day, all the rebels, surrendered to the authorities in Brazil, and there they obtained political asylum. Later the passengers were transferred to the Vera Cruz, which left Recife on the 5th of February. The transatlantic, Santa Maria left for Lisbon only on the 7th of February, entering the river Tagus on the 16th.

Regardless of the political hijacking, the incident reinforced the popularity of this Portuguese passenger ship, and it maintained the regular journeys between Portugal and USA.

At the same time of the hijacking of the ship, serious incidents started to happen in Luanda, capital of Angola, which led to more conflicts in the north of the country.

The Portuguese attachment to the colonies has been going on for several centuries, but the overseas war began based on the Portuguese dictatorship, to prevent their independence and the situation got even worse.

The popular movement for Angola, which was supported by the Soviet Union and Cuba, started by attacking in Luanda, a police station. Several police officers were killed. In the North of the country several attacks also began unleashing against the white population. Angola was the first Portuguese colony where the armed struggle against the Portuguese domain began.

In June a group of sixty students from Mozambique, Angola, Cape Verde, and other colonies, escaped from Portugal and the Portuguese dictatorship, to join the war for freedom. This clandestine escape changed the course of Portuguese speaking countries and some of those nationalists came to have high positions, such as generals, presidents, ministers and many more important ones, changing a very relevant path on the destiny of their own country.

These wars worsened the country's economic situation and weren't very popular throughout Portugal. The nation fought against groups from Angola, Mozambique, Guinea-Bissau, Goa, and Timor-Leste, that wanted independence. It was quite rare for a Portuguese family not to have one of their own fighting in those colonial wars, because military service lasted for four years, any opinion against the regime and the way they conducted everything was severely repressed by censorship and the police. Even so 1961 was marked by the failed military coup attempt against Salazar – who was by then the defence minister.

Chapter 20

One week before the religious ceremony, the young couple had the civil wedding, just with their parents and godparents, but for them it was like it wasn't. Sara started with the help of another two women to prepare the hall where the reception was going to take place. There was plenty to be done, and she wanted everything to be perfect for her daughter and future husband. She prepared everything apart from the wedding cake, and one or two different deserts.

Two of Ana's best friends were going to prepare the rice and the rose petals to throw at the bride and groom when leaving the church after the wedding. It was all very exciting, but Ana started to be nervous about it, but her mother told her that all brides get nervous. Some lose weight and the dress is slightly big after, but it is all part of the occasion.

The day before, Sara didn't stop. She needed to have everything ready and the two women and another one (who they asked to help too) had a few waiters for the day, and Sara would only be back to help in the kitchen after the religious ceremony.

Ana didn't have much to eat the evening before, she felt like she had a knot in her stomach. The next day was going to be intense; she would be the centre of attention for everyone. In the morning while she gets ready, her parents will hold a brief buffet in their house for some guests from their side, just before the ceremony, Peter would do the same, it's part of the tradition.

The buffet consisted of some traditional pastries, little sandwiches, coffee, and tea, because weddings take long. After the church services the newly wedded head to the sun doors to have some pictures taken and only after, they go to the hall for their lunch, but no one starts without them.

Around ten o'clock in the evening, Sara went to her daughter's bedroom to have a chat. Not long after, Torres knocked on her door too.

"You can come in." Ana said, not knowing if it was her dad or brother.

"Dad! Is anything the matter?"

"Little heart...tomorrow is going to be a very important day for you... and for us too. So, I want to give you some advice as your father. Everything that happens inside the four walls of your room, after the wedding, is for you and you alone, no one must ever know, understood? Only if there is something you are not sure of, you can talk to your mother, and after she will talk to me. I want you to keep this in your mind for the rest of your life, ok?"

"Yes dad."

Jonny saw all of them in her sister's bedroom and he asked if he could join them too.

"The four of us together for the last time, I will miss that. Don't worry sister I'm used to your...Peter now. I just want to say that I'm very proud of you, and tomorrow will be an amazing day."

"Jonny is everything ok tomorrow for the car and..."

"Calm down Ana, Joe is going to be here after 9.30, chill and all will be perfect."

Joe will drive the bride and father to the church, and later the same day he would take the newly married couple to his parent's flat for their honeymoon, in Lisbon. For one week they will have the flat for themselves, it was the wedding present they had agreed before. Joe's parents were taking one week to stay in the countryside.

Torres put his arm on Jonny's shoulder and both men walked away from Ana's room. As soon as they left, mother and daughter had an enormous cuddle, and Sara whispered to her daughter. "If one day you need me darling, I will always be here, no matter what...I just want you to be happy." Both had tears in their eyes.

"Mother do you think tomorrow I will be ok..."

"No doubt about that, you know it's going to be a big day, you will be the centre of attention for everyone, but everything will be good."

"Do you think I will be pretty in that dress?" she pointed to the dress hanging outside of her wardrobe."

"Ana, tomorrow is your day...You will be a Princess for the day, everything is under control, just take a deep breath."

Ana was anxious, but what bride isn't?

Just before Sara left her room, she told her daughter to try to sleep, but an hour later she couldn't, and her mother gave her a camomile tea. They chatted for a little while and then each of them headed for their own room.

At six in the morning, Sara was already up to set the dining table for the buffet. She called Jonny to help; everyone was a bit nervous. Torres got up too and went to get ready. Ana joined them in the kitchen for breakfast, she still in pyjamas, and couldn't eat much, so she went to have a shower. When she finished, she went to her bedroom to start preparing herself, but instead she sat on the bed looking out of the window and tried to feel calm about the day she had ahead of her. Since she met Peter, deep in her heart, she always imagined this day. He was her first and unique love, the one she wants to share her life with, the only one she ever kissed on the lips. Her mind was a whirlwind of thoughts, but all very good, she was very happy to be getting married to the love of her life.

After she had been in her room, deep in her thoughts, she called her mother to help her get dressed, before the hairdresser arrived to do her hair and put the tiara and veil on, and she was thrilled when Sara came in with the flower bouquet. The bouquet was simple but chic, with 10 roses, like a champagne colour, with plenty of green around it and a satin ribbon looping the bouquet. Sara kept spraying the flowers to keep them fresh and alive.

Torres was looking very well, with a dark suit, white shirt, dark tie, and shoes with a rose the same colour as the bride's bouquet, in the blazer top pocket. Sara saw him and thought he was looking very well. Jonny was more or less the same as his father, with a rose in his blazer too, looking very handsome. Sara finally got a bit of time and went to get ready. After she let the hairdresser and Ana's two friends join the bride in her room.

Sara got ready very fast. She wasn't vain. She had a simple dress with a jacket all in navy blue, the same colour shoes, a white necklace, and a little handbag. She went to check on the bride. As soon as she opened the door she was lost for words after seeing how beautiful her daughter was.

Torres and Jonny were entertaining the guests, but one hour before the church service he advised them to go to the church. The house was needed for the photographer to take pictures of the bride with her parents, and brother alone. They needed time to do this and to get to the church in time. The girls and hairdresser left for the church as well and Torres, Jonny, Joe, and the photographer were in the living room when Sara appeared with Ana. Torres looked at his daughter and his eyes filled with tears.

"You are absolutely amazing...you make a beautiful bride." Jonny also had his mouth open when he laid eyes on his sister. The girl of the family looked like a princess indeed.

After several pictures had been taken, Torres had to tell the photographer that was enough because they needed to go to church.

The church was all illuminated, full of people, most of them invited, others just went out of curiosity. Peter was at the end, near the altar with his father. On the front bench his godparents were sitting, his stepmother was on the other side where Ana's godparents, Jonny and soon her parents would be sitting. Peter looked at his watch and told his father to sit, so his godparents could stay at his side. Sara came in with Jonny, meaning they were only a few minutes away from the bride coming in. Her godparents stood up and went to their position next where the bride would stand.

The music started, and everybody looked back. Torres started walking his daughter down the aisle, with a little girl walking in front of them dressed in a short white embroidered dress, with little socks and shoes and a fluffy little basket carrying the wedding rings. Just behind the bride and Torres was another girl dressed like the one walking in front, and a boy, with navy trousers, shoes and waistcoat, white shirt, and a navy tie, carrying two cushions in white for the new couple to kneel on when getting married.

It was very special, Peter was keeping still, till Torres handed his daughter to him with a very deep look into his almost son in law's eyes.

Peter was stunned when he saw his future wife, he couldn't believe in what his eyes were seeing. In his mind there was just one thing...in a few hours she will be all his, without being afraid of being caught by anyone, now they just needed to get on with this day.

The moment Peter lifted the veil from Ana's face and was allowed by the priest to kiss the bride, her parent's eyes were full of tears. All the memories they both had from their daughter's childhood were flooding into their minds. Sara remembered when she met Peter for the first time, it was love from the very first minute, and she had the feeling that he was the right man for her.

It was a simple and beautiful religious ceremony. While leaving the church, they had rice and petals thrown at them, followed by the guest's congratulating the new couple. The sun doors were the next destination to have some pictures taken, while the guest's and family headed to the hall. One hour and a half later, the bride and groom arrived at the hall. More pictures were taken before, during and after the marvellous lunch. In Torres's opinion, it was to many pictures, but he left the decision for the new couple to take care of.

After the long lunch, it was time for dancing. The newly wedded started with the first one, and just before the end of it all it was time for the single girls at the party to get together. With her back turned, the bride would throw the bouquet and whoever caught it would be the next to get married. It was one of the traditions people liked to keep alive, and girls feel very excited about it. Only after it is thrown, some girls feel a bit jealous, because everyone wanted to be the lucky one.

The bride and her husband were very happy about the day, and finally they belonged to each other. There was not long to go till they could be in each other's arms, enjoying each other's body, fulfilling their desire, their dreams, being completely crazy and wild under the sheets.

The party was over, and it had been a very long day, but just before they left to go and change their clothes and start their honeymoon, Ana cuddled her lovely mother, and thanked her for all her support and hard work.

"Mother...I will never forget everything you have been doing for me... I love you." She said with her eyes full of tears. It had been a very emotional day for all of them when emotions are very superficial.

"Don't be silly...I'm your mother, it explains everything, all parents do the same for their kids, it's the best we can do."

The next few days Sara still had lots to do, she was very tired, but she didn't want to stop till everything was done. She was very proud of how the wedding went; it could not have been better. Even so, she could put aside the anger that she had towards her husband.

Now the next chapter in their lives would be the hard one. They needed to learn how to live without having their daughter around. Ana made a house full with her presence. Sara didn't look forward to seeing the emptiness left by her daughter, but she had no choice now, there was nothing she could do to avoid it.

The time was flying, and soon her beloved daughter will be going to live away in a different country, for Sara it will be the hardest thing to face. But she would need to hide her feelings very well, for Ana's sake.

One week after the wedding, Ana and Peter returned to Santarém after exploring their love in full and the city of Lisbon. They went everywhere, from seeing all the gardens, parks monuments, and the birth place of Pasteis de nata. They also spent one day on the coast of Lisbon visiting some amazing places at the seaside. They took advantage of the honeymoon enjoying every minute.

Back home it was a different story. They stayed at her parents' home, and it was handier to get things done for their next adventure. Peter and his new wife needed to get all their documents ready with their new status situation. In the beginning he thought it was a simple matter, but when he started putting everything together, he felt confused; there was lots to be organised before both of them could head off. In England his sister was taking care of the acceptance letters, for them to be legally working there, and she would lend the money for the trip.

Getting the new ID cards and passport took longer than they expected, but after some weeks, they finally started to have all the pieces together. Meanwhile they were getting everything sorted with their jobs, their bosses and working colleagues were sad to see them go, but life is just like that, everyone goes in search of a better life if they are not afraid of doing it. No one is prepared, they need to learn during the adventure, keeping strong and being positive about the target outcome. No one said life was easy, but for sure in Portugal there was no future at all for people who wanted more from life than being stuck in a country with no rights to anything and no life quality, just a dictatorship that scars everyone.

The country doesn't invest in people, the leader wants them to be ignorant. No education, no better life, nothing of anything. He once said that one sardine and a piece of bread was enough for people, they didn't need anything else. For him and his cabinet it was a different story. In fact, Portugal had the largest gold reserve in the world, but it was a backward country.

No one understood why Salazar was conducting the country the way he was, because he was born into a humble family of small agricultural landowners.

His journey in the Portuguese State began when he was the one chosen by the military to be Minister of finance, for the very brief period of a fortnight, after the revolution of 28th May 1926, and subsequently he returned once again as Minister of Finance between 1928 and 1932, following by ruling the country with his authoritarian way since the beginning.

The day for the new couple's departure was approaching. Both mother and daughter's hearts were getting tighter by the day. Torres never said a word, his way of dealing with it was working long hours and educating himself to be strong and watch his little heart go.

Jonny was all good, he wanted to be in his sister's shoes, he loved travelling but the longest trip he had ever done was to Spain but just on the border. Since he knew she was going to England, he gave her an old English vocabulary book, from when he was learning many years ago, and she already knew a few words.

Peter's sister told him about the severe weather in the Winter. She advised them to take warm clothes.

Two days before, some of Ana's friends came over to say goodbye, they couldn't believe she was leaving. Maria knew Ana since she was born - for her it was very difficult to see her go, she was like a daughter to her.

Joe was supposed to pick them up from Santarém and take them to Lisbon, but before that, Sara and Torres had organised a special dinner, the day before, for all the family; they didn't know when this was going to be happening again, to have everyone around the table. The couple had all their family's support, both sides welcomed the new member, which did not always happen.

That goodbye dinner was very intense for all, only Jonny was a bit jealous because of all the attention his sister had had these last few months. Torres was very curious about their trip to the Land of her Majesty, like people call it. Peter and Ana explained they were going by ship, from Lisbon to the South of England, Southampton.

"Father, we have the tickets, and the name of the ship is on them. It's big and nice, but I would prefer it to be the Santa Maria." Ana said. Torres explained to his daughter, that maybe it is better to travel in an unknown ship, with not such a bad story attached, and even so Santa Maria never navigated to North Europe, but always to America, like the Vera Cruz did to Africa and a few trips to America as well.

Sara entered the conversation saying the most important thing, is for the trip to go well, and Peter agreed, of course.

They ate, laughed and drank and Ana said they would get together again when possible, and looking to both parents, said she would miss them very much.

Throughout dinner, Sara kept very quiet, but her mind was all over the place. She was reflecting on what her own life would be like from now on, without the reason that made her live with someone who treated her so badly during all those years. Now she had no incentive to keep living this difficult life...but...leaving her husband was something that she wasn't prepared to do, not yet at least, maybe because she didn't want to be the subject of others gossip. One thing she absolutely knew that moment in their life was like a new chapter of the book that life is. For her it was an old book, but for her daughter it was the first chapter of a new one. Her daughter was going on a new path in life, and she truly hoped it was a good one. In many ways Sara was sad that she was not going to be a present presence in her daughter's life; what if she has kids? They wouldn't know her; she would be unable to help them if they needed her support The only thing she would do for sure, was from now on, she would hide her own life. So far away, she didn't need to worry about me, she thought. When people are far away, normally they imagine the worst, and no need for that. She wants her kids to be happy, now, and always. She couldn't go and visit them in England now, but who knows what would happen tomorrow? Life is a closed book, full of new surprises, some good others less so, so the best thing is to wait and see how things go.

At the end of the dinner, Torres proposed a toast to the couple and told Peter to take care of his daughter, because for him his son in law was becoming a son too. Jonny didn't like his dad's comment. In fact, he never liked Peter that much, and listening to this was a bit too much, he felt like Peter was getting along better with his dad than himself.

They all said good night, and while Sara cleaned up, Ana wanted to help her, but she said no. They just cuddled and kissed goodnight.

No one really slept well in the house, apart from Jonny. This last night was life changing for everyone

On the next day, they all got up early. Joe was on time, like always when they needed his help, and they all had the breakfast that Sara had prepared.

The time for goodbyes had arrived, but it was hard. While Peter and Ana were with their respective families. She cuddled her father and thanked him for everything, but when it came to her mother, she started crying. She cuddled her mother, but there was nothing she could do. She never thought this situation could happen before, living close to her mother was always part of the plan, but since she officialised her relationship with Peter, England was on their horizon.

"Ana don't...please...you are a married woman now. Just be strong, you know where I am, if you both ever need me."

Ana didn't have words; she was too sad about leaving. She and her mother were best friends, they were very close, her mother knew all her secrets, the coming months were going to be hell. Inside Ana's young mind, there was lots of confusion, but she was aware that it was the best thing to do if she wanted a better life. She understood all that, but it didn't mean that she wouldn't miss her beloved mother, she was also worried about Sara. What if her father continues hitting her mother? What if her mother gives up her own stupid life and leaves? It was too many Ifs. For Sara the major concern was the trip... she couldn't wait till both were safe and sound in England.

After the suitcases had been put in the boot of the car, Sara urged her daughter to give news as soon as possible. Joe, Jonny, Ana, and Peter got in the car, and they drove off while they all waved goodbye.

Sara stayed outside waving till the car disappeared at the end of the street. She was very sad but didn't cry. Torres was silent and went to his office, Sara went in the house, and stood in the middle of the kitchen for a while. After, she headed to the room that had belonged to her daughter since she was very little. She stood at the door, hesitant. Then, she pictured her daughter as she went in, touching everything that belonged to her. Suddenly, she burst into tears. It was the first time ever she cried the way she did. She was in Ana's room for a very long time, crying till she lay down on her daughter's bed. The sadness of the distance and when she would be seeing her daughter again, her move to England, tiredness and worry of what her life would be like from now on, while her kids are away. All that made her fall asleep.

She lost control of time, and when she woke up it was late. She didn't even make lunch for her husband, but she was not very concerned about it. In the evening, she made dinner just for him, but he didn't turn up. He was probably dealing with his own feelings at his office, but she didn't care. For once in her life, she was putting herself first, not thinking about others. They were all getting on with their lives, meaning that she needed to do the same. That night she went to her daughter's room again and slept there all night.

The next couple of weeks were the hard ones. The house seemed haunted, no noise, laughter, or conversations. The silence was deafening, even at meals there was no noise at all, not even a fly could be heard.

A few weeks had passed since Ana and her husband had left for England. They had had a good trip and it was less of a worry for Sara. Torres has been more muted than ever since the departure of his daughter. Days were passing by without Sara hearing his voice. They were more distant from one another than ever before. He was not sure if she would stay at his side after everything, he did to her, but he was not very concerned anyway. For him, having the dinner on time on the table and his clothes being cared for was the main priority.

The house was still monotonous and sad. One afternoon she was in the kitchen with her head between her hands, thinking about her life, thinking of the possibility of leaving Santarém for good and moving back to Coimbra. She could ask her sister at the convent to see if there was a place for her there. It was worth asking, there was always lots of things to do there, helping children in need was the most important for her. She was looking at the possibility of living in a place where she could feel useful to help others, and Coimbra was still very close to her heart even after all those years, it was the place she had never forgotten. Even if she decided to move back, her kids could visit her there if they wanted to, and they would.

She was deep in her thoughts, when she was interrupted by a knock on the front door. She almost jumped out of her seat. She went to see who it was, and it was the post man with a letter from her daughter. The letter was thick, and she couldn't get rid of the postman fast enough open the letter and start reading.

Dear mother and father, I hope you are both well with Jonny. Peter and I had a good trip. It was too long but we met good people. We met a couple from the North that were coming to England as well. We had meals together, and the lady was always very scared if the ship would sink, but my Peter was amazing to her. He told her that she needs to control her nerves, because it was not the way she feels that was going to prevent anything bad happening, so it was better if she enjoyed the trip.

The funniest thing was she listened to Peter, and she was less nervous. It was nice to meet them, they were nice, and we exchanged addresses, in case of any of us needed help to get jobs, if things were not well with the ones who gave us the acceptance letters in the first place. There were so many other Portuguese people going abroad. Most of them kept quiet and always looked a bit suspicious like they were afraid of something. I felt sorry for some, because they looked so poor...I bet some didn't even go to school, when they were kids, I noticed the way they talked, ate and behaved; it was very limited. It was a new experience for us to be along people that are going to try new opportunities far from home too. They were very courageous; we must admire them for such a decision.

When we arrived in the South, where Peter's brother-in-law was waiting for us. He acted like we were hosts, the way he looked at us, then we went to take the train to London.

It was so strange to hear a different language and not understand a thing.

Reading this, Sara imagined the funny face her daughter would have had.

You know I like to talk, and not being able to is a big thing for me. I don't speak English yet, but I will, but from what I have seen, Peter's brother-in-law doesn't speak much either. He likes to show us that he does, but I can see he feels very jumbled every time he needs to speak, but...it's not my problem.

When we got out of the train station here in London, it felt very weird because the traffic circulates in the opposite way than in Portugal. It can be really confusing; we need to be careful if we don't want to be Ironed by a car.

The English are very polite. They don't talk much, apart from saying please and thank you, but with time I will teach them to...

Sara laughed.

They smile but they are shy; they call me darling; can you imagine? In Portugal if a man calls a woman darling, her father or husband makes them spend a night in hospital.

"Darling? Oh, it must be their culture." Sara murmured.

The weather is rubbish, at least it is so far. There are some streets where the houses all look the same. Peter's sister has a very big house in South London where we are staying. I will lose weight because there are plenty of stairs. Their house has four floors, and they live on the ground floor. Peter and I are on the 3rd and there are more Portuguese people on the 2nd and the 4th, but they all look nice.

A few days after we arrived, Peter's sister took us to the police station; we had to register ourselves there, with name, address, job address. At the end they gave us a little green book, that we need to keep with us always, it's our identification.

Peter and I have started to work in the restaurant where our brother-in-law works. I know what you are thinking, but my sister-in-law told me that her boss doesn't need more employees at the moment, but as soon as he does, I will be joining them, but for the time being I need to earn some money.

We work very hard in the kitchen, and he is a nasty person to us at work, but for the moment we just need to carry on. Peter's sister is so good, she doesn't let us buy any food, we eat all together, because her stupid husband brings food from the restaurant and it's enough for all of us. One day I was off work, and she asked me if there was any place here in London that I would like to visit, and I said I would love to see Westminster and the Bridge that opens,

Tower Bridge, and she took me! Wow there are amazing monuments, I wish you could both be here to see it, but you will one day. If God helps me, I will bring you two here to this wonderful city. One day I will buy my own house like Peter's family did, and then I will bring you both to London. You will see then what I'm talking about – It's a very beautiful city. There is something called the underground – it is a train under the ground. We use the underground train every day; it's very different from Santarém where I used to walk to work. At the moment we both have the same shift. I'm good but Peter is a bit sad; I thought I was the one suffering more, but I'm not. Peter is the one having trouble with adaptation.

Now I'm going to tell you something that is going to make you laugh. The other day Peter was coming up the escalator from the train in Piccadilly Circus, and an Indian man bowed when he saw him; I think he thought Peter was Prince Phillip, they are so similar that he can pass well as the Queens husband.

Sara smiled.

My room is very cosy, and we have everything we need here. My sister-in-law is always asking me if there is anything I need. She is the sister I never had.

How is Jonny? I hope he has matured.

Mother and father, you are always in my heart, can't wait to have a letter from you too. Mother I miss spending evenings talking to you so much.

Keep well...miss you lots. Ana.

After finishing reading the letter, Sara started to look distant and less worried, even her earlier thought had gone. Now she knew for sure, that she would never leave her husband. This letter was all she needed to make up her mind. Their kids need to feel secure if something doesn't go right, they always have a home to come too. All these years she has been suffering at the hands of her husband, but she never left because of her kids, but now they are all grown up and living away. In the end she feels sorry for the man who keeps hurting her for no reason. She kind of forgot about herself, she always put others first. If her daughter becomes a mother, the grandparents need to be together to support the family.

Talking to herself, she said if Jesus suffered for all of us, she can too for her own family. She was very pleased after finishing the letter. She put it inside the envelope and left it on the table to give to Torres later for him to read too.

Since Sara received the letter from her daughter, she was more happy and less worried. She started helping Maria again and spending some afternoons with her. She was always happy to help her friends when needed.

Elizabeth opened a big restaurant, in the place where the agricultural fair was happening during that time. Sara worked very hard.

The restaurant had a big room on the ground floor and another one on the first floor. During the fair, every single day, they served plenty of meals. There was always plenty to do. Sara's help was always dealing with washing the plates, dishes, pans etc. Lots of people worked there, the confusion was enormous. Some evenings after getting home, Sara had a shower and went straight to bed. At least she was not spending much time with her husband and not having time to think about the fact that Ana had left. Jonny never missed one weekend in Santarém during the fair, but apart from that he avoided going back home. She understood his reasons, and now he was growing his own roots in Lisbon, like he told his mother more than once. His love was the capital, fado and seafood. Sara didn't know if he had a girlfriend, but she thought he was too immature to have a proper relationship.

Twice a month Ana sent a letter to her parents. She was missing them a lot. They always replied that she needed to be strong because her place was always by her husband's side. She knew that, but in one of the letters they received, after they had both had been away for 18 months in England. Ana was very concerned.

Ana was devastated after Peter fell very sick, he was off work, and she asked her brother-in-law to not to give Peter's position at work to anyone, till he was able to return, meanwhile she would do both jobs. She was very tired, and the worst thing was her brother-in-law being very mean to her. He oversaw the kitchen, but he was always a pig to the ones working under him.

Every day, when she got home after work, she cried in the bathroom, so Peter could not hear her. It was a very delicate phase for the young couple, she only had help from Peter's sister. Ana never understood why Peter's sister got married to such a plonker.

Ana's parents were very worried about it and asked their daughter if she wanted to come back with Peter, but the reply they got from her was that she believed in her prayers, and Peter would recover.

It was three months of complete worry. Sara was waiting for the postman every day; she was desperate for good news. She was too far away to help.

Finally, one letter from England, this time it was much better news, but before she opened the letter, she blessed herself with the sign of the cross.

My dear parents, I hope you and Jonny are well.

My Peter is much better, and he has already returned to work; he is still very weak, but he is not so pale anymore. I still do part of his duties at work, but we need to get another job, our brother-in-law is the worst person I have ever seen. He keeps saying that Peter made up his disease just so he didn't have to work; he is a horrible person, and he thinks he is very important. To me, he is less important than a dog poo which I avoid not to step on.

While my Peter was unwell, the beast did everything he could to splash me when he was washing the floor and made me do things more than once saying that I was stupid and never learned anything properly. Peter and I are saving money, as much as we can to move out of the house and get another place to work. Peter speaks calmly and says that with perseverance, and time we will. I can't wait to get away from that place of work. Peter's sister is encouraging her boss to give me a chance and in her opinion he will very soon. The customers are increasing, and the coats (visons, is the name) are very, very expensive. If I can get in, it would be amazing because the wages are great.

Every evening Peter and I have been learning English from the books we have, the vocabulary Jonny gave us is very useful, I'm getting better at it.

Now I'm going to send you lots of kisses, regards from Peter, and pull Jonny's hair for me. By the way, is my brother still crazy?

Sara smiled.

This letter had better news, at least they are both very positive and close.

That evening at dinner Sara and Torres talked about the problems their daughter and Peter were facing.

"I never thought Peter's sister was married to a beast like she is." Sara mentioned.

"Maybe he is like that because of what he has been through since he had to leave Portugal to live in a different country. Immigration is a hard thing."

"If so, he has good reason not to do these things to others. Portuguese abroad   must look out for each other. It's difficult for everyone, but I think what he needs is a good beating."

"A real man never gets beaten; you don't know what you are talking about. Women. Woman shut your mouth."

"A man?" she smiled. "Do you agree with what he is doing to our daughter? If I was closer, I would teach him a lesson."

The following day, when Sara went out, she had bruises on her face and body, and her lower lip had a cut on it. She wasn't ashamed anymore, unfortunately she was used to having this appearance, but her friend Clementino didn't like to see her like this.

"Sara darling...don't tell me...he did it again!"

"Yes, but...don't worry I'm fine."

"Fine...How could you say that? Why does he keep hitting you? For God's sake!"

"We were talking about Ana, and we disagree about some problems...his answer to me is always the same."

They talked for a bit longer, and he asked about the new couple in England then they both went their separate ways.

Torres was in his office when he heard a knock on the door.

"May I come in Mr Torres?"

"Clementino...Nice to see you. What brings you here?"

"You, Mr Torres."

"Me? Why?"

"I want to ask you, please stop hitting Sara...she is a lady, you don't have the right to do what you have been doing to her."

"Clementino, this is not your business, its nothing to do with you. Just leave it."

"I will, but not before I make this clear. The woman you call your wife is a Saint to put up with you."

He was furious with this man that everyone respected but was actually a criminal. No man should hit their wife; they do because it's the tradition of weak, cowardly men. They know their wives never hit them back, that's why they feel free to continue the violence time and time again.

After he left, Torres sat back on his chair; he was surprised about what had just happened. Clementino never interfered in anyone's life, but he cared so much about Sara and seeing her through the years, hurting but always smiling. It was hard even now that her daughter was away. They were very best friends, and Ana's departure left a huge void in Sara's life.

Torres never told Sara about it, but he clearly felt ashamed of himself, she never understood why he was this way. She always put her family first, forgetting herself, and never let it go if anyone took advantage of her. Not to have her kids at home was big. But at least she could still see Jonny occasionally when he came home for weekends.

He was coming this weekend, so she was cooking his favourite menu. That Friday evening soon he came through the door, by the aroma he could guess what the dinner was. Roasted leg of lamb with potatoes and vegetables.

"Mother...you are unique, I love that food." He said, he didn't realise that it was his sister's favourite as well.

Every single day since her daughter left, Sara never went to bed at night without going to her bedroom. It was her weakness. Behind her strong appearance she could have a sensitive side. Her love for both her kids had no limits, and she was eager to have news from Ana about a new addition to the family. She couldn't wait to be a grandmother; however, she knew it wasn't the time, they needed to settle down first. Her daughter and son in law have dreams, but now they have lots of things to deal with.

The three of them had dinner, and just as they were finishing, Jonny surprised everyone by saying he was thinking about getting married. His parents stopped eating and looked at him in surprise.

"Son, do you realise that you need to have a girlfriend first? And know each other first before the big decision?" Torres told his son.

"But I have a girlfriend, we have known each other for a while now." Sara was looking incredulous.

"Son...Marriage is a very important step...are you sure about this?"

"I'm sure, but father you don't look too happy...don't I deserve a party like my sister had?"

"Don't be stupid son...of course you do, but this is about you knowing the women that you are committing the rest of your life too. I think you should wait a bit longer before any major decision."

"OK, if you don't agree, I will marry her just with the godparents...don't worry. I love her, that's all that matters."

"Stop their son.... can we meet her, at least?" His mother's mouth was open, she couldn't believe in what was going on. How Jonny could be so stupid as to marry a woman he hardly knows?

"Let's meet her first and talk about marriage after, shall we? Is she from Lisbon?"

"No, no, she is from the North, but she has been in Lisbon for a while. It's incredible because she likes most things that I like."

"Can I bring her next weekend father?" Torres looked to Sara, and she made a positive sign.

"You can, Saturday, just for the day."

It seemed obvious to his parents that he was jealous of what his sister had, from the way he pointed it out, but his sister and Peter had years of dating. Jonny was a pure joke. He must have known this girl for only a few months, not more. He had known some nice girls from good families here, for years, where he was brought up.

The following Saturday came fast, and Sara had prepared a good lunch for the four of them. Jonny was like a kid with a new toy, but the girl, Sophie, didn't convince his parents. The lunch went well, but her demeanour was fake in Torres's opinion. From his experience, his future daughter in law was a good actress, but maybe it was destiny wanting to give Jonny a lesson.

Sara found her nice, and she loved seeing her son happy. However, she wanted to have a talk with Jonny - marriage should wait a bit longer. It's not a decision to be taken lightly. Jonny needs to give time to time, but unfortunately, he was in a hurry. The following weekend he was home again, but this time alone. His parents didn't get why he wanted to get married so urgently. At one point Sara asked her son if Sophie was pregnant. Jonny was angry with that question.

After a hard discussion they agreed, the marriage was to go ahead, but in Lisbon, not in Santarém. Jonny was too vain, it was easy just to ask his parents to do his wedding, to spend a lot of money. They didn't have money and they were resigned to but not convinced about this relationship. They didn't mind all this in a different context, in which their son had a different vision of the future, more responsible.

Everything was organised. Sara worked like crazy once again to give a nice wedding to her son, because the last thing she wanted was for Jonny to accuse her of not providing him with a wedding like his sister had. Normally parents spend more money with daughter's wedding than sons, but for Jonny it was a different vision. On more than one occasion his parents had the sensation that he wanted to get married just to be the king of the party. Because of his personality, his sister was always the one to confront him. She didn't understand why her brother was so different from her.

One week before the wedding, Jonny was at work when one of his colleagues called him.

"Jonny go to the office because there is a lady who wants to talk to you."

"Good morning, ma'am, can I help you?"

"I'm Sophie's mother."

"Nice to meet you... what is your name?"

"My name doesn't matter!"

"Are you here for the wedding?" The woman gave Jonny a hard look.

"I just came to Lisbon to ask you not to marry my daughter, that's all."

Jonny looked astonished, facing his future mother-in-law.

"I love your daughter, and you should too."

"She doesn't love anyone, but herself. I warned you..." Saying that she turned back and left. Jonny was bemused after what had just happened, but he didn't tell anyone about this visit. Maybe he was really in love, or so he thought, but he decided not to tell anyone.

The wedding happened in Lisbon in a small church, not many guests, not even his sister and husband were there, and just a very few people from the bride's side.

Jonny and Sophie rented a small flat in Central Lisbon, and now he was back to his parents' home less than ever, and six months after the big day he started to go just on his own. His parents asked him why she was not with him, but he always said the same thing, that she was busy working. Torres didn't believe it, but he never said a word, his son thought he knew everything, never accepted an opinion from his parents, now it's his problem to deal with the mess he was in.

Sara asked her son if everything was ok; his answer was always positive. They never invited anyone to go to their flat, even family. Jonny avoided questions about his relationship with his wife, and he was always smiling and ready to go out with friends enjoying himself, as long as no one talked about his wife.

One Friday evening he turned up at his parent's house, had dinner, and halfway through he told them he was preparing everything to go to England. His parents were puzzled.

He had everything planned, he wanted to go by train to Paris first, stay there a while, afterwards Munich and then London. He told them he was going on his own first and then he would prepare things to take Sophie too. When he said that, Torres looked at him with a look in his eyes that any mature person would understand straight away, but not Jonny. Their son was still very immature, living in a fantasy. His parents were getting the feeling, he was distancing himself from his wife, but there was nothing they could say or do.

Jonny left Santarém only on Sunday at the end of the day.

Another letter from Ana had arrived, and this time she was happy about a few changes in their lives.

She had finally started to work with her sister-in-law at the high-class ladies' coats shop. Peter left the kitchen because his boss wanted him in the restaurant working as a waiter, his nice physique was the cause for the change. Peter was thrilled with that decision, firstly because he was going to be away from working with a nasty man like his brother-in-law. Secondly, in the restaurant he could see people, learn English and it's a cleaner job. Still, while working in the kitchen he learnt how to cook, make sauces, and do most of the recipes. He was a good learner, always paying attention to every little detail. He was very happy because for a very long time he was thirsty to evolve in what he did, he loved the change, so he was giving everything in his power to please the boss and the customer, but most importantly, to feel happy about his personal evolution, in this recent change of professional path. They had opened a bank account too at Halifax building society. They managed to raise a considerable sum of money for the opening of this account. They wanted to do everything they could to have stability and independence in the near future. They were still living with his family, but in a more private way. The first week after Peter's promotion was a bit difficult. Every time he was at home at the same time as his brother-in-law, he heard him making jokes about his promotion at work. Sometimes it was hard to listen to, but like Ana mentioned in the letter, donkey voices don't go to heaven.

Things are improving and looking promising, and Sara is much more tranquil about it. She wished Jonny could have a much more stable life too, but only time can show that. Now his new adventure to go to Europe worried Sara but she couldn't interfere. He was a married man and not a boy anymore, if he wants to run away from his problems it is something he needs to deal with, nobody else.

A few times she wanted to talk to him but gave up. He made up his mind to go away, never asked for financial support from his parents, and if he did, they didn't have money to help him. Not his father, but Sara once asked him about how he would survive without work, for her it was difficult to understand, but Jonny - always with his silly smile – said he would work here and there to get going. He thought he spoke enough French and English to keep going.

He organised everything to leave the country, and his wife behind, he couldn't hide his happiness about it. His father wasn't very pleased about this event, but the only thing he could do was watch where this decision could take Jonny. They knew what he was doing, but now instead of running away he should sleep on the bed that he made. Their parents tried open his eyes about marrying someone that he didn't know, but he was too proud of himself to listen then. At least they didn't have children.

The day before he left for Paris from Lisbon by train, he went to Santarém for goodbyes. He was excited to be leaving, and all the advice his parents gave him entered from one ear at five km an hour and left from the other at much greater speed, but that was Jonny.

Sara grabbed her son and cuddled him very tight; she didn't know when she would be doing that again. A long time had passed since he was a child and she always knew where he was, like any other mother towards her children.

On the next day, he left his flat alone with a little suitcase. His wife was working or maybe she just didn't want to be there to avoid seeing what he was doing. Her opinion didn't matter for him, it was a normal practice, women didn't have a say about anything. Sara once said to Maria who would had been the first son of a bitch, to invent that woman are less than men, he should have rotted in hell. They need us more than we need them. They don't know how to survive without us, they only need a hole to rub what's inside their pants. They should have been rubbing it on a stone.

The weeks were passing by, and no news about their son, even their daughter in law didn't have any. Torres wasn't very concerned, but Sara was a different story. She was working at the market again, sometimes helping Maria, trying to keep busy as much as she could. One Thursday after returning home, after a very long day, she opened the front door, and she found a letter on the floor from her daughter.

She put all her shop that she had brought on the table, sat down, and opened the letter. The news this time included her brother. After three long months in Paris, Munich, and Berlin, he had arrived in London.

One evening he approached my house in Clapham North, South London. He saw me with the family having dinner through the window, but he just walked away without them seeing him. The next day he turned back and this time he knocked on our door.

He told me of a horrific situation where Portuguese people were living in Paris. One day he went to a place where there were lots of old cars on mud with pieces of wood making bridges where they can walk without mess and saw people living inside. Jonny told me when he left the place he had tears in his eyes, and I did too when he told me. I never thought people could live in such poverty. Mother can you imagine children living like that?

Even Sara had tears in her eyes reading the letter.

Jonny told me he was staying in a room in Central Paris and worked for a while in a cafe. Then he went to Munich. He said it's a beautiful city, but the Germans seem to have their mouths full of hot broad beans when they talk. He travelled to a few places in Germany; he loves the country. He went to Berlin, and the only reason he didn't stay there was because of the language, it's too hard. But now he is here. He can't live without me...

Ana told her parents that Jonny was already working, and she told him that he needed to bring Sophie to be with him. He had agreed and said that as soon as he had enough money to make that happen, he would. He too rented a double room in the house, now preparing things for Sophie to join him.

Ana was doing very well at her job; she was learning all the tricks to make perfect ladies fur coats. The only thing she mentioned in the letter was about the poor animals that needed to be killed to make the very expensive coats, to please a bunch of women because the only thing they know about is spending and spending. She worked in this sector because it was good money and a good work environment, and there is no perfect job in the world.

Eventually, Jonny went to Portugal to take Sophie to London with him, but as soon as he got to his Lisbon flat, he was completely mad when he found out that as soon as he had left for Paris, Sophie had sold all his good bottles of wine and whisky as a punishment for what he did.

He took her to London, and she got a job almost immediately, but Jonny was always finding excuses to be away from her. He used to say it was work, but his sister knew him too well.

In London Ana and Peter were doing just fine, working very hard, but it was paying off, because finally they were thinking about asking the bank for a mortgage. One day, very late at night both were talking about it, when Peter told her that on their day off, they would be going to the bank to see if there was a chance for them to buy a house.

Everything looked promising after they visited the building society for help with a mortgage. Since they opened the account, they deposited the same amount of money every single month, but they never withdrew it, and it was certainly a good thing towards this important investment. a North London estate agent was their next step.

Ana was very surprised, why did they need to go so far from where they were now to get a house. Peter said he wants to be far from his family. When families are only visiting, they all have a good relationship, but when they live on top of one another, there is always trouble, and in their case, they need to detox after almost six years. They were very organised about it, and good ideas were fertilising in their minds.

Three months after they started working on their new project, they finally found the house that touched their heart and seduced them in Northwest London.

The house had a little front garden, with a tree and a big garden at the back, with lots to do. On the ground floor, was a big kitchen, a big living room, corridor, and a small storage cupboard. Upstairs they had three rooms, a double, single and a very little bedroom with a bathroom.

The house needed a few things to be done, and the bathroom needed a new floor, and a new mirror with storage just above the lavatory. The whole house needs a good painting, and one or two things need to be done in the kitchen. That was the motive they used to have the price reduced. Obviously, they needed to get all the furniture, but in the beginning, they just needed a bed, wardrobe, table, and chairs – the rest they would be getting later. Peter and Ana would be the ones doing all the repairs around the house, to save money.

When Sara received a letter from Ana, she was very pleased about it, now they can start to have their own space and independence and they could start their own family. Ana was so excited in the letter that she was making plans for her parents to visit them. In all this time they had been away, they had only returned to Santarém once. It was not enough time for her to see the relationship between her parents, and she wouldn't know for sure how things were, but she assumed that all the hitting had probably stopped. She never asked her mother about it, and even in the letters from her she never read anything that made her think the situation kept going. Sara never dreamt about going to London; her feet were well placed on the ground. She was pleased with what Ana had achieved in life so far, unlike Jonny. His relationship with his family was growing more distant every day. He had criticised his sister and Peter for buying a house so far away, but Ana immediately put him in his place. Since he became a man, his favourite subject was criticising his sister, but Ana has a strong personality most of the time just by keeping her eyes wide open, and her brother gets the message straight away.

Sara had lived for her kids, all through the years she worked for their benefit, but now the only news she had about Jonny was through Ana. He never contacted his mother in any way. If it wasn't for her daughter, she couldn't know if her son was alive or not. Sara knew her son couldn't blame others for his behaviour, but he clearly forgot he had parents. Many times, she blamed herself for it, she gave him too much time, she always had excuses for him. In the end he hadn't been prepared for life the way she thought he was.

Sara's days started to be just meat to fill up chorizos. Apart from Ana's letters, her life at home now was just routine, a stupid one. She still works at the market every morning very early and when Elizabeth needs her for harvesting the olives and grapes and to help in the restaurant during the Ribatejo fair. She is always looking for ways to earn some money. She never says no to a friend when they ask her for help, she always makes herself available to help. She has a little box hidden in the room that used to be Ana's where she keeps some savings that were left over from the month's purchases. Even if is not too much, she keeps doing it. Sara always thinks in case one of her kids needs help; she has to be prepared.

The only two present people who made her feel alive in town were Clementino and Maria. In one way or another, they were there for her.

The last letter Sara received from Ana made her realise that there were always people with worse problems than her.

Mother, two weeks ago Peter and I were shopping, when we saw Victoria! Do you remember her, from the dress maker? She was a seamstress apprentice when I started to have my dresses made, but she was a bit quiet, though she had good taste to choose fabrics. I don't know why, but as soon as I saw her, I recognised her straight away. Mother if you saw her now...she is so different...poor woman. How this world is so small...Her husband is very violent; he hits her constantly. She left Santarém 18 months ago after her brother wanted to create justice with his own hands, because of the way he treats his sister.

Now they are here, but she is very unhappy, she didn't want to leave Portugal, but he made her do it anyway.

Mother, she works very hard, and he keeps her money – he hits her with his belt. He is a monster...Do you remember her having long nails? He cuts them very short just from one hand, he does all this because he drinks a lot. Mother I felt so sorry for her. They are living in a room not far from where I have my house.

Mother...Peter and I booked some tickets.... yes, we are going to have holidays, and Peter wants us to take a break from London. We are so excited...It's like the days are now taking longer to pass. If everything goes well according to plan, we will have dinner with you and dad on the first Wednesday of July. Mother do you need anything from London? I know what I want to bring from Portugal - sun, lots of it. My peers at work are so jealous of me, because of my holiday. But they are so good, all of them, they have helped me since the very first minute I entered the workplace, teaching me how to do my job properly, and always with a smile on their faces. Sometimes I bring some of our delicious food to work and we all have a party. Lately even Peter's sister brings something too, especially on Fridays and it's so much fun mother. There is this friend, she works just next to me, and her name is Doris. She is very pretty, and she has been my English teacher since the beginning. We talk and laugh all the time. Our boss said the other day that before I joined them, every single day was grey, but now it was a beautiful summer day. The other day I didn't work in the morning because I needed to go to see my doctor, so when I went after lunch, they all were so happy to see me. You should have seen them laugh that afternoon after I told them how my doctor's appointment was.

I had a problem with one of my fingers, but here in England mother, fingers are on the hands, because on our feet its toes, so to explain myself to the doctor I told her that I had a problem on a fingernail on my foot. The doctor said excuse me, and she turned her face away and laughed very much. Later I told my friends here at work, and they laughed like crazy, and I did too. One thing is for sure...I will never forget how to say it again.

But they are all very friendly mother. Life here is very different from Portugal, but I love it.

Sara was very excited about her daughter and husband coming home, and she started to organise her old bedroom, and the dinner for the day. It was not only Ana and Peter counting the days; Sara was too. It was very rare for Sara to write to her daughter, there was nothing important to tell her. When people are near one another, they always find things to talk about, but when they need to write, that is when the pig twists its tail, she thinks.

During all the time left before she could see Ana again, Sara got two sets of new bed linen embroidered by hand, a tablecloth embroidered by hand too and towels to give Ana and Peter to take home with them. She was getting all the goodies home and ordered a big leg of lamb to roast for their first meal.

The morning before they arrived, Sara was doing the last-minute shopping and getting the Pasteis de Belém fresh - they couldn't be missing. It was very important for her as a mother to please her daughter on this special day.

The moment Ana arrived home, she and Sara cuddled each other so intensely with tears rolling down their faces. It had been a long wait, but finally the day was here. She cuddled and kissed her father too, but it was slightly different. He loved his daughter very much, but he was not the type of father to be doing that, a kiss and a single cuddle was enough.

Sara helped them with the luggage to their room. As soon as Ana got in, she admired her old room, saying that her mother keeps everything just the way it was when she was there, before her wedding.

The two women talked for a bit, the saudade was too much.

That evening Torres and Peter talked in the kitchen for a long time about their life in London while the two women in Ana's room talked and unpacked the suitcases.

"I can't believe you are here...Ana are you happy?" Sara asked.

"Of course, I am mother, why are you asking?"

"It's a simple question...mother's like to know these things. You got married, and moved to another country, I have your letters, but it's not the same thing as if you had been living here." They looked at each other. "Tell me...are you and Peter going to make me a grandmother?" Ana looked very seriously at her mother, with a negative look.

"No... we are not."

"OK...there is a motive for that decision? I'm sorry, I know it's not my business...but..."

"Mother, do you remember when I got pregnant, and Peter didn't want me to have an abortion?" Sara nodded her head. "Peter told me he wanted that kid so much, and because we didn't have him, he was done. We didn't have the first one... there is no space to have a second one." Sara understood, once again because of her husband, lives were changed forever. She passed a hand on Ana's face and smiled to her daughter. "Are you sad Ana?"

"Not really...we have a very busy life now, even if he wanted to, it is a difficult time. We have to rely on each other, nobody else."

"Tell me about Victoria, how is she?

"Mother, she has a horrible husband...he does such bad things to her...I don't understand why she keeps living with him! She works hard, but her stupid husband takes all the money away from her."

"Who would say when she was here that she would end up with such a man by her side. Good Lord Ana. I noticed that she was always very quiet, I understood she didn't like to talk much."

"When we met, she was so happy to see someone that she knew, she was starving to talk. Since she had gone to London, the only Portuguese she discussed was her stupid husband. Even Peter was feeling sorry for her. She has a very well-paid job, and she does what she likes most. She said sometimes she takes home some very expensive dresses to finish in the evening. She works for a stylist and meets very important and rich women. They pay her very well, but her husband keeps all her money, and when she needs to get something for herself, she can't. It's a stupid life I must say. Changing the subject, have you been seeing Clementino? "

"Always, why?" Ana giggled.

"I brought him some eye shadow and can't wait to give it to him."

"He will love it, I'm sure."

Both women talked till late, while Torres and Peter talked as well in the kitchen. It was a very pleasant evening, long awaited from all of them.

The next day, they all had breakfast together in the kitchen before they went to see Peter's family.

The next two weeks were very busy, seeing all the people they hadn't seen for a while, and being invited for lunch and dinner. When Ana met Clementino and gave him his present, he was so moved that he cuddled her and kissed Peter. Like always he was very polite, and it was not every day that he got a present. He too invited the young couple and Sara to go to a coffee shop.

It was always so good to go home, see their families, friends, eat their favourite food, drink the good homemade wine, and visit their favourite places. They enjoyed every minute of their holidays, but one day in particular was great fun. They were invited by some friends to have a nice meal at their farm. They made this dried cod fish roasted in an outdoor wooden oven, seasoned with hot olive oil, and sliced garlic, and roasted small potatoes only with salt, and after they are punched and go again to the oven for a few more minutes. The wine was gorgeous too, from their farm. They all had a good lunch, under a big tree. Sara was very happy, just wishing Jonny was there too. Before they left, they all agreed next time Ana and Peter came to Portugal, they would repeat this wonderful day again.

They had two full on weeks of pleasure without being worried about work. But like everything in life, there is a start, middle and end for everything, and it was time to say goodbye once again, till next time probably the following summer. It was always hard, plenty of tears from mother and daughter, but the distance didn't separate their good relationship. They missed each other tremendously, but life is just this way; everyone needs to find their own path.

Chapter 21

During 1968, Salazar was replaced by Marcello Caetano, who didn't have a good reputation to lead the country because he became very sick after a fall. He had been in power since 1932, but now was in no condition to keep doing what he had been doing since then.

Salazar had a very good education, from being an economist to a statesman, but he abused his power throughout his life, making the destinies of millions of people miserable and scared. But even so, he has been a Catholic fanatic practitioner all his life.

His disease made him very week by the day, and on the 27th of July 1970 at the age of 81 he died in Lisbon. The man who had led the country for four decades, doing everything he wanted, without justifying anything to anyone was no longer in power. The fascist, egocentric dictator and religious fanatic was lost forever.

His body was in the Mosteiro dos Gerónimos in Belém. The country was mourning, people needed to show they were sad; they must because it was the way forward but despite his death and the new leader, the country's regime remained unpopular with its people. No one was allowed to have an opinion, there was still no freedom of speech and every time people said something against the government, they simply vanished without leaving any trace. The International Police and Defence of the State (Pide) was created on the 22nd of October 1945, at the peak of the Salazar dictatorship, and the function of this police force was to pursue people who they knew had ideas against government. These people were seen as enemies and would be arrested and questioned, tortured and killed (most of the time).

Those people, just because they had a different political view of the regime, were taken to prisons in the country and Cape Verde. In these horrific prisons, people were isolated, sleep deprived, starved and they did not have any conditions of hygiene. When the sea tide was high, they would have water up to their necks.

His body travelled all the way to Santa Comba Dão, further North of the country where he was born and now where he was being buried, on the 30th of July.

However, the country was mourning Salazar as their resident, even though he wasn't their president anymore.

When alone with Maria one day, Sara told her, one bastard had gone, but another had replaced him, and the shit continues, till people wake up, get together, and get rid of him for good. Maria told her to shut up in case anyone could hear her, but she said she didn't care. She was fed up with living in fear, first from her husband and then from her own country. Both women through the years knew new people, who had their lives and suddenly vanished. One of Maria's friends had a husband and a son. One day both left for work in the morning but never came back. The woman was in shock for a long time. Years later, she got married again. One day she was at home, and she heard a knock on the door. When she opened the door, there he was standing, her first husband who had disappeared before.

And almost four years after Sara said that to her friend, the regime of dictatorship in the country suffered a wonderful shake up that would change the lives of many for ever.

Before April 25th, 1974, Political parties and movements were banned, political prisons were completely full, leaders of the opposition were in exile, strikes were prohibited, unions were tightly controlled, and cultural life was strictly monitored. People were starved of education, deprived of food, but had pain in abundance.

Lots of families around the country lost loved ones, because they simply vanished for good. It was like the walls had ears, most times people thought it was safe to talk, and soon after that they were picked up by secret agents, "PIDE", then they just disappear. No one could be trusted; these secret agents were everywhere. Even at home people needed to be careful about what they said.

Despite the change of the country's leader, there were very Conservative wings that simply refused to allow reforms to take place and help promote the regime to be a bit more flexible to give a little freedom to the people. 42 long years were more than enough.

Almost four years after Salazar's death everything changed and freedom in Portugal began, with the carnations of revolution, enough was enough, people were having the courage to make the difference, to change the destiny of the country for ever and to end this authoritarian system once and for all.

Shortly after midnight on April 25th, 1974, a song that had been forbidden until then started to be transmitted on the radio. "Grândola Villa Morena", was the main key for the much-deserved freedom of the people. After so many years of fascist dictatorship and wars in our colonies, the army organised a coup to overthrow their leader (Marcello Caetano) out of power.

This coup became known as the carnation revolution, because on the day, carnations carried by the population in the soldiers' rifles ended up becoming the symbol of the revolution.

On that day, Portuguese troops occupied strategic locations all around the country. When the sun rose, crowds were already surrounding the radio stations waiting for the latest news. The operation was very well calculated, and taking the regime by surprise, Marcello Caetano was cornered by his people and military and with no other solution he resigned as the leader by telephone to the coup leader, General António Spínola. Then he was transported by an army tank to Lisbon Airport and sent to Brazil with a one-way ticket to start his new life, in exile. In eighteen hours, the oldest dictatorship in the world had come to an end. Four people died in the conflict from the takeover of their headquarters. The only ones to offer resistance during the revolution were the government's elite police.

Mário Soares, founder of the socialist party, one of the most dissident of Salazar's regime, returned from exile in Paris. He was received by thousands of people at Lisbon train station, with carnations and much more thrown by a helicopter over the city, and the famous, "Grandula Vila Morena " key music was played, it had become the anthem of the Portuguese revolution.

Álvaro Cunhal, the founder of the Portuguese communist party, emerged from exile a few days after, joining Mário Soares on the streets of Lisbon to celebrate the country's freedom. The two together later created the first temporary government.

There was reckoning after this coup, life slowly started to be normal, lots of people who had fled the country before started to return from exile. Politicians and artists were the first ones to arrive, and the democratic regime of the country was rebuilt. There have been jokes about this revolution being the revolution of red flowers, never in any other part of our planet had there been anything like this. A coup so well organised and with carnations stuck in the barrels of rifles, was unique.

The Portuguese could now live without looking over their shoulders, they needed to learn how not to live in fear anymore. They started to invest in people's lives, like reforms, education, and health. The country was well behind compared to the rest of Europe, meaning there was a lot to be done to push Portugal forward. Mentalities needed urgently to be upgraded, but it was a tough job. Even so there were a few people who still talked about missing the dictatorship, not allowing themselves to taste the flavour of freedom. Sara couldn't understand people who think this way. She thinks they are not normal at all. It's very bad when they don't know how to distinguish right from wrong. How can anyone prefer to be oppressed, scared, and feeling fear to having freedom? She felt very cross every time she heard about it.

The next letter she wrote to Ana, gave a very detailed explanation of everything about the carnation revolution, she couldn't hide her happiness about it.

Torres never talked about it to anyone, he kept very quiet about it, the only thing that made Sara sure he was very pleased too was the fact that from the 25th of April onwards, his favourite flower was a carnation.

Everyone had a different way of showing their feelings about this landmark of Portuguese history, that will live in the hearts of those who had played the most important part in it and will be celebrated for many generations to come.

Chapter 22

Ana and her husband were keeping the same jobs in London, and they were very pleased. Their house looked wonderful, and whenever Peter had time, he dedicated it to his garden.

One evening, Ana was alone at her place, the weather was bad, the storm had given no respite, and she was sat at the stairs covered in a blanket. The noise caused was tremendously scary. There was heavy rain and wind banging on the windows, causing the sensation that they would be breaking soon. The lightning from the thunderstorm was illuminating the whole house, making her cover her head and shake. Suddenly she heard a knock on her front door. She felt even more scared, but the knock went on and on, till she got the courage to go down the stairs, get closer to the front door and ask who it was.

A very familiar female voice replied shouting, letting Ana know who it was.

Ana threw her blanket back and opened the door quickly helped by the strong wind, and there stood Victoria, all soaked, crying and shivering, in her night dress. Ana didn't believe what her eyes were seeing. She pulled her friend into the house. Victoria apologised but she had to run away from her husband after a violent evening. She was looking very different from what Ana knew. Victoria was normally a tall woman, with her black hair short but always well combed, and nicely dressed, but at this moment she looked different. She had half of her head shaved, she was completely ashamed with the state she was in, but Ana was her only chance to get help in this difficult time.

Ana felt so sorry for her and didn't want to waste any time, she took her upstairs to the bathroom and prepared a hot bath. She needed urgently to remove the wet clothes and warm her up.

She stayed in the bath for a while. Ana went to her wardrobe to get some of her own clothes for her friend, and a scarf for her to cover her head. An hour later both women were sat in the kitchen having a hot drink. The storm was a little better, but Ana was still worried because Peter should have been home by now, but with this weather she was more concerned than ever.

Victoria couldn't take it anymore, her husband was the worst of the animals, she left him for good, the only thing she needed now was help till she could be on her feet. Ana wanted to know why Victoria got married with such a prick. Victoria explained that her husband was a friend of her family, and while her own father was alive, he was always a good person, now she thinks he might have been afraid to show who the real him, was in case her father put him straight on a pair of roller skates and pushed him down a hill. Her father was a very nice man, she explains, but very protective of his own family. He used to say his family was sacred. There was no way he could see one of his children being hurt, without doing anything. The problem was he had passed away three months after her wedding, and since then, Victoria's life changed from being a beautiful summer day to the worst miserable Winter one. She always tried to hide her suffering, but now things got so bad. She hates sleeping in the same bed as him, but he makes her. It's like her body doesn't belong to her anymore - when he wants her, he has her. Even looking at him was painful. Since they arrived in London, Victoria has been her husband's slave, working for him indoors and at her job, giving him all her money, and if for any reason he thought she wouldn't give him the amount he had in mind, he simply went to her bag and spread everything on the floor. Most times, he was drunk. It was a pity he never drowned in his alcohol. She concluded to Ana. Victoria was a woman with too much suffering, too much pain, her eyes showed to Ana that she was in complete despair.

While they still having their hot drink, Peter arrived very wet and cold too, the weather didn't give any sign of stopping, and in a few hours, he would need to head back to his work again.

When he saw Victoria at this hour of the night, he had the feeling that something was not right but after he had a hot shower and went downstairs. Ana explained to him what had happened, and immediately he turned to Victoria and told her she could stay as longs she needs. Victoria apologised but Peter told her to stop, that it was not her fault, he just wanted her to lift her head and look forward, because the way to go is always ahead.

Two days later Victoria went to her flat, but she took Ana with her. She went to pick up some clothing and her documents, her husband was still under the influence of alcohol, but he didn't say anything.

Peter and Ana supported Victoria and helped her in everything they could, they let her stay in one of their bedrooms. Slowly she became herself again, working hard, always helping at home and contributing for the meals. Peter and Ana never accepted a penny of rent. A few months later she asked them if she could bring a sewing machine to put in her room to work on the weekends and evenings when Peter was not in. They agreed, but not to put it in her room, but in the smaller one. Later Ana started to help her sew hems and buttons, and they got along very well, and extra income started to make a big difference for them both.

Every time Victoria's boss gave her remnants of fabrics that couldn't be used for anything else, she gave them to Ana, and she knew that she would make nice skirts and tops.

If Ana talked to her about probably one day getting a new man in her life, Victoria felt sick. It was the only thing she knew for sure, no man ever again.

That year Peter and Ana decided to have the big Christmas party, on Christmas Eve like Portuguese tradition demands, at their house, inviting all his family, Jonny, and Sophie.

All the preparations started very early, gathering all the ingredients they needed for the occasion. Every day off Peter and Ana had, they dedicated to doing some recipes for the occasion, and put them in the freezer, so it would be much easier to do it on the 24th.

Peter brought a big Christmas tree and assembled it in one corner in the dining room, with all new decorations he was about to pick, so Ana left all the work for him and vanished from the room, laughing.

There were two days to go, but still a few things to be done. Victoria surprised everyone by getting the Kings cake with the little surprise inside and the traditional big bean inside of it too, meaning the person who got it when eating must pay for the cake next year. They celebrate the season in the Portuguese way on Christmas Eve and English on the 25th, even the crackers won't be missing.

On the 24th neither of them had to work, so they had plenty of time to organise all the food. Peter had a lot of refinement setting the table, a home-made embroidered tablecloth, beautifully made placemats with English cottages on them, nice, beautiful crystal glasses, and the cutlery and dinner set all only used for special occasions. He wanted everything to be very precise and in place. In the place he had been working at since he got to London, he learned how to do all of this perfectly. He was very professional, but at home sometimes he was a bit too much of a perfectionist regarding meals and table setting. Ana knew him so well that she gave him space.

That day was freezing cold outside, but in their house, it was nice and warm, not to mention in their hearts. Peter was happy to have all the family in, so he wanted to make sure everything was good. Ana was happy too, but she wished her parents could be there.

The family started to arrive, and the confusion and noise was intense, but it was part of Portuguese culture when they are happy. All of them brought presents, wine, and deserts. There wasn't enough space to put so many things.

Slowly Peter had things organised, and all of them had a drink, snack and sat down.

Dinner started at 8 pm, after they burst the crackers and put the paper crowns on their heads, only Victoria didn't want it, because she thinks it's foolish.

They all enjoyed dinner, drinks, presents and each other's company, but it was 11.30 pm and the visitors were preparing to go home when Peter's brother-in-law opened the house's front door and was confronted with a white blanket covering everything he could possibly see. While they were enjoying the evening, no one noticed it was snowing and now all the cars were covered in white.

Ana and Peter organised for all of them to stay there for the night. They moved some furniture out of the way in the dining and living rooms and made some beds on the floor for their visitors to sleep. They all were in a good mood and made fun of the situation.

On the Next day, they all had breakfast followed by cleaning the snow off their cars and left.

Chapter 23

Since her kids left, Christmas for Sara hadn't been much fun. She spent the evening dinner with Torres, but after it was very quiet. The 25th after lunch she always met her friend Maria, so she had someone close to talk too, it was like a normal day. She didn't feel sorry for herself, she was happy because both her kids were good. One month before Christmas, she always sent a box of things to London for Ana and Jonny, but he never remembered to send a letter to his mother thanking her.

Every year when the new year turns Sara starts to count the months till her daughter and husband come for holidays. There is something to look forward, but she is thinking about going to see her sister in Coimbra at Easter. She doesn't know how to tell her husband, but she knows she wants to do it. She tried to find the best time to tell him, but his scorn towards her was intense. Sara only represents a housekeeper for her husband. They haven't slept together for years. The only thing that still happens, but not every day, is having meals together. Even when her daughter used to ask her about it, she says that Torres doesn't hit her anymore. She doesn't want her daughter to be worried. She told Maria once, when people are far away, they must receive good news, because if they tell us something is not quite right, they always imagine the worst and there is no need for that. Torres never stopped hitting her, and he never will, unless he or she dies, or one of them disappears, but it's unlikely. Sara stopped dreaming a long time ago, life turned into monotony. When her kids were little, she thought lots of times of leaving her husband, but it never happened. Now they are not at home, but she still thinks being with him is the best thing for her family's sake.

In London Jonny and his wife were having lots of problems, and she gave up on him. One day when he got home, late at night, she had gone, but he only noticed the next morning. She took her clothes, and she didn't even leave him a note. His only problem was towards his family - what was he going to tell them when they found out.

Sophie had prepared her escape very well with a live in job as a private chauffeur, driving a Rolls Royce. She was working for a very wealthy old lady for a while now. and when she invited Sophie to live in the house, she didn't think twice and accepted. Since they got married, Sophie and Jonny had a very stormy relationship, very rarely they agreed about things, both were rowing in different directions. She was very organised, he was completely the opposite, they had different prospects for life, she wasn't the type of women to sit in doors waiting for her husband, she had dreams too, and she went for it.

The first month after she left, he was trying to find excuses in case Ana found out, but it had to be a good one, because his sister already had suspected things were not good between them.

Ana invited Jonny and Sophie to have dinner on Easter Sunday at her house, but he declined, left her with a flee behind her ear, like she used to say when she was suspicious something was not right. So, when he declined the invitation, she said he could come alone. Jonny with his eyes with open, asked her.

"You know?" She said yes, but she was bluffing, she couldn't possibly know, but he fell straight into his sister's trap.

He explained things his own way to Ana, but in the end, she told her brother that he dug himself the grave of his marriage.

They talked, they disagreed, but in the end, he accepted the invitation for Sunday lunch. Ana was strong in her words, sometimes a bit aggressive but she loved her brother and she wanted to see him happy, but for that to happen, he needed to have his head in good place. Jonny agreed with all his sister said, but she was used to it, he agreed because he didn't want to be criticised. He hardly argued with her, but now at least she knew.

In Santarém the day Sara was supposed to travel to Coimbra, Torres lost it and almost killed her. She had her small suitcase and the minute she was going to leave, he grabbed her from behind by the hair, pulled her hard from side to side, pulling out lots of hair, slapped her on each cheek till he threw her on the floor kicking her anywhere he could, and opened her suit case and spread all her clothes on the floor and stepped and spat on them, saying now she could go anywhere she wants, then he left.

Sara was on the floor, surrounded with all her clothes crying in silence. She was there all morning, her body was in pain, every bit of her body was hurting. It was late afternoon when she got up and headed to the bathroom before she washed her face. She looked at herself in the mirror and talked to it.

"You cow, how can you live with this bastard!!! I hate...I hate you...I always hated you you...you son of a bitch. You are a piece of shit!" She screamed and cried and cried. Finally, she washed her face, combed her hair, went to pick up her clothes from the floor and washed them, hung them outside and went to Ana's room, locked the door and lying on the bed she stared at the ceiling and fell asleep digging into her own thoughts.

Torres had disappeared from the face of earth, without leaving a trace behind, finally she was a free woman, not being afraid of anybody. She could work, she could stay or go when she felt like to go anywhere. She could breathe freely. She was flying into a completely new world without being hurt. The painful days are long gone, her world now was very warm, her kids were coming home with their respective other half for a very special meal in a beautiful garden under a tree, the flowers have all sorts of different colours and shapes. Suddenly lots of small children started to surround them, and calling Sara, Sara, Sara... She woke up. She stands up and looked around...it was a dream. She looked at the clock...It was

2.30 am, she lay back into bed and closed her eyes. It was too good to be true.

For another few days, she didn't lay eyes on her husband, and she started to wonder if the dream was a sign of something, but later realised the dream was just a dream. The days passed by, she cooked for him, she washed his clothes but didn't talk much, they were complete strangers, but she preferred it this way. They hadn't spent much time in the same room. She spent much of the time out working, she didn't have much free time, Elizabeth kept her busy and she liked things this way, at least she had peace.

Sara was counting the days to see Ana and Peter; she didn't know about Jonny. It was like he had forgotten his mother. All her sacrifice for that boy, a man now, and he simply doesn't care if his mother is alive or dead. Ana always says something about him in her letters, just to make her mother feel a bit better about it, but she didn't tell her about Jonny's separation from Sophie. She thought Jonny would tell her and their father when he was ready.

In London she was doing some shopping occasionally, so that she didn't have a big impact on their financial status.

Victoria was doing well too, and after everything that happened to her, brought the three of them very close together, like a family. A few times she thought of moving out, but Ana asked her to stay longer with them, because she was the sister she never had. Peter was still working very hard, even on his day off, he spent time improving little things in their home. The garden was just perfect, with a flower bed around it, grass in the main part with stones marking the way that led to the end of the garden barbecue. They had made a canopy for their summer barbecues out of wood and roof tiles.

Three weeks before their holidays back home, Victoria was upstairs in the little room doing some last-minute alterations on a dress to be collected the following day, when Peter took the opportunity to be alone with Ana to tell her something that he was thinking for a very long time now.

"Ana, I need to ask you something and now I think it is the perfect time for me to do it." Ana was concerned when he said that.

"Is everything ok darling?"

"Of course, why are you asking that…just because I want to ask you something? Ana it is very important not to stress about something when you don't know what is going to be said." She opened her dark eyes with an expression saying, "Go on, talk."

"I have been thinking about getting our own house in Portugal."

"You have? Why?"

"Why? Because I love my country, because on our holidays I do prefer staying in our house than at your parents. Also, when we retire, we are going back. Do you think it is enough for us to step out on our next adventure?"

She cuddled and kissed him, and he knew what that meant. They were very organised with all their expenses, and they never purchased things that they didn't really need. They always combined their income and every month after paying their bills, they always sent to their joint bank account in Portugal a sum of money too. In so many ways they started preparing for this giant step towards their dream quite some time ago. The pound was strong, compared with the escudo (Portuguese currency), and the money they had been gathering back home in the bank had earned good interest, if things kept going this way, it would be easy to pay the mortgage, so the dream was becoming a reality very soon. They were planning when in Portugal to go and talk to the bank for a mortgage.

Ana couldn't believe everything they had achieved since they left their country, they worked hard but it was worth every minute. Peter loved his country to bits. He always tried not to get too attached to London, so he didn't suffer too much one day when deciding to go back, but Ana was a different story. She loved everything about London and had made very good friends. Now she was trying the taste of being involved in fashion when Victoria asked her to go with her to a fashion show. Her boss knew about Ana, and they needed someone else at the show, so Victoria asked if it could be Ana. The boss agreed and Ana was making some extra money. She loved everything about fashion, it was a different world for her that brought lots of knowledge and meeting new people. So far, she had seen important people. She loved going to the west end; she had her favourite shops in Oxford Street.

Jonny was living with another woman, but his aspect was very bad indeed. He was brought up in a very different way than he was now. Sara made sure he always had clean and good-looking clothes and nice clean shoes, but now he was looking like a very poor man despite earning enough money to keep looking well.

One day he met his sister in Central London, but she couldn't believe her brother was looking so bad. He was smiling like a silly person, but Ana told him if he decided to go home to see their mother, to just get some nice clothes. It would be very sad if she saw him so miserable. He didn't care much about it, and he was not thinking about going home anyway. He was a different person from what he used to be, making Ana wonder if it had been worth their mother spending her whole life in awful conditions with a man who beat her, when the boy she did all this for doesn't care about her. He was always protected by her, he was her little Jesus, but if she hadn't done what she did, all those years ago, he would still in this position, but at least she would have a different life, a happy one.

Sara was organising Ana's bedroom for them to stay in during their holidays, and she was moving to the room that used to belong to her son.

The last two weeks were crucial, and the time didn't seem to pass. Sara was getting very anxious, and her nerves made her eat when she wasn't hungry, so she put on some weight, but only realised when her skirts started to be too tight. She went to help Elizabeth one afternoon and she couldn't bend the way she used too. She was really concerned about it, but she couldn't control herself when she was at home thinking and being worried about things. Maria tried to talk to her about it, but she replied that food made her do this. Sara was clever enough not to believe in what she was saying, but she needed to come to terms with herself and put a full stop to her worries. Sara hadn't told Maria about the last time Torres had hit her, but her friend suspected that something must have happened for her to have such behaviour. She tried to ask Sara, but she couldn't rip out any words about it.

The day before Ana and Peter arrived, Sara was preparing the last-minute arrangements and she was very happy about having them back home.

In this time of the year, July, and August most of the Portuguese people who lived abroad were returning home for their holidays. Very often in the country during this season kids of those people who were born in the countries where they had lived talked their different languages. Their holidays always had the same destination: going home to see their families and friends. Most of these people who decided to leave Portugal in search of a better life were natives of the countryside in the North.

Most of them went to countries in Europe that after WW2 had lost so many men and needed labour. France and Germany were the countries which met a phase of prosperity and who most opened their doors and attracted the Portuguese, with much better salaries and better life quality. And in the 60's was when huge numbers of populace immigrated, it was quite alarming, leaving some poorer parts of the country deserted but later that result brought a significant increase in investment. Most of those people who had the guts to do what they did - running away from poverty and the political situations – were part of illegal immigration that took place in extremely difficult conditions.

Elizabeth had a niece who was invited by her relatives in France to join them, but when she tried entering the country illegally from Spain through a desert field, she fell and hurt herself badly. Her relatives were on the other side waiting for her, and when she didn't turn up, they went looking for her. They found her later, but she was in a bad way. She was left with bad scars on her face.

Chapter 24

The big day had arrived, and Sara had been working at the market since 5 am, but her mind couldn't think of anything else apart from the moment she would see her daughter. She got home and saw her husband waiting for her in the kitchen. She had a bad feeling about it, but she tried to relax and carry on with her business.

"Sara, while they are here, I want you to move back to my room, understand?"

Sara looked horrified.

"I beg your pardon?"

"You heard me!"

With her very strong voice she replied, "No, I won't ever!"

"I'm not asking you; I'm giving you an order!"

"No, you will never touch me again." He pulled a chair throwing it to the floor saying she was going to regret what she just said.

Torres grabbed her by her hair, pulled her back and slapped her numerous times on her face, waiting for her to say yes, but she never said it. Then he threw her against the table. She fell, and he kicked her everywhere he could, but she didn't say yes.

Furious, he left the house slamming the door behind him. It was getting very difficult for her to keep going like this. She felt too weak to stand up straight after what she had been through.

She heard a knock on the door, and a second one. She got up, passed her hands on her face, walked towards the door and opened it.

"Mother....what happened?" She didn't blame her father, she simply said she had fallen, but of course Ana didn't believe it. It was not a good way for them to start their holidays. For quite some time all of them imagined a nice warm welcome, but nothing like this was expected. Sara was ashamed about the way she received her daughter and son in law, but it wasn't her fault.

Peter carried the luggage to their bedroom while Ana passed a damp cloth on her mother's face. She told her mother that she loves both her parents, but this situation can't go on.

"I thought my father had stopped this situation a long time ago, but from what I can see he didn't."

"It was only today, Ana, he has been good, don't worry."

Ana cuddled her mother and made her a cup of tea. When she met Peter in the bedroom, he told her they needed to put this behind them and not let this interfere with their plans. She agreed but she told him she was going to have a conversation with her father about it.

That evening Torres didn't join them at dinner, but the next day at breakfast he came through the front door, saying hi to his daughter and Peter. Peter shook hands with Torres and Ana cuddled him. Before any other subject, Ana told her father that she was very sad and disappointed to come home after all this time and find out he never stopped hitting her mother.

"Why father? I love you but I don't want you to treat my mother like this. She is a wonderful woman, mother, wife, and friend. I told you many years ago and I'm going to tell you again. If she wanted to, with just one punch she could make you fly." Peter was surprised, and her father had his elbows on the table covering his face with his hands. He knew she was right.

"I want you to stop hitting mother!" Torres removed his face from his hands, stood up, walked away from the table, turned around facing his daughter and spoke.

"You can take her away; I don't want her anymore."

"What are you saying father?"

"What you just heard...I don't want her anymore." Ana stood up as well, facing him.

"I will take my mother away with me, but you will never, ever ask me to bring her back, because I won't. I will give you my word...from the moment my mother walks from that door, I will make sure that she will never return.

"I don't expect anything less, but she is not allowed to take anything from here apart from her clothes; all the rest is mine."

"She won't be needing it, but I thought you could have more respect for the woman who brought up your son putting her own life aside and who had your daughter."

Sara's head was down, and Peter was shocked by everything he had just heard. Torres left, and Ana turned to Peter and apologised for her father's behaviour. All three of them were shocked by what had just happened. Peter had a different approach to the situation.

"Sara, it looks like I need to contact the travel company to get you a ticket to go back with us to London." Said Peter.

Ana looked at her husband, smiling and thanked him.

"Mother, I love my father, and I always will but your suffering ended yesterday, I will make sure from now on, that no one in this world will ever hurt you again.

Those first two days of holidays were far from what they expected their holidays to be like, but at least they sorted out a very old problem, that had needed to be done a long time ago.

As a child Ana felt very sad every time her father hurt her mother. She wished many times her mother could have the courage to hit him back, so it might make him stop, but growing up, it made her realise women never hit men; It's not part of the culture, so men do whatever they want, like her own father did. With time she understood why plenty of women never wanted to marry again after losing their husbands. Some because they had a bad experience, others who were happy before didn't want to risk not finding a man as good as their first husband.

Peter contacted the travel agent and luckily, they got a ticket for Sara to be travelling with them on the same flight, but they needed to get her a passport too. That same day she asked her son in law how much the ticket was, and she gave him the money to pay for it. At first, he didn't want to receive it, but she insisted, saying that she is not the kind of person to be a burden, she has savings, and she will pay for it. She told him and her daughter that once in London she wanted to get a job too, but Peter immediately said she can do whatever she wants when in London, but neither he nor her daughter would accept any money, they just want Sara to be happy from now on.

Ana told Sara, they are doing everything they can to get a mortgage to buy a house in Santarém, and they had an appointment at the bank. Sara was very happy for them, at least it was something to look forward to.

They took all the documents the bank asked them to, and everything looked very promising. It was a race against time, and they had to use their time well. The lady at the bank had known Ana since before she moved to London.

In the meantime, they started to be looking for a flat, in the city, and it gave them pleasure doing it. They tried to take Sara with them several times, when looking to take her mind of things. She was not used to this new phase of her life, she wasn't feeling very comfortable being with her daughter and husband, though she was looking forward to this new experience.

Sara quit her job at the market and said goodbye to a few people there. Elizabeth wasn't there, she was always very busy with her multiple businesses. She always wanted to make money, she never stopped, even on weekends she worked and if someone asked her why she was not going to church on Sundays, she replied that she needed to make a life for herself because God never gave her anything.

Sara understood her friend and never criticised her.

Walking away from it she stopped outside looking at it and for an instant her mind travelled back in time, to when she saw the market for the first time. She got closer to the white and blue tiles and passed her hand through them, like saying goodbye.

Later that day she went to Maria's house, to tell her friend that she was leaving for good. They had a cup of Melissa tea, two pasteis de nata, talked for a bit and then said goodbye.

Sara could never leave without saying goodbye to Clementino. She knew what time he got home, so she went.

This farewell had some tears on both sides. They had known each other, for many years and they talked about everything and anything. Lots of times he opened up to her. They were two beautiful souls who made others happy, despite their personal experience and hurt. Clementino made Sara promise that every time she came home, she must visit him, and she replied that he can't be rid of her. They cuddled and she said another goodbye, but not before he told her that it was a tremendous honour to know her and her big heart. He said he knew why she was leaving, and he would love her forever and he would never forget her as long as he lives.

After leaving his house, she walked around to the places she liked the most. The departure date was approaching, but she couldn't leave without going to the sun doors. The day was very hot, but the garden had this impressive way of making its visitors relax and feel in a place of hope. When Sara entered it, she walked slowly to the edge on the end of the garden and had a look at the amazing panoramic view of the River Tagus and the lezirias. She looked down and saw the train passing towards Lisbon. She closed her eyes, and she took a very deep breath like she wanted to take all this air with her. Then she looked to the fields and thought like a bird, if she could fly freely to feel the wind from above and from there leave all her unhappiness and loneliness that was eating her alive, drop and disappear in the air. She was tired of suffering, and it was good that she was going to change places, make new discoveries, new places. Her friends would all be there for when she comes back, apart from her lovely Coimbra that lives in a particular region of saudade in her heart. That, no one can take away from her.

After she let her mind travel to another dimension, she sat down at the wall and still looking down, her memories from all over the years were coming and going at a very high speed. She remembered when she first came to Santarém, surrendering her own life for the life of a little creature. The thoughts of baby Jonny made her smile, she kept looking down at the lezirias and thinking, in life nothing is permanent, from one minute to the next, things can take a huge turn. She never expected to be homeless like that, after all those years, losing everything that used to be hers, but she didn't care, it was the price she was paying to have the passport to freedom. She needed peace to live, not objects.

She walked for a bit around the garden and sat on one of the benches below a tree, and a whirlwind of thoughts were in and out of her mind. She knew she was doing the right thing in going to London but living with her daughter and husband was another worry. Sara was a very easy person to live with, she knows her daughter, but Peter? He was a good man, Ana loves him, but Sara never spent time with him more than the holidays every time they came over. She smiled at a little girl who came close to her and offered her a flower.

"Is that for me? Thank you." The girl nodded her head saying yes.

"What is your name? Sara asked.

"Joana." Sara was delighted with the little girl when a grown woman approached and called the child.

"Is she disturbing you lady?" The woman asked.

"Absolutely not... Joana is very sweet, look what she gave me!" Sara showed the flower.

"Do you want to be my mother?"

Sara was overwhelmed by what the child had just asked her. She was so young, fragile, and unloved, what could possibly have happened in her little life to make her ask for a mother.

"Don't you have a mother darling?"

She shook her head, but the woman explained to Sara that Joana's mother died when she was still a baby, and her father relied on some neighbours to help him bring her up.

Again, life was taking Sara to a place where a child was in need of love much more than food. How could God be so cruel to take a baby's mother away when they needed her most? Why does he allow such things to happen? Why does a woman get pregnant in the first place if it's not to be present in the baby's life? Sara felt her heart shrink, but she couldn't help...not now after she had a ticket to leave the next day. But how to explain all this to a young human being? She picked up the child, sat her on her lap and explained to her that she can't be her mother because the next day she was leaving for a place too far away. Sara's heart was shattered when Joana told her, that she can ask her father to let her go too.

Sara pulled her close and cuddled her saying that won't be possible. The woman took Joana from Sara's lap and told her not to be silly, because her father was never going to give her away to anyone. Sara gave some coins to the girl and told her to get some chocolate, then she saw them walk away.

Her heart was playing games with her, she couldn't see a child suffering, and now with everything that was happening, why did she have to feel so worried about it, there was nothing she could do.

She stood up and kept walking towards the main gate. When got there, she looked back and whispered.

"Goodbye, see you when I see you."

Since the talk he had with his daughter, Torres never went home. He kept sleeping at his office and eating elsewhere. Peter and Ana took him a few times to restaurants, but without Sara. Her name was never mentioned to Torres. He knew his daughter, and he knew she only has one word. He looked distant and his sad look was more obvious than ever. He liked his son in law like a son. One evening during dinner he told Peter that he was the son he never truly had. Ana asked her father, if he didn't love Jonny but he simply lowered his face and never answered. They all said the farewells two days before the departure. Torres grabbed his daughter very tightly and kissed her on one of her cheeks. And she told him not to be sad because next year she will be back and if there was anything he needed to just let them know. He told her, he won't need anything, he had everything he needed and apologised to her. She thought it was because of the way he treated her mother.

Later Peter told Ana, Torres's true love was Rosa and because he lost her, he couldn't cope. For Ana it was hard to understand why her father loved his first wife, when on their first day as husband and wife, he hit her hard. It was a funny way to love someone. She defended his behaviour by the life he had as a child. He hates women generally; in his opinion they only have duties not rights. Women don't have the right to be happy or to have freedom. He was the kind of father that preferred death to scandal, and they all knew that, back when his daughter and Peter started to date.

Torres was a hurt bird who was never happy, never made his wives happy and changed the live of some forever. Since they had to hide from him when Ana got pregnant, Peter put aside the idea of becoming a father. Torres changed their lives forever, because of his way of making others afraid of him. Peter wanted to have the first baby with Ana, he wanted to prove his love for her and for their child.

The day before their departure, Sara had prepared a nice lunch for them, and she was sat in the kitchen when they came in. Her daughter was giggling, and that only happens when she is excited about something.

"Mother...I think we found the right flat for us; it's going to be perfect!"

"Did you?! I'm very happy for you. Where is it?" Ana explained to her mother the location, it was quite central and not too far from Sara's home.

"Mother it's a first floor building, still being built, it has 110 square metres, two bathrooms, two bedrooms, a big kitchen with a storage room, living and dining rooms open plan, and a space in the loft, it and has an outside space for us to have a table and chairs, but the contractor wanted me and Peter to go next week with him to choose the tiles for the bathrooms, kitchen and corridor and we need to choose the kitchen cabinets too, but when we told him tomorrow we are leaving, he asked us if we can go this afternoon, of course we agreed. Mother I want you to come with us, ok?"

"No, I won't." She said smiling.

"Why mother?"

"Because it's your home. You two need to choose what you like, not me. It's going to be your house, your nest, it should be decided by you. But thank you for asking, I will wait till the house is ready and yours. My advice is, if I might; sometimes we need to pay a little more to have what we like, whatever you choose, make sure you don't have regrets later, because tiles can't be changed so easily like a dress. Another thing: are you going to have dinner here or out today?"

"After choosing the things for the house, we will be coming home, we need to pack, but we are going to have dinner here."

"What do you want me to do?"

"Whatever you feel like doing." Ana said.

It took four hours to choose everything, there was so many different tiles for the walls and floor. Peter told Ana to look around for the floor on the corridor, rooms, living and dining rooms. He liked terracotta tiles very naturally, and she agreed. For the kitchen she chose white cabinets with blue handles, white tiles with a blue decoration just around the middle. They chose for the smaller bathroom dark green tiles; the master bathroom was in white and blue. The corridor was going to have tiles half height in blue and white. Everything they chose was going out a bit from the price of the house, but Peter and Ana were willing to pay, they just wanted the house to look great when finished, and even that day they signed the contract of promise purchase and sale with a 2000$00 cheque to secure the business.

That evening Sara in her bedroom pulled the suitcase she had from when she came to the city, from the top of her wardrobe, and put it on the bed. All her clothes - there weren't many - and shoes fitted inside. Ana came into the room to ask her mother if she needed to put anything in her suitcase, but there was no need.

"Mother are you sad to go to London with us?"

"Don't be silly, I just don't want to make Peter feel uncomfortable with my presence in your house."

"Now mother it's my turn to say, don't you be silly. Victoria is living with us too, you both need to share the same room, because the little one has Victoria's stuff. Mother we will all be happy, look on the bright side. Peter is going to live with three women, he will be a happy man." They laughed.

"Mother, I understand this is an enormous change in your life, but you cannot keep being father's punch bag." Sara was silent and listening. "No one will ever know why he's doing that, but one thing is for certain, I will never let you go back him. I know it's hard for you to leave all your possessions behind, but you won't need them anyway."

"Ana if it is the price, I have to pay to end this stupid marriage, I can tell you that I will never look back."

"Good mother. I know you always respected him, but I also know that if you ever hit him back, you could finish him off, and in this aspect, I will thank you, because I know he is a good father, but a terrible husband. I never say that but...thank you for being my mother and for staying all these years."

On the next morning, they all had their breakfast at eight, because at ten thirty they needed to take a bus to Lisbon.

They got into the bus, and Peter told Ana to sit with her mother, but Sara refused saying she doesn't need a babysitter. The bus started to move and headed towards the exit of Santarém, and shortly after it stopped at another two places to pick up more passengers. In

Lisbon, the first stop was the airport, where the three of them with another couple exited the bus.

Everything was new for Sara; it was the first time she was there. It was the first time she heard people of other nationalities talk. They all joined the long queue for the check in. It took some time, but after they all went through the duty-free. Ana and Peter got one perfume for each other, one bottle of whisky, chocolates, and cigarettes. Sara didn't want or need anything.

Two hours later, they heard the call for the TAP flight to London. They boarded the plane, and just inside, Ana asked Sara if she was nervous, but she said no.

When the plane took off, Sara felt sadness deep inside her heart, while the plane flew over the capital to take the route towards London. It was a lovely view.

That day after lunch, Torres went to the house and in every room, he picked up Sara's framed pictures and smashed them to the floor. He went to get some bags and put inside everything that belonged to his wife including the bedding sheets and blanket, everything that reminded him of family went in the bags. He took all of it and left it at a church close by. Just a few hours after Sara left, her house looked like a war zone. He opened the kitchen cabinets pulled plates, glasses and other dishes onto the floor and broke everything. Then he banged his head against the wall, followed by going to his room. It was the only room in the house that was clean and tidy. He opened the first chest drawer and took a plain paper, envelope, and a pen.

Ana my little heart, you are the best thing your mother gave me and that happened to me. Since I took you in my arms for the first time, I fell in love with you. I tried to be present in your life as much as I could. I taught you to walk, to talk and read. I protected you as much as I could because you were my darling daughter. I'm sorry about your mother, I couldn't stop it. I love your husband like he is my son. He is a true gentleman and good man for you. Ana always be a good wife to him; respect him all your life, be faithful. No woman should shit on her husband. Women are just to belong to their husbands and do what they say.

Ana, you will never see me again, but I'm asking you to remember me in all the good times we shared. I'm sorry but my time has come to an end. There is nothing left for me. Be happy and... love you always little heart.

He put the letter in the envelope, wrote Ana's address, put a stamp on it and went to the nearest letter box, and posted it. He knew the letter would take days to get to the delivery address, but it was the way he wanted it to be. He went back to his house, without speaking to anyone, put a hand full of tablets in his mouth, opened the sink tap and with his to hands together, gathered some water to swallow. After, he went to his room, lay on his bed, with his arms and hands crossing on his chest like a body in a coffin. He put an end to his life while his family were travelling to London. He didn't want Sara to see him like that. He calculated his daughter and husband would be coming back to deal with the situation, but he also knew Ana wouldn't let her mother come. Obviously, he never loved Sara, he needed her to take care of someone that through the years had forgotten about him. He could never overcome his childhood; his mother was the one who made him the way he was.

He loved his first wife, but never knew how to treat her, he loved his children, but his daughter was the one who conquered his heart. He never hit her, he respected her and her religion. He was always very proud of her, but from now on, after she discovered what he was doing, he wasn't so sure if she would still have the same feelings that she used to feel for him.

His departure was taking him to the one he loved.

Chapter 25

Sara tear's rolling down her cheeks, but she kept looking out the window seeing the shape of Portugal's silver coast. Her mind was racing with lots of thoughts.

My country is left behind, my strange husband will be drowning in his misery, he doesn't have me to blame anymore, to hit and hate. I left behind my Coimbra with its charm. I will never again want a man in my life. I will start a different journey to help my daughter and husband in everything I can. I will do my best to learn the language or at least the main things. I will have a whole city to discover, I will have a new life finally. I never regret falling in love with my Jonny, if it was today, I would have done it again. Thank God I didn't have money to do the abortion, so my daughter came along. These were all her thoughts while looking down through the plane window.

Their trip lasted 2h 30 minutes, then another 2 h to get home. Sara was feeling relieved and very curious about London. When they arrived at their Street, she looked around and said all the houses looked the same.

They went in and Victoria already had dinner ready, but she was upstairs, when she heard them come in.

"Hi Sara, long time don't see you!"

"Hello Victoria, it's good to see you."

"Welcome to the club of single women!" Victoria added.

They took all the luggage upstairs, and Victoria took Sara to her room, saying from now on it's their room. Sara was delighted with the house. It was strange for her to be at her daughter's house, but the tension she had felt the last few weeks was leaving her mind.

They all savoured the delicious meal and talked about the new flat that Ana and Peter were buying back home. Ana noticed her mother was very quiet, so she asked if she was alright. She responded she was better than ever, but now she needed to get used to her new life and having new routines. Everything was different, but she was very positive about it. Her daughter and husband told Sara the next day they would be at home, but the following day Both went to work, apart from Victoria who was going the next day. The most worrying thing for Sara was the fact she wanted to work too.

They all talked about it, the problem was that she didn't speak English, but Victoria told them she was going to have a look for something for her to do.

Sara was going to do the house chores, and cook, but she wanted to be out of the house, and do something productive.

That evening both women were in bed talking about their husbands and their personal lives.

Victoria told her friend, when Ana was organising her wedding, she used to date a boy from Santarém, António and she loved him, but one day he wanted to have an intimate relationship with her, but she didn't agree, so she told him only one day if they got married. He was a very tall and slim, dark eyes and hair, very attractive, and he was studying to be a lawyer. He told her he would marry her but first he wanted to see if she was a virgin. She said no, no way, he felt disappointed, and he said if she changed her mind she knew where to find him and ended their relationship. He was from a good family, and his father was a lawyer too, and his mother was descended from a very wealthy family. They had a big house on the street to the sun doors with a big garden. She carefully told Sara all this.

"Victoria why did you end up with your creep of a husband then?"

"You know, I was a complete idiot. After he left me, I was in pain, I couldn't believe he was so stubborn, if I had agreed with his wishes who knows what could happen? So, after a while, my father introduced the one who I ended up marrying. He was the opposite of António I didn't like him, but my parents did. They were friends and always talking about him, that he was a good man, and that I needed to forget António, because he was rich. At one point I felt like taking revenge on António and started to date the one my parents wanted. We dated just for six months, and he wanted to marry. My parents were overjoyed with the proposal. Sara, I remember it like it was yesterday, my mother told me if I didn't seize the opportunity, I would start to be the motive for people to talk about me, and I could end up on the shelf. Fed up with everything, I accepted. We got married, but still local people started to say that I was getting married too soon, that maybe I could be pregnant."

"Always people putting their nose where they shouldn't." Sara said.

"I got married and he was very good to me, but I felt something wasn't right. One day I had a very serious health problem, and I was admitted to a hospital in Lisbon. The only person who went to see me a few times while I was there, was António."

"No..." Sara said.

"Yes, but it was too late for me. With his visits I realised he really loved me. But what could I do? One month after I left the hospital, my father died, and my husband started to hit me. The rest is history. Things went from bad to worse, and now here I am."

"I didn't know Victoria...He was a jerk like Ana's father, but in his case, I think he was sick, all the years we lived together I noticed lots of times, for some reason he liked to unload his problems on me."

"You are going to be ok."

"Of course, I will be, I do not doubt it."

"You will have fun with me and your daughter."

They talked till midnight, when Ana popped into their room and asked them to be quiet, it was not a decent hour for them to be talking. Sara and Victoria looked to Ana and said,

"Yes captain!" And gave a salute. The three laughed and went to sleep.

The next day was going to be a challenge for Sara, her daughter was going to take her to look around the neighbourhood, and to the local shop. The owners were a very nice Indian couple who had been living here for a few years now. They had three kids, and they were very nice to Ana and Peter.

Sara was introduced to the couple, but not knowing how to speak English, they all agreed that it wasn't a problem. Sara was very practical, and she told her daughter she didn't need to speak the language to do the shopping, as long as she knows how to say good morning and thank you, the rest she will learn with time. Learning it is easier when people are younger because their minds are fresh and ready to travel in new adventures, without even noticing. Nature has a course for everything in the living world and makes people have phases. She knew in her own actual phase, things could very well be stressful, but it wasn't anything that time couldn't cure.

Ana hadn't told her mother about Jonny's separation from Sophie; she wanted to give some time for Sara to adapt first. It had been a very difficult time for her mother, too many chaotic situations to take in, however Sara didn't show her disappointment, everyone around her knew that it must have been hard to deal with Torres all those years and now just being disposable. The problem involving her son was just another one to add to the long list.

The first day Sara spent on her own at home when everybody else went to work, was the key she needed to make them understand, she really needed an occupation too. Victoria was trying to find something, but it wasn't easy.

But one thing she was finally sure of – No man would have control of her ever again.

THE END

Acknowledgements

I would like to thank the amazing Sara Alegria, Paulo Alegria and Christopher Hunter, because this book would not have been possible without their hard work.

I have been so fortunate to have had family and friends to help me with this book.

I would also like to thank my special Lynne Dawson, who unfortunately will never get to see this book come to life.

This process took a long time, but it was all worth it.

I would especially like to thank the people around me who let me have my own space and respected me, even when I was going through hard stages.

Make sure to look out for my

next book

coming soon!

Printed in Great Britain
by Amazon

76257010R00251